SIMPLY
CARNAL

Books by Kate Pearce

The House of Pleasure Series
SIMPLY SEXUAL
SIMPLY SINFUL
SIMPLY SHAMELESS
SIMPLY WICKED
SIMPLY INSATIABLE
SIMPLY FORBIDDEN
SIMPLY CARNAL

Single Titles
RAW DESIRE

Anthologies
SOME LIKE IT ROUGH
LORDS OF PASSION

Published by Kensington Publishing Corporation

SIMPLY CARNAL

KATE PEARCE

APHRODISIA

KENSINGTON PUBLISHING CORP.

www.kensingtonbooks.com

APHRODISIA BOOKS are published by

Kensington Publishing Corp.
119 West 40th Street
New York, NY 10018

All Kensington titles, imprints, and distributed lines are available at special quantity discounts for bulk purchases for sales promotion, premiums, fund-raising, and educational, or institutional use.

Special book excerpts or customized printings can also be created to fit specific needs. For details, write or phone the office of the Kensington Special Sales Manager: Kensington Publishing Corp., 119 West 40th Street, New York, NY 10018. Attn. Special Sales Department. Phone: 1-800-221-2647.

Aphrodisia and the A logo Reg. U.S. Pat. & TM Off.

ISBN-13: 978-0-7582-6945-4
ISBN-10: 0-7582-6945-5

First Kensington Trade Paperback Printing: February 2012

10 9 8 7 6 5 4 3 2 1

Printed in the United States of America

*This book is dedicated to all the readers
who have enjoyed the "Simply" series over
the past years. I wish I had the space to
name you all, but rest assured that I appreciate
each and every one of you.*

1

London, England, 1826

"May I speak to you, sir?"

"Of course, Ambrose. What is it?"

Christian Delornay looked up from the accounting book he was studying and considered the worried face of his normally unshakeable aide-de-camp. According to the clock on the mantelpiece, it was already well past midnight, but the noise from the upper floors of the pleasure house had not yet abated.

He directed a frown at Ambrose. "Why are you still here? You are supposed to be off duty."

Ambrose shrugged. "Because there were matters that required my attention. Why are you still here?"

"Because my mother is not, and she's left me with all the monthly bills to pay."

"You like it when she's away. You fight less."

Christian found himself smiling reluctantly at that truth, but Ambrose didn't smile back. "What *exactly* kept you?"

"There's a woman in the kitchen."

Ambrose's upper-class drawl held a hint of the warmer cadences of his West Indies homeland that emerged only when he was perturbed.

"There are always women in the kitchen." Christian put down his pen. "Should she not be there?"

"She is asking to speak to Madame Helene."

"Did you tell her my mother isn't here?"

Ambrose hesitated and came farther into the room. "I did not. I think you should see her yourself."

"Why?"

"Because she is sorely in need."

"Of what? A man?" Christian grimaced. "Then she hardly needs me. There are plenty of willing guests upstairs for her to choose from no matter what her tastes."

Ambrose shut the door behind him with a definite click and advanced on Christian's desk. "That wasn't the kind of help I had in mind."

"Does she want money, then, or worse, a shoulder to cry on?" Christian's smile wasn't pleasant. "I'm not known for my soft heart. I leave that to my mother and sisters."

Ambrose held his gaze, his warm brown eyes steady. "I would still ask that you see her."

Christian leaned back in his chair. "She obviously had quite an effect on you."

"She . . ." Ambrose hesitated. "She reminds me of how I was before you took me off the streets and offered me a job and a home."

"She's a pickpocket and a thief, then?"

Ambrose's smile flashed out, his teeth white against his dark skin. "I doubt it. She seems to be a lady, but there is something in her eyes that reminds me of how it feels when you can see no future for yourself. I'm not sure if she has the will to last another night."

Christian sighed. "A lady you say? I can scarcely fail to help a damsel in distress. Send her in."

Ambrose paused as he opened the door. "You will be gentle with her, sir?"

"As gentle as I was with you when I caught you picking my pocket all those years ago."

Ambrose chuckled. "You threatened to strangle me and drown me in the Thames."

"Ah, that's right." Christian nodded. "I promise I will listen to what she has to say. Will that satisfy you?"

"I suppose it will have to. I'll go and fetch her from the kitchen."

Christian returned to his account books half hoping that the woman had taken off, preferably without stealing anything too valuable. He was soon engrossed in the complex figures, and it was only when he heard Ambrose gently clear his throat that he remembered to look up again.

The sight that met his eyes wasn't unexpected. Working, as he did, on the less salubrious edge of society, he'd seen plenty of desperate women. But Ambrose was right—she was different, and he'd been trained to notice the smallest details. Her clothes, although soiled, were of high quality, and her skin was as pale and unlined as a lady's. She briefly met his gaze and then raised her chin as if he was beneath her notice and looked beyond him to the window.

Her profile was quite lovely and reminded him of a Titian angel. Christian yearned to stroke a finger down her jawbone and touch the shadowed hollow of her cheek. Her hair was dark and braided tightly to her head. She was far too thin, of course, and probably on the verge of starving.

"Mr. Delornay," Ambrose said. "This is Mrs. Smith."

Christian nodded. "Thank you, Ambrose. I'll call if I need you."

He received another stern look from Ambrose but refused to respond to it, his attention all on the woman in front of him.

"Mrs. *Smith*, it is a pleasure. How may I assist you?"

Her gaze came back to meet his, and he noticed her eyes were slate gray without a touch of blue to redeem their steel.

"I was expecting to meet Madame Helene."

Her voice was low and cultured with a slight French accent that only underlined her status as a lady.

"My mother isn't here tonight. I'm Mr. Delornay. May I not help you instead?"

She swallowed and brought her hands together into a tight clasp under her breasts. She had no gloves, pelisse, or bonnet. Her only outer garments were a thick woolen shawl and muddied half boots soaked through with filth. She'd probably pawned the rest of her clothing. The question was why? What had brought her to living on the streets?

"I need employment, Mr. Delornay."

Christian sat back and studied her. "And you thought my mother might provide it for you?"

"I was told she might, sir."

"With all due respect, ma'am, you look a little frail to manage a job in either our kitchens or as an above-stairs maid."

She moistened her chapped lips with the tip of her tongue. "I understood that this was a brothel." She glared at him. "Doesn't a brothel always need new flesh?"

Christian slowly raised his eyebrows. "You are a whore?"

"I am whatever I need to be to survive, sir."

Christian poured himself a glass of brandy. "But my mother does not run a brothel. She runs an exclusive pleasure house, which is available to the very rich for an extortionate fee, and even then she personally vets every member."

"But surely these men still need women to . . . to . . ."

"Fuck?"

She flinched at the word, and he wondered whether she might run. "If you are indeed a whore, my dear, you should hardly be shocked by my language."

"I've heard that word before, sir. I'm no shy virgin."

"That might be true, but you are scarcely a common trollop either, are you? You look more like a rich man's mistress." He waited but she said nothing. "What happened? Did your lover abandon you?"

Her smile was small and desperate. "Alas, I almost wish that were true."

"Then what is the truth?"

She pressed her lips together and stared at his desk.

"You expect me to employ you without telling me anything?"

"I was widowed. My husband's family was unwilling to support me, so I left."

"You left?" Christian frowned. "What an incredibly stupid thing to do."

"I had no choice, sir."

"I find that hard to believe."

A small choked laugh escaped her and Christian tensed.

"Do you truly believe I would be standing here begging you for the opportunity to sell my body to any man who wants it if I had another choice?"

"As I have already told you, this is not a brothel. No one sells themselves. In truth, they all pay a great deal for the privilege of having sex with anyone they want."

"Why would anyone want to pay for *that*?"

Christian smiled. "Because they can?"

She shivered and wrapped her arms around her waist. "Then you have nothing to offer me?"

She was shaking now, her whole body swaying like a willow tree in a storm, and he feared she might swoon. "I can offer you a hot meal and a decent bed for the night."

She raised her head to look at him. "Your bed?"

He considered her for a long moment until a faint blush stained her pale cheeks and then he smiled. "In your present pitiful state, I fear you wouldn't survive the night, my dear."

"But then you know very little about me, don't you?" She stepped forward until she was almost at his side. "I am quite happy to prove my worth to you."

She started to descend to the floor. Christian reached forward and grasped her by the elbows, bringing her back to her feet. He kept hold of her and stared into her gray eyes. Ambrose was right. There was no hope there, only desolation and desperation.

"I'll keep your generous offer in mind. When did you last eat?"

She blinked at him. "What does that have to do with anything?"

"I can scarcely throw you out on the street in this condition. My mother's reputation would be ruined."

"Not yours?"

"Mine is already beyond redemption." He patted her shoulder and moved away from her to ring the bell. "We will talk again when you are rested."

While he waited for Ambrose to reappear, Christian retreated behind his desk and picked up his pen again. His visitor was visibly shivering now, one hand gripping the back of her chair as if she would fall without the support. He kept a wary eye on her until he heard Ambrose's welcome footsteps in the hall.

"Yes, Mr. Delornay?" Ambrose asked.

"Would you provide Mrs. Smith with a warm meal and a bed in the servants' quarters? I will see her again when she is restored to health."

Ambrose bowed. "Of course, sir." He smiled encouragingly at the woman. "I would be delighted to assist you."

Mrs. Smith continued to stare at Christian. "I'm not sure why you are being so kind to me, sir."

"I'm not being kind. As I said, you appear to be at death's door. I cannot afford to cast you out and have your lifeless corpse found anywhere near my mother's pleasure house. It would be bad for business."

She nodded and Ambrose took her by the elbow to lead her gently out of the room. Christian sat back in his chair and contemplated the silence. Mrs. Smith, and somehow he doubted that was her real name, was a mass of contradictions. Her blunt offer to sexually service him had confounded his previous opinion that she was a well-brought-up woman down on her luck.

And he didn't like being wrong.

He found himself smiling. As Mrs. Smith said, desperation made a hard master, but he wasn't sure how he could help her within the confines of the pleasure house. Luckily, his circle of acquaintance was extremely wide, and he was certain he would be able to find her some form of employment if he couldn't persuade her to rejoin her family.

The thought of trying to convince her of anything made him smile again. Despite her bedraggled state, he'd sensed a core of steel that had impressed even his cynical, cold heart. For the first time in a long while, he was looking forward to meeting someone again and matching his wits with theirs.

"Mrs. Smith? Are you well?"

Elizabeth struggled to focus on the anxious face hovering over her. The struggle not to swoon in front of the obnoxiously handsome and silver-tongued Mr. Delornay had used up the last of her meager resources. He'd seemed far too perfect to be real—until he'd revealed a dark sense of humor that she'd been unable to deflect in her present state. Now all she wanted to do was lie down in the nearest gutter and give up.

"I am quite well, Mr. Ambrose."

He guided her down onto a bench in the warm kitchen where she'd accosted him earlier. The smell of baking bread and pastries curled around her, and she was suddenly nauseous.

There was no sign of any of the staff she'd seen before, and she was glad not to be observed.

"Call me Ambrose. I don't have another name. Now bide here while I fetch you something to eat."

That stirred her interest, but she didn't have the resources or the energy to question him now. She folded her hands on the solid pine table and stared down at them. Her nails were ragged, and despite her best efforts, her skin was never quite clean. She'd never considered water a luxury until she'd been forced to do without it.

"Here you are, ma'am."

Ambrose slid a bowl of porridge topped with brown sugar and milk in front of her. Elizabeth swallowed convulsively as he handed her a spoon.

"Take it slow, ma'am, and you'll be fine."

"I'm not sure if I can eat anything anymore."

Ambrose took the seat opposite her and smiled. "Yes, you can. Your stomach is probably the size of a walnut, but you can at least manage a few spoonfuls."

Her eyes filled with tears at his unexpected kindness. "How do you know that?"

"Because I've been starved myself." His smile died. "If it hadn't been for Mr. Delornay, I would've died on the streets."

Elizabeth licked the rough brown sugar from the spoon and some of the porridge and wanted to moan at the influx of rich tastes against her tongue.

"Does Mr. Delornay make a habit of rescuing waifs and strays?"

"Despite what he might claim, he follows his mother in that respect. No one is ever turned away from the pleasure house without a crust or a coin."

"Or a bed for the night in my case." Elizabeth ate two whole spoons of porridge, and for the first time in weeks she felt warm inside. "I am very grateful for that." She glanced across at

Ambrose. "I had no more coin to pay my rent, and my landlord took all my remaining possessions until I could come up with the money."

"We can probably get them back for you."

"I'm not sure how." Elizabeth sighed and ate another spoonful of porridge. "I still have no money."

"I'm sure Mr. Delornay will have some ideas about that, too, when you talk to him."

Elizabeth put down her spoon as her appetite deserted her. "He said I was too weak to work here in a menial capacity and that he didn't employ whores."

"With all due respect, ma'am, he does have a point. You are indisputably a lady."

"And ladies whore in different ways, don't they?" she whispered. "They are sold into marriage and cannot deny their husbands sexual congress." She stared at him. "I think I'd rather whore *myself* and at least receive some financial compensation in return for my efforts."

Ambrose stood and came around the table to her. "I think you should go to bed, ma'am. I will escort you."

She took his proffered hand and looked up into his face. She reckoned they were of a similar age. "If you are just Ambrose, will you call me Elizabeth?"

"If that is your wish, I would be honored." He kissed her hand. "And now let's get you somewhere safe and warm to sleep. If you leave your clothing outside the door, I will arrange for it to be laundered and returned to you tomorrow."

"Safe . . ." Elizabeth sighed as he walked ahead of her. Mr. Delornay was right. She'd been a fool to run away without taking the things she valued the most. Getting them back seemed impossible now—unless she could truly earn enough money to return. She swallowed down another inconvenient wave of tears. It was impossible to think in her current state, but at least she didn't have to worry about anything until the morning.

2

"*Maman* ..."

Christian tried to interrupt his mother again, but she was in full flow and quite unstoppable. Not that she looked old enough to be anyone's mother as she paced the space in front of his desk, her face flushed, her hands eloquently emphasizing each point. He sat back and just admired the sight, his irritation dying.

Helene stopped and stared at him. "Why are you smiling at me? Were we not fighting?"

He shrugged. "We were, but I was struck anew by your magnificence, and I decided to hold my tongue and save my arguments for something I really care about."

"You do not care about the future of the pleasure house?"

"*Maman*, we are hardly discussing its demise. You still have ten applicants for every place and our coffers are full."

"I know that." Helene resumed her pacing, the blue silk panels of her dress kicking out behind her as if she were a sailing ship in a gale. "But we have always prided ourselves on offering something *more* to our clients, and I fear we are no longer doing so."

"Because you've left the general management to me?" Christian sat up, his good humor evaporating. "I am quite capable of running the business and turning a profit, ma'am."

"I do not doubt that, but . . ." She hesitated and Christian tensed. "I'm not sure if you have the soul to truly understand this place."

"The soul?" Christian laughed. "Whatever you choose to call the pleasure house, it's a high-class brothel, *Maman,* and I could run it blindfolded."

"But it's not just a business. There's an art to it and a personal element, which I fear you lack."

A flicker of heated emotion clenched in Christian's chest and made it hard for him to breathe. There was a slight movement as the other occupant of the room, who had so far remained silent, cleared his throat.

"Helene . . ." Christian stared at his father, Philip, who was watching his mother with a frown. "I hardly think that is fair. Christian has proved an exemplary manager."

Although Christian resented his father's quiet interjection, he managed not to show it. He'd learned to his cost that sometimes Philip was the only person Helene would listen to.

Helene sighed. "Of course you would side with him. You are a man. You do not see things the way that I do."

Philip walked over to Helene and took her hand. "I see that you are worried about your business. I'm just not convinced Christian is the cause of your concerns. You have been closely involved in this place for many years and have only recently attracted some competition. Madame Helene's is not the only pleasure house available to the rich and sexually adventurous anymore."

"That is true." Helene looked up at Philip, and he brought

her hand to his lips. "You have a terribly annoying habit of being right, my dear."

Christian cleared his throat before his parents forgot he was present. "I do agree that we need to formulate some new strategies for the pleasure house. Ambrose and I were talking about it just the other night."

"What did you envisage?" Helene asked, her face alight with interest.

"I'll let you know as soon as I have something more definite to share," Christian said neutrally, and then took a deep breath. "If, however, you have lost confidence in me as your manager, I would be happy to step down." He would be damned if he'd bow down to all his mother's whims. He was twenty-six and had been involved in the running of the business since his nineteenth year.

"You do not mean that," Helene said sharply, her blue eyes flashing. "You are just attempting to put me in my place and I will not have it!"

Christian stood up and rested his hands on the desk. "And weren't you just trying to do the same to me? I'm tired of this, *Maman*—either let me manage the place in my own way or take it back and run it yourself."

Helene glared at him. "Perhaps I will do just that!" She turned toward the door. "If you cannot come up with a comprehensive plan to improve our business within the next week, I will be forced to reconsider both my position and yours."

Christian bowed. "As you wish, ma'am."

Helene swept out and Christian stared after her. He cursed eloquently in French and sat down with a thump. Philip closed the door and turned back to him.

"That did not go well."

Christian raised his head to look at his father, who seemed his usual pleasant self. Although Christian favored Helene in looks, he had his father's hazel eyes and calmer temperament, for which he was secretly grateful. "As you know, my mother is rather overemotional about this place."

"Do you think so?" Philip contemplated his boots. "She founded it from nothing and under great adversity. I suppose she is entitled to have some attachment to it."

"I know that, but surely she must realize that she cannot control every damned thing? She questions every innovation I suggest, countermands my orders, and confuses the staff." Christian shoved a hand through his blond hair. "You cannot wish for her to take complete control of the place again."

"You are right about that." Philip smiled. "In truth, I would prefer her to hand over control of the house to you entirely."

Christian went still. It was the first time Philip had been quite so open with him about the matter. "You would?"

"I've waited a long time for your mother, and as you've taken more on your shoulders, I've enjoyed the last few years immensely." His smile this time was rueful. "So it seems that for once we are on the same side, Christian."

"I would be more than willing to work with you, sir, to achieve our aims."

"I'm sure you would. You've always shown remarkably good sense when needed." Philip checked his pocket watch. "I will find your mother. We are supposed to go and see Lisette and Gabriel this afternoon."

Christian stood, too, and came around the desk to shake his father's hand. "Give them my best, won't you?"

"You don't wish to accompany us?"

"With my mother in this mood? I think not."

Philip's answering smile died. "Families can be very complicated sometimes, can't they?"

"Well ours is certainly unconventional." Christian studied Philip's face. "Is there something else I should know about?" He thought of his younger half sister. "Emily's well, isn't she?"

"Emily is very well, although she spends far too much of her time in the kitchens here for a young unmarried lady." Philip hesitated. "I had a letter from Richard. He's decided to come to London."

Christian's eyebrows rose. Philip's legitimate son had previously scorned to know his father or his half siblings, preferring to roam Europe and live as a permanent houseguest with his friends rather than deal with his father's scandalous second marriage.

"Aren't you pleased?"

"I'm terrified. He's never hidden his distrust of me, or his displeasure at my marriage. He idolized his mother."

"Perhaps he's realized the error of his ways and wishes to make amends." Christian couldn't quite believe he was the one trying to reassure his father. Their relationship had scarcely been less complicated than Philip and Richard's. "By the way, I'm quite willing to meet with him if he wishes to do so."

Philip clapped him on the shoulder. "I appreciate the offer. It can't be easy for you either."

"Do you think Richard fears I'll kill him in a rage over my illegitimate birth?" Christian shrugged. "He's more than welcome to your titles." He walked away from Philip and opened the door. "Now go and find my mother and use your exceptional talent for soothing her ruffled feathers."

"I'll do my best, but I suggest you come up with a plan to transform the pleasure house as well."

"Agreed."

Christian went back to his desk and sat down. With a groan he put his hands in his hair and stared at his blotter.

"Am I interrupting something?"

He slowly raised his head to find his eyes level with Lieutenant Paul St. Clare's amused brown gaze.

"What do you want?"

He'd inherited Paul from his brother-in-law, Gabriel Swanfield, when Gabriel had transferred his club membership into

Paul's name. It had been Gabriel's suggestion that Paul should explore his sexuality at the club. Paul had embraced the opportunity with great gusto and seemed to be always under Christian's feet.

"Marie-Claude said I should check with you that I am allowed to play the part of a Roman centurion in the orgy room this week."

"Why does she need my agreement?" Christian asked irritably.

"Because I believe it is to be an all-male affair."

"I don't care who or what you fuck, Paul."

"Well that's good to know." Paul crossed one booted foot over the other. "Your brother-in-law still keeps urging me to try new things."

"Gabriel feels responsible for you."

"And I keep telling him that is nonsense. My sexual choices are my own."

Christian held Paul's heated gaze. "And I agree with you. Do whatever you want."

"Thank you, Christian." Paul rose to his feet. "Did you know there is a woman in your kitchen?"

"God, not you as well," Christian groused. "Another one?"

"I'm not sure what you are talking about, but there is a woman picking very daintily at a croissant in your kitchen. In truth, she reminded me of one of the wax dolls my cousin used to play with—all glossy perfection and tumbling ringlets, but fragile as hell if you dropped them."

"Ah, that woman."

"You know of her?"

"I know about everything that goes on here," Christian snapped at Paul, who looked remarkably unrepentant. "She arrived here about a week ago. Her name is Mrs. Smith and she is seeking a job. She has been recovering from exhaustion. I was unaware that she was up and about."

"Well, she's talking to your mother." Paul yawned as he sauntered over to the door, his uniform coat unbuttoned and his cravat wrinkled. Christian suspected he hadn't been to bed at all that night. "They seemed to be getting along very nicely. Her French is excellent."

Christian shot to his feet. "My mother?"

"Well, we all know your mother's French is excellent, seeing as she was born there. I meant Mrs. Smith's." Paul yelped as Christian shoved past him into the hall. "I take it you didn't wish for them to meet?"

"I . . ." Christian stopped walking and stared down the hall-way. He had no idea what Mrs. Smith might be saying to his mother, but he had no doubt as to the outcome of her little chat.

"I cannot go back, madame. There is no question of it." Elizabeth swallowed hard and forced herself to keep her gaze on the beautiful blond woman sitting opposite her. "As I mentioned to your son the other night, I truly have no option other than to remain in England and earn my living."

Madame Helene nodded, her blue eyes full of sympathy. "France is not a particularly tranquil place at the moment, especially if you are English. There is much resentment over the demise of that upstart Napoléon. I am glad that he was defeated, but there are many who are not." She reached across and took Elizabeth's hand. "You must not despair, my dear. Are there any members of your own family who might take you in?"

"I fear they are all deceased, madame." Elizabeth manufactured another sigh, fairly certain that the astute woman sitting opposite her would not be fooled. "I am truly on my own."

"Ah, there you are, *Maman*. I believe Philip is looking for you."

Elizabeth tried not to jump as Christian Delornay's silken

voice came over her shoulder. Madame Helene kept a firm hold on her hand.

"Christian, I think I have a solution to your dilemma."

"*My* dilemma, ma'am?"

Helene stood and smiled at her son, and Elizabeth suddenly wished she could hide under the table.

"Indeed. I've said all along that you lack a woman's sensitivity for this place."

"Perhaps because I'm a man? I can scarcely help that, can I?"

There was a snap to Mr. Delornay's words that made Elizabeth stiffen.

"And you do not need to worry about it anymore." Helene pointed at Elizabeth. "Mrs. Smith will come and work as your assistant and help you reinvigorate the pleasure house."

Elizabeth closed her eyes and anticipated the explosion of wrath that was sure to come. Instead there was a frozen silence, and she finally had to turn her head to stare at Mr. Delornay. He appeared to have been struck dumb, but his hazel eyes were brimming with fury.

He bowed and Elizabeth flinched.

"As you wish." He turned to Elizabeth. "Perhaps you might accompany me to my office and we can discuss your duties. I am glad to see that you have recovered."

Madame Helene gave her an encouraging smile. "That's right, my dear. Go with Christian. He is an excellent teacher."

Elizabeth reluctantly followed Mr. Delornay's broad, black-coated back out of the kitchen and along the many hallways to his office. He held the door open for her and waited until she took the chair in front of his desk before going to sit himself.

"Mr. Delornay, despite how it might appear, I did not ask your mother for a position here."

He raised his eyebrows. "Why not? I believe that was your original intention."

She stiffened. "You'd already told me there was nothing I was sufficiently qualified to do here."

"Does that still rankle?"

She took a deep breath. "Are you angry?"

"Do I look angry?"

She studied him carefully. He was dressed immaculately in shades of black and white; his cravat was modest and held in place with an unobtrusive jet pin. His guinea-gold hair was cut close to his head but still displayed a tendency to curl up at the ends. He looked like any other young man of fashion, apart from his hazel eyes, which were still radiating with cold fury.

"You do look rather displeased, and I can understand why. No grown man wishes to be told what to do by his mother."

"How very astute of you." He leaned back in his chair, one arm angled along the gilded top, but his relaxed posture didn't reassure Elizabeth at all. "I am glad to see you have recovered both your appetite and your mettle."

"And I am very grateful to you for offering me that opportunity, sir." A week's worth of good food, warmth, and safety had taken the edge off her desperation and given her hope again.

"Grateful enough to take the job?"

She met his gaze. "Are you offering it to me?"

He shrugged, the elegant motion utterly French. "I am my mother's son. She still owns the pleasure house. I just work here."

There was a hint of bitterness beneath his airy words that made Elizabeth wary, but she had no choice. She needed to find employment too badly to complain about how the offer was delivered.

"What exactly do you wish me to do?"

Mr. Delornay's hazel eyes met hers. "I'm not quite sure yet. I doubt my mother's vision of your usefulness is quite the same as mine."

"I am willing to do whatever you require, sir."

He continued to study her. "So you said."

"That includes use of my . . . of my person, sir."

"You seem remarkably eager to get into my bed, Mrs. Smith. Do you think to influence me more easily between the sheets? I can assure you that will not happen." He leaned forward, his hands clasped together on the desk. "I've had every kind of sexual encounter imaginable. Nothing excites or entraps me anymore."

"Then we might suit very well, sir."

His smile was charming and made her set her teeth. "You are a woman of experience, then, Mrs. Smith?"

"More than you might imagine, sir."

"Yet you look quite untouched."

"Which I understand is an asset." She had to look away from him. "Apparently, my husband married me for that very reason."

He didn't answer her immediately. She stared down at the floorboards, aware that he had the ability to unnerve her, something she'd sworn she would never allow to happen again.

"May I ask you something, Mrs. Smith?"

She gathered her resolve. "Of course you may. And as you are to be my employer, I will endeavor to be as honest as possible."

"As possible." He considered her again. "You have lived abroad?"

"For most of my life, sir. My father liked to gamble and I believe my mother was Italian, so they spent many years on the Continent."

"Was your husband English?"

Tension coiled in her gut. "I would rather not answer that. I can tell you that he lived in France and considered that country his home."

"Do you consider France home?"

"I've never had a home, sir, but I consider myself English."

His smile was slight. "And I consider myself French, but I was born here." He glanced down at his pen and picked it up. "Are you certain there is no one in England I can contact for you?"

"There is no one, sir. My father was disowned by his family. I have never met any of my English relatives, and I doubt they would want to meet me either."

"Are you so certain of that? They do say blood is thicker than water."

"I am quite certain. I would rather stay here and earn my own keep."

"In whatever manner I suggest to you?"

"Yes, Mr. Delornay. I am willing to agree to anything."

A smile flicked up the corner of his mouth. "You should be careful what you promise, Mrs. Smith. You are in the most licentious pleasure house in London, where any sexual fantasy can become a reality."

"And I am more than willing to embrace every single one of them." She smiled into his skeptical face.

He rose to his feet and looked down at her. "Then perhaps you might enjoy a tour of the establishment. If you manage to survive that, we'll discuss the terms of your employment."

3

"This is the main salon where the guests tend to congregate when they first arrive."

Christian flung his arm wide to indicate the two large interconnecting gold and crimson decorated rooms that took up most of the first floor of the pleasure house.

"Is the house open all day?"

He glanced down at his companion, who seemed remarkably unperturbed by the display of naked flesh on view and the pile of heaving bodies on the velvet cushions in the center of the room.

"From around two in the afternoon and for most of the night." He glanced down at a well-endowed countess who was slowly sucking one of the footmen's cocks. "As you can see, it isn't very busy yet. Most of our guests arrive late at night after they have exhausted all the other avenues of pleasure available to them."

She nodded as if that made perfect sense and walked farther into the room, stepping neatly over an outstretched leg and avoiding a groping hand. She wore a plain blue, obviously borrowed, dress that was a little too large for her slender frame and had a tendency to slip from her shoulders. To Christian's critical eyes, she looked as out of place as a nun in a brothel.

"We also provide a buffet and beverages that are constantly refreshed night and day."

"That is very thoughtful. Who is in charge of the food?"

He came up alongside her as she studied the large tables crammed with every dish imaginable. "Madame Durand cooks, and Ambrose and I deal with the process of serving and ordering the food."

She picked up a trailing bunch of grapes and rearranged them carefully on a gold plate. "I should imagine there is a lot of waste."

"Not that I know of. The staff are permitted to take anything home that is returned to the kitchen, and the rest goes to a pig farm."

For the first time, she looked impressed and Christian fought another smile. "My mother is French, Mrs. Smith. She is not about to let good victuals go to waste when others are in need—particularly the pigs."

She glanced up at him, and he thought she almost smiled back. Her expression quickly returned to one of neutral mild interest, and Christian began to wonder what it would take to fluster her. There were plenty of places within the pleasure house that would shock the most experienced of upper-class matrons, and Mrs. Smith was hardly that.

"Despite your mother's benevolence, I still think you should have less food out at once."

Christian's smile disappeared. "I beg your pardon?"

"There is too much."

"The pigs certainly don't think so."

She didn't back down but continued to stare at him. "Have you not been paying attention to current dining fashions?"

Christian leaned back against the silk-covered wall and studied her. "I can't say that I have."

"Recently, in France, there has been a yearning for simplicity in all things rather than the ostentation of the aristocracy or the failings of an emperor."

"Ah, and you believe that fashion will soon be followed here in England?"

"I believe so."

He nodded. "Then I will gladly remove myself from dealing with the buffet and leave it in your capable hands. Talk to Ambrose."

He turned away from the table and walked swiftly back toward the entrance hall that separated the two main areas of the first floor. She hurried to catch up, her slippers making no sound on the soft carpet.

"Are you sure you wish to entrust me with this?"

She sounded a little out of breath. Belatedly, Christian remembered that she was still far from well and felt an unaccustomed and disquieting twinge of guilt.

"Indeed, it is not a task I relish and you seem quite capable of taking it over."

She stared at him, her head angled to one side. In the sunlight streaming through the hall window, he noticed her tightly braided hair was black rather than dark brown.

"I have never met a man who makes decisions so quickly."

"Your husband was a ditherer?"

"My husband was a dictator. He never asked for my opinion about anything. He just expected to be obeyed."

"And how did he enforce your obedience?"

She bit her lip. "How do you think?"

"He beat you?"

She shrugged. "Usually his valet beat me. My husband was several years older than I was when we married."

"How much older?"

She raised her eyebrows at his abrupt tone and probably at his curiosity. "About forty years."

"Christ." Christian almost forgot to breathe as he stared into her calm gray eyes. "And exactly how old were you when you married?"

She lowered her eyes and he found himself staring at her long eyelashes. In her perfection, she really was ridiculously like a doll. "Sixteen."

He touched her shoulder, and she went still under his hands. "Who permitted that to happen?"

"I believe my father was in his debt. I was his last remaining asset."

There was no emotion in her words, only a lightness of tone that failed to deceive Christian. He of all people knew how to lie about his past, how to present it as an amusing farce rather than as a painful, sordid reality. She moved away and turned to look back at him over her shoulder.

"Are we going to visit these more private rooms?"

"Indeed we are." He shook off his disconcerting thoughts, caught her up, and pointed to the small, framed card on the first door. "Each room has a sexual theme. The themes change on a regular basis depending on the popularity of the room. There are several scenarios that rarely change, but we do try to revisit those and make sure they are fresh and original."

"Such as?"

"The Roman era." He tapped the handwritten card on the second door. "Tonight, for example, there will be an all-male Roman banquet with an all-female serving staff and entertainment."

"If you insist that you do not employ whores, who plays the female slaves?"

He smiled at her pointed question. "Female guests directed

by our staff, who assign the roles and make sure that everything is moving along smoothly."

"And is that a role you would wish me to play?"

"I haven't decided yet."

He opened the door and ushered her inside. There was no banquet progressing at this point in the day, but there were some couples lying around and idly making love. Christian halted behind two men, one of whom was naked and on his knees pleasuring the other. A slender gold chain encircled his neck, the end held by the other man who pulled gently on it in time to the man's sucking.

In front of him, Mrs. Smith had gone still. He leaned down to whisper in her ear and inhaled the lavender-scented soap his mother bought for the whole household.

"Have you ever seen two men fornicate, Mrs. Smith?"

She turned her head until her lips brushed his cheek, and he found himself suddenly erect and aching. "Yes."

He directed her attention to the other side of the room. "How about two women?"

"Yes," she whispered again.

"And which scenario do you prefer?"

"I have no preference."

He wanted to bury his face in the hollow between her shoulder and her throat but only allowed himself the luxury of tracing the line of her jaw with his thumb before straightening up. "Your husband must have been an interesting man." She didn't reply, but he felt her instant withdrawal. "Perhaps not. Shall we move on?"

He walked along the whole corridor, showing her the different scenarios, watching her reaction to each sexual situation, but nothing seemed to shock or embarrass her. She nodded at his comments and seemed to be absorbing the information. There was no doubt that she was intelligent. For Christian, the interesting part was that he couldn't avoid reacting to her physical presence. The more he showed her, the more remote her expression became and the more he wanted to shock her.

Eventually they were back in the center of the house at the foot of the staircase. Christian pointed up the stairs.

"On the second level, things become a little more risqué. The rooms are smaller and the groups involved are more intimate too. Part of my job is to help guests find others who have the same, more select sexual tastes. Sometimes they find each other, but sometimes an introduction is necessary."

"I should imagine that some guests do not even know what they desire."

"That is true and that is where my mother excels. She has an uncanny ability to discover a person's true sexual nature."

She paused at the top of the stairs and looked down at him. "Madame Helene told me that you were even better than she was."

"She did?" Christian smiled. "I wonder why she said that when she patently doesn't believe it to be true?"

Mrs. Smith didn't say anything and he wasn't surprised. Despite her calm exterior, he'd deduced she was as watchful as a cat and just as careful. He wondered what it would take to dislodge that calm, to make her show any emotion other than dutiful smiling politeness. Poverty and near starvation had put a hard edge on her composure but obviously hadn't broken it.

He walked her through the almost empty salons, explaining how things worked and nodding to the staff who were dealing with the few guests who lingered. In the farthest salon he came across Marie-Claude, who greeted him with a smile.

"Good afternoon, Monsieur Delornay. Were you looking for me?"

Marie-Claude had been at the pleasure house for many years and had risen to her current position through a combination of extreme common sense and the ability to make the wildest of sexual scenarios a man or woman could imagine come true.

"Marie-Claude, this is Mrs. Smith."

Marie-Claude smiled. "Welcome to the house of pleasure, Mrs. Smith. I understand that you will be working here."

Christian groaned. "I suppose everyone knows that by now."

Marie-Claude switched to French. "News does travel fast, sir, and Mrs. Smith sounds like an excellent addition to our staff."

"You think my mother is right and that we need a more feminine point of view?"

As he had expected, Marie-Claude didn't avoid his direct question. "I think she has a point, don't you?"

Christian wasn't going to start an argument in front of Mrs. Smith. "Be careful what you say, Marie-Claude. Mrs. Smith has lived the majority of her life in France. I expect she can understand you perfectly."

Marie-Claude's smile grew even wider and she winked at Mrs. Smith. "I'm delighted to hear that. Perhaps you might come back another day and spend some time with me, and I'll explain the way this floor works?"

"I would be glad to do so," Mrs. Smith answered in French, and curtsied to Marie-Claude. "I fear I am already taking up too much of Mr. Delornay's time."

"Oh, no, ma'am." Christian bowed. "I am enjoying myself immensely." And the surprising thing was that despite his sarcastic tone, he was telling the truth. He hardly knew anything about her, but she already intrigued him. Something about her lack of emotional involvement with the excesses around her reminded him of himself and made him understand for the first time why his lovers found him so exasperating.

And they would be lovers. He'd already decided that would be one element of her duties he would be happy to involve himself in. He nodded a good-bye to Marie-Claude, took Mrs. Smith by the elbow, and walked toward the next set of stairs. She stopped and leaned against the wall, fanning herself with her hand.

"Are you tired, Mrs. Smith?"

"I am a little fatigued, sir." She used the tip of her tongue to moisten her lips, and he stared at it, transfixed.

"Do you wish to retire?"

She straightened her spine. "Not at all, Mr. Delornay. I am eager to see more."

"The top floor is not to everyone's tastes. Very few of our members venture up there."

"I doubt I will be shocked, Mr. Delornay."

"I doubt you will." He paused. "You are quite extraordinary, Mrs. Smith."

She smiled at him properly for the first time, and he bent his head and licked a slow path along the seam of her lips. She went still but she didn't pull away, and Christian tugged on her lower lip until she opened her mouth to him. The kiss was short but surprisingly erotic as she met the thrust of his tongue with the languid curl of her own.

Christian drew back and stared down at her composed face. "I look forward to your mouth on other parts of my anatomy."

"You have decided that bedding you is part of my job?"

"Consider it a perk." He cupped her jaw in his hand and stared down into her eyes, which betrayed nothing except polite interest. "I dislike sharing my bed with women who want me to make promises to them and expect my emotions to be involved."

"I will expect nothing from you, sir. I can assure you of that."

"And give nothing in return?"

"I am highly skilled, Mr. Delornay. I doubt I will leave you unsatisfied."

He pictured her beneath him, her naked body rising to meet his thrusts, her fine skin flushed with pleasure as he fucked her. Would her composure break then? He took her hand and kissed her fingers. "I look forward to it, Mrs. Smith. Shall we proceed?"

Elizabeth allowed him to escort her up the narrow flight of uncarpeted stairs. She found the idea of bedding Mr. Delornay because she *wanted to* rather erotic. She'd earn the money she needed from her other duties and would consider his attentions as an additional benefit to be experienced and enjoyed at her leisure.

She touched her mouth. The kiss had been expected, her reaction to its gentleness and brevity quite *unexpected*. Most of her lovers hadn't bothered to kiss her, their intent being to get themselves between her legs or into her mouth as quickly as possible to gain their release.

She pushed that thought away and studied her surroundings. The hall was narrower here and pitched at an angle. There were less than a dozen doors leading off the space and only one entrance at the end of it guarded by a large man dressed in the house's livery. She jumped when Mr. Delornay touched her shoulder.

"The rooms are all similar." He reached around her to open the nearest door, his arm brushing against the underside of her breast. She inhaled the scent of leather and sawdust and fixed her eyes on the wooden rack that dominated the room.

"The guests who frequent this floor enjoy the more painful aspects of pleasure," Mr. Delornay murmured. "Sometimes the more painful the better."

"I have met people like that." Elizabeth nodded as she surveyed the whips on the walls along with the chains and gags.

"And is it something that interests you?"

She turned slowly to face Mr. Delornay, who leaned up

against the door frame. His expression was as inscrutable as she suspected her own was; only the thick bulge of his cock visible in his buckskin breeches displayed his interest. She allowed her gaze to linger on his groin until he smiled, shifted his stance, and his fingers caressed his hardening shaft.

"You are teasing me, Mrs. Smith."

"As I said, sir, I am willing to do whatever you wish."

He walked toward her, filling the small space with his presence and his clean, laundered scent.

"Even if I wished to tie you up and whip you before I fucked you?"

She shrugged and her gown fell off her right shoulder. "As long as you didn't kill me in the process."

He chuckled and bent to kiss her exposed skin. His hazel eyes were more gold than green and narrowed with lust. Her faint hope of his actually liking her died. She'd never understood what it was that made men want her, but it seemed Mr. Delornay was no different. She braced herself for his touch, but he stayed still, an arrested expression on his face.

"Let's go and look at the main salon, shall we?"

He turned and walked out the door, leaving her feeling breathless and unsure. She'd been certain he was about to take her, to force her, and yet he'd turned away. Was it possible that he meant what he said and was capable of bedding her without expecting more than she was willing to give?

In her experience, men were contrary creatures who simply took what they wanted from her until she no longer appealed and then discarded her. She'd learned not to be surprised by that, had been glad of it by the end, after the horrible episode with Gaston. . . .

"Mrs. Smith?"

Elizabeth hurried after Mr. Delornay, nodding at the red-headed man guarding the door, who let her pass with a smile.

As she had expected, the room was a glorified version of the more intimate chambers. An array of leather, chains, whips, and sexual instruments was displayed on the bloodred walls, and the floors were bare boards.

In one corner, a man was wielding a long whip over the back of a woman strapped to one of the leather horses. She moaned with each crack of the whip, her body arching against the lash and then falling. The man talked to her in a low soothing tone as he beat her, one hand fisted in her long brown hair.

Elizabeth walked around the edge of the room until she could see the woman's face, see the tears dripping from her eyes as she moaned the man's name. With a sudden exclamation, the man threw the whip away, ripped open his breeches, and shoved his cock deep into the woman's sex. He braced his hands on the edge of the leather and pounded into her, his words muffled as he kissed her neck.

"She isn't being forced to do anything she doesn't want to do."

Mr. Delornay's quiet voice brought Elizabeth out of her memories and back into the present. The smell of sex permeated the air as the man continued to fuck the woman.

"I know that. I saw her face. She was in heaven."

"Yet it disturbed you."

She glanced back at him. She really needed to be careful. He was already far too astute at reading her face.

"Not at all." She took a deep breath and turned toward him. "You said you would like to do that to me. Do you intend to start now?"

"Nicely done, Mrs. Smith. For how many years have you been perfecting the art of distracting men with the promise of sex?"

She allowed her gaze to rest on his cock. "I never realized men needed distracting from their primary aim, sir."

His low laugh surprised her yet again. He bowed and turned back toward the door. "Shall we return to my office, Mrs. Smith, and discuss the terms of your employment?"

"Did I pass muster, then, Mr. Delornay?"

"As if you need to ask that."

He bowed and held the door open for her. Behind them the woman screamed in release and the man groaned her name. Elizabeth allowed herself a small, complacent smile.

"I'm glad I didn't disappoint, sir."

He gazed down at her. "If you have no objections, I'll arrange for your belongings to be placed in the room opposite mine."

So it was to begin, then, their sexual liaison. She couldn't say she was surprised, and he was a lot more palatable than many of the men she had been forced to bed. She nodded. "I have no objections, Mr. Delornay, but I have no belongings."

"I believe Ambrose has had some success retrieving your things from your landlord. Go and find him in the kitchen and then meet me in my office."

4

"Welcome to the pleasure house, Mrs. Smith."

"Thank you, Lieutenant."

Elizabeth smiled as Lieutenant Paul St. Clare toasted her with his tankard of ale and then brought it to his lips and drained every drop. It was late in the evening, and she was sitting at the large pine table in the kitchen. Madame Durand was shouting orders at her staff, and the smell of roasting chickens and spices filled the lofty basement space. To add to the noise level, the second shift of upstairs waitstaff was assembling for Christian to give them their orders for the night.

Elizabeth glanced uncertainly over at the crowd and put down her bread. "Should I be attending Mr. Delornay?"

Ambrose shook his head. "You've already done enough for your first day, Elizabeth. Mr. Delornay said to tell you that you are free to retire whenever you wish."

Elizabeth smiled at Ambrose. "Thank you for all your help."

He shrugged. "I did very little. You learn quickly."

"Indeed you do, Mrs. Smith," Lieutenant St. Clare said. "I was most impressed. You seemed to be everywhere tonight." He held out his hand and firmly shook Elizabeth's. "And, please, call me Paul. I hate being reminded of my army rank."

"You shouldn't be down here, sir," Ambrose said without much conviction. "You're a guest."

"I'm practically family." Paul snorted. "Has Christian been telling you to chase me off again?"

Ambrose opened his mouth to speak and then glanced up as the back door opened. His smile became warmer and he rose to his feet.

"Miss Emily!"

A tall girl with brown hair and brown eyes came into the kitchen. She was dressed in a cream satin ball gown that Elizabeth immediately coveted.

"Good evening, everyone!"

"Good evening, Miss Emily."

Paul stood, too, and bowed. Dressed as he was, in a toga and crooked laurel wreath, he didn't look much like the military man he claimed to be, but more like a slightly rakish fallen angel.

"How is it that you welcome Miss Emily and not me? She isn't exactly staff either, is she?"

"She is *family*." Ambrose fetched a bowl of hot chocolate from the cook and slid it across the table to Emily, who had taken the seat beside Elizabeth.

Emily studied Elizabeth and held out her hand, her brown eyes full of interest. "Good evening. I'm Emily Ross."

"Emily is Christian's half sister," Paul volunteered as he helped himself to more buttered bread and ale. "Despite what Ambrose says, she's not supposed to be here either."

"Oh, do be quiet, Paul," Emily said, and Paul winked at her. "I've done my duty and attended a terribly dull piano recital with my chaperone. Now I just want the opportunity to drink some of Madame's delicious hot chocolate and relax for a while."

Elizabeth shook the proffered hand. "It is a pleasure to meet you, Miss Ross. I'm Elizabeth Smith, a new employee at the pleasure house."

"Mrs. Smith is Christian's assistant." Paul grinned wickedly as Emily's eyes opened wide.

"Christian's *assistant?* However did that happen?"

Ambrose went to say something, but Elizabeth answered for herself. "I fear he was persuaded into it by Madame Helene."

Emily studied Elizabeth and then nodded decisively. "I think it will be good for him. He spends all his time here these days and never seems to smile anymore. Despite what he claims, I believe he misses Lisette quite dreadfully." She picked up her bowl of hot chocolate and sipped it with a sigh. "Madame Durand is such a treasure. . . ."

As a headache threatened behind her eyes, Elizabeth rose to her feet. Who on earth was Lisette? The complicated relationships of the Delornay-Ross family were too confusing for her to deal with right now.

"I think I will take Mr. Delornay's advice and seek my bed. I am quite fatigued."

Three pairs of eyes filled with speculation fastened on her, and she fought an unexpected urge to blush. "It was a pleasure to meet you, Miss Ross, and you, too, Lieutenant."

The men rose and Paul came around to her side. "I have to get back to my all-male orgy, so I'll escort you upstairs."

"That won't be necessary, Lieutenant, but thank you," Elizabeth said, and headed for the door.

He kept pace with her on the stairs anyway, chatting easily about the weather and the excellence of Madame Durand's cooking. Elizabeth hesitated when she reached the second level and looked up at him. His skin gleamed faintly with oil, and his right shoulder and arm were completely exposed in his Roman garb. His build was slight and he wasn't particularly tall, but she sensed the strength in him.

His smile was devastatingly sweet.

"Are you worried I'll see where you are sleeping and tell the others?"

There was no malice in his question or anything other than gentle interest.

"I have my own room, sir."

"I'm sure you do."

"And I intend to sleep in it."

"I do not doubt it. Have we embarrassed you with our interest about your sleeping arrangements?"

Elizabeth shrugged. "Not at all, sir. Your interest is not unexpected. I *am* living in a bawdy house."

"Don't let Madame Helene hear you call it that and, please, call me Paul." He touched her cheek, the caress so light it was almost nonexistent. "If you want some company in that bed of yours, I would be happy to oblige you."

"That is very kind of you, Lieutenant, but—"

"Paul, please." He placed his finger over her lips. "But you are already taken."

"It is part of my employment."

His soft laughter made her tense up. "Oh my word, I can't believe Christian had to resort to that."

She raised her chin and gave him her most confident smile. "Perhaps the conditions were mine, sir."

"Christian has been known to share his lovers."

"Living here, as he does, I can quite believe it."

"He didn't grow up here. From what I can piece together, he was brought up in France and came over at the age of eighteen to find his mother." He chuckled. "I believe the existence of the pleasure house was something of a surprise to all of Madame's children."

Elizabeth considered that interesting snippet of information and shivered. No wonder the relationship between Mr. Delor-nay and his mother appeared a little strained.

"Don't worry, Mrs. Smith. Christian is perfectly respectable now." Paul caught her hand and kissed her knuckles. "You might be seeing me again one night. Christian has taught me a lot about making love to a woman, although it is not my nat-ural inclination."

"Then why do it?"

It was a strange conversation to be having with a man she barely knew in the stairway of a pleasure house. She couldn't seem to prevent asking the most impolite of questions. Perhaps her husband's death had liberated her in more ways than one.

"Because I find I do not wish to bring my family into disre-pute. If I am seen consorting with a woman here occasionally, they can avoid the disgrace of having a known Molly in the family."

"And what about you? What do you want?"

His smile was charming but quite devoid of emotion. "I've realized that making love to a woman can be quite . . . pleasant. So, perhaps my friends' and family's attempts to widen my horizons have met with some success." He let go of her hand. "And I have been monopolizing your time quite dreadfully. Good night, Mrs. Smith."

She watched him walk away with his lithe grace and natural elegance. Despite his best efforts to disguise it, his aristocratic breeding showed. She bit her lip. And now he had made her worry again. She truly had no idea of Mr. Delornay's sexual tastes. For all she knew, he might invite forty men to share her. She shivered at the thought. He struck her as a very private man, but she of all people knew that a man's sexual tastes were not always obvious or conventional.

She took out the key he had given her and unlocked the door that separated the public part of the house from the pri-vate. It was much quieter here, the colors less garish and the artwork more soothing than stimulating. Her slippers sank into the thick carpet as she moved like a ghost through the deserted halls.

Her room came in sight and she opened the door with a relieved sigh. Someone had laid a fire in the grate, lit some candles, and turned down her bed. She stared at the blue satin counterpane. Would Christian join her there tonight? It seemed more than likely.

She wrapped her arms around herself. He'd given her more than a week's grace, so she should consider herself lucky. Most men would've taken her up on her first desperate offer in his study and not cared about the consequences. In truth, it would be no hardship bedding Christian Delornay. He was unlikely to see her as more than a passing diversion, and he expected nothing more from her than gracious compliance.

She sat down in the large wing chair, kicked off her borrowed slippers, and contemplated the flames. And she was good at complying. She'd learned the hard way that it was possible to allow her body to be used and yet set her mind free. She yawned and studied the turned-down bed. A minute here before the fire to warm her and then she would undress and await his appearance. He probably wouldn't be long. . . .

She awoke with a start to the sound of the door opening and opened her eyes to see Christian, his blond hair gleaming like a gold coin in the candlelight. His gaze drifted from the empty bed to the fire, and she blinked at him.

"Did you fall asleep, Mrs. Smith?"

"I must have done." Elizabeth rubbed hastily at her eyes and tried to untangle her stockinged feet from her skirts. "What time is it?"

Christian approached the fire, and she noted that he still wore his immaculately fitted evening clothes. "It is a little past midnight." He paused. "If you are tired, I can leave."

"No, that won't be necessary. I'm perfectly ready to receive you." Elizabeth fixed a smile on her face. Better to get it over with now rather than endure another night of uncertainty. She struggled to her feet and found his hand already waiting to aid her. "Thank you, sir."

He cupped her cheek and stared down into her eyes. "I fear you must find me a little autocratic in our dealings. I wish to make it clear that your employment is not dependent on you sharing my bed."

She didn't believe that for a moment and wondered what he would do if she actually dared to send him on his way. "That is very kind of you, sir, but I'm still happy to proceed."

He studied her for a moment and then kissed her forehead. "Then may I help you undress?"

"Of course, sir."

"Christian." His long fingers stroked down from her chin to her shoulder and she shivered. His thumb settled on the lace at her bodice and slipped beneath the borrowed silk to caress her flesh. "We must have some clothes made that fit you. This gown is far too big."

"I had to borrow it from Marie-Claude. I sold most of my gowns in order to afford to eat." Elizabeth managed to keep her voice calm as he continued his maddeningly slow exploration of her throat and shoulders. "I will purchase more when I earn sufficient funds."

His fingers met at the back of her gown, and he started to unhook it, causing the short puffed sleeves to fall to her elbows and trap her arms against her sides. He made no effort to free her, his attention all on the upper curves of her small bosom. He bent his head and licked a wet path down between her breasts, his hands busy again at her back unlacing her corset.

Elizabeth made no effort to grab at her stays as they came away from her skin. She allowed him to look his fill, to touch and cup her breasts through her thin shift as the corset fell unheeded to the carpet. He murmured his appreciation as he

pushed the rest of her gown down along with her simple petticoat. His thumbs came back to rest on her breasts, and she
closed her eyes as he rubbed and circled her nipples into hard,
aching points.

"Mrs. Smith?"

She reluctantly opened her eyes to find him looking at her.
Up close, his eyes were more golden than brown.

"Don't close your eyes. I want you to watch me taking you.
I want you to see it all." He slid his hand around the back of her
neck. "Unpin your hair for me."

She raised her hands and set about the laborious task of unpinning and unplaiting her long hair. While her fingers were
busy, his wandered over her body, touching and learning every
inch of her flesh.

"Your hair is much longer than I first imagined," he murmured as he smoothed a long strand through his fingers. "And
a thing of beauty. Put your arms around me and kiss me."

There was a note of command in his soft request that made
her want to obey him. She went up on tiptoe and kissed his
chin, then the sensual curve of his lips. His mouth descended,
taking possession of the kiss and deepening it until his heat
consumed her. He lifted her against him, the hard press of his
cock rubbing against her sex.

He wrenched his mouth away and set her back on her feet.
"Help me undress. I want to be inside you."

She hastened to obey, her eyes never leaving his, her fingers
busy untucking and unbuttoning him until his cock was a hard,
thrusting presence in her hand. She started to go down on her
knees but he shoved a hand into her hair and kept her upright.

"Later. I want to be inside you."

He drew her over to the bed and followed her down onto
the soft mattress, his body covering hers, his hard thigh sepa-
rating her legs and rubbing against her already-wet sex. Eliza-

beth anchored her hands on his shoulders as he continued to kiss her, the slick wet presence of his cock sliding against her belly. She reached for his shaft, but he drew her hand away and pulled back from her.

"Wait one moment." He turned to the bedside cabinet and took out a bottle of tansy oil and a small piece of sponge tied with thread. "I want my come in you. This will prevent conception."

Elizabeth didn't bother to tell him that she already knew that. His intentions were good, and she didn't want to destroy the promising mood. He took the sponge and slid one long finger deep inside her, and she arched against the bed. His thumb settled on her bud and she sighed his name.

With a growl, he came down over her and his cock penetrated her sex. She let herself relax as he rocked deeper and deeper until his whole length throbbed inside her. His mouth returned to hers, advancing and retreating in the same rhythm as his cock, a slow demanding dance that invited her participation.

Elizabeth kissed him back and allowed her body to share his rhythm and absorb his thrusts. She kept her eyes open, noticed his expression intensify and reacted accordingly. She tightened her inner muscles around his cock until he groaned her name and lost his smoothness. He gathered her buttocks into his hands and thrust harder.

"Come for me, come with me."

Elizabeth tightened her muscles even more and began to pant and writhe beneath him, her fingernails biting into his flesh as she bucked and rubbed herself against him as if in the throes of passion. He went rigid and then she felt the hot gush of his seed deep inside her and obligingly screamed his name and made her body go limp.

He collapsed over her, his shoulders slick with sweat and his breathing uneven. After a little while, he rolled off her and lay on his back staring up at the ceiling. Elizabeth stayed exactly as he had left her, her legs parted, her arms over her head. Experience had taught her that men liked it if they thought they had exhausted her with their passion.

With a soft curse, Christian rose from the bed and went to light some more candles. He glanced back at Elizabeth Smith, who despite the speed of his lovemaking looked well satisfied, her pale body relaxed against the sheets, her nipples still hard from his mouth and hands. His cock jerked and he touched himself, enjoying the quick return to form that had eluded him for quite a while. There was something about Mrs. Smith that made him hard.

He set the candles down beside the bed and crawled back in between the sheets, his gaze on the luscious wetness of Elizabeth's now-swollen sex. She'd taken him easily, her body as welcoming as he'd hoped. . . .

"You are obviously as skilled as you claimed."

She turned her head to look at him. "Thank you."

"I'd almost say that was a command performance."

A small frown appeared between her brows. "Did I not please you?"

She sat up and came toward him, her gaze fixed on his half-erect cock. He watched her approach and waited until her tongue flicked out to circle the tip of his crown. He imagined her with a collar around her throat like the man in the Roman room, imagined himself guiding her to do his bidding.

"Do you want more, sir?"

"Of course I want more." He fisted his hand in her long hair and held her still, the crown of his cock jammed against her lips. "Suck me."

She opened her mouth and he surged inside her, groaned as she let him cram himself down her throat, taking all of him and starting to suck. God, and he wanted it hard, liked it hard, and wanted to fuck her mouth like this every day whenever he wanted it.

Her hand cupped his balls, her long fingers caressing them, circling the pucker of his arse and making him even stiffer and more eager to come. He groaned her name and surged deeper, felt the kick of his climax deep in his balls and the back of his spine and spent himself in her warm and willing mouth. She released his cock with a small kiss and retreated to the other side of the bed, her gray gaze fixed on him as if daring him to suggest he found her wanting now.

He eased back against the headboard and waited for his breathing to settle down, waited to see what she would do next. She did nothing but watch him, her eyes calm, her expression dutiful and politely willing. He knew that if he wanted her again, she'd take him, and that excited him despite what he'd begun to suspect.

She fingered the sheet and he tensed. "Is there something else, sir, or may I go to sleep?"

He held her gaze. "What if I wanted to lick and suck your cunt? Would you allow that?"

She shrugged, the motion as graceful and as empty as anything he could achieve at his most annoying. "I have not told you no yet, have I?"

"Would you ever?"

Her smile didn't dim. "Most men seem to enjoy a woman who allows them to use her as they will."

"Do you feel used, Mrs. Smith?"

A faint flush colored her cheeks and she looked away from him. "What else can I do for you? Do you wish to fuck me again?"

His cock liked that idea, but his mind did not. "Do you always befuddle men with sex?"

"Befuddle them?" She raised her eyebrows. "Isn't that what I'm supposed to do?"

"That's not what I meant." He gestured at the rumpled sheets. "You use sex to distract a man from asking questions about your pleasure."

"I took my pleasure, sir. Perhaps you were so engrossed in your own that you failed to notice my small efforts."

He almost wanted to smile at that. "Unfortunately for you, I'm not quite that conceited. You were very convincing, but I know you didn't climax." He paused to make sure that she was listening to him. "Do you ever climax?"

"I have no idea what you are talking about." She licked her lips and started toward him again. "I'm sure I can show you that you speak nonsense. You are a superb lover and you know it."

"I *am* a superb lover, and that's why I know when a woman is faking her pleasure." He caught her by the elbows and held her still, their noses almost touching. "Don't try and pretend otherwise."

She swallowed hard. "You are wrong, sir. I am perfectly satisfied."

"And apparently an excellent liar—let's not forget that." He disengaged himself and climbed off the bed. "I'm going to my own room to sleep now. Good night, Mrs. Smith."

She knelt on the bed, her hands clasped together in her lap. She looked the picture of hurt confusion. Part of him admired her acting abilities; the rest felt an unaccustomed sense of annoyance.

"I have disappointed you, Mr. Delornay."

He didn't bother putting on his clothes. His room was only across the hall. "You haven't disappointed me at all. I enjoyed myself immensely. In truth, what man could be dissatisfied with a woman who gives everything and takes nothing in return?"

"Most men would agree with you." She raised her chin, and

he was glad of it. Had he finally managed to needle her into a fight? "Perhaps that is what I intended."

He faced her and she held his gaze. "Then you have succeeded in your aim. I can only hope that your current state of sexual frustration is satisfactory to you. Or was that the whole point? Do you prefer to take your satisfaction into your own hands?"

"I . . ." She stopped speaking and simply stared down at the floor. "Good night, Mr. Delornay."

"Good night, Mrs. Smith."

He nodded and left the room before he entered into a conversation he was certain he would not win at this hour of the night, or ever, if he was honest. The real question was whether Mrs. Smith was incapable of achieving a climax or whether she was deliberately choosing to withhold her pleasure from him.

Christian carefully closed the door to his room and stared at his untouched bed. It was ironic that she'd given him exactly what he'd asked for, excellent sex without cloying emotions, and here he was fuming over it. He smiled. Mrs. Elizabeth Smith would soon find out that he was not the sort of man to accept defeat in any area of his life, particularly in the bedroom.

5

Christian stared down at the parchment on his desk and carefully underlined the date for the third time. It was almost nine on a typically cold, gray autumn morning, and he was supposed to be meeting with Ambrose and Mrs. Smith to discuss their new proposals for the pleasure house before he shared them with his mother.

Helene would insist that all women were capable of experiencing pleasure. She believed that men were the problem because they were too selfish to make the effort to bring a woman to orgasm. Had he been too fast? He grimaced as his pen spat out an ink blot. He hadn't exactly taken much time getting between Mrs. Smith's legs. . . .

"Mr. Delornay? Are you listening to me?"

He looked up to find Ambrose staring at him.

"I wish you to make some inquiries about Mrs. Smith."

Ambrose looked resigned. "I assumed you would. I did talk to her landlord when I went to retrieve her belongings, but he had very little to say about her."

"Did you look through her bags?"

"Of course not!" Ambrose frowned. "But from what I saw, I doubt her few pitiful pieces of clothing held many secrets."

"She had no papers or letters?"

"As I said, I didn't search her bags. If you really want to find out more about our mysterious guest, you will have to ask your mother. Her social circle is immense and extremely influential."

"Perhaps I'll do that," Christian muttered, and glanced again at the clock. "Where is Mrs. Smith anyway?"

"Don't you know?"

Christian frowned. "Don't make it sound like an accusation. I am hardly to blame for her tardiness. I left Mrs. Smith early last night to sleep peacefully in my own bed."

"You left her bed?"

"Yes. Why do you sound so incredulous?"

Ambrose regarded him intently. "Because it is not like you. When you take a new lover, you are normally insatiable."

"This is hardly normal, is it? I haven't taken up with one of my employees before."

"That is true." Ambrose sipped at his coffee. "And I'm still not sure if it is a good idea."

"I don't believe I asked you for an opinion," Christian retorted.

Ambrose grinned. "I'm offering one anyway."

"And it is not welcome." Christian shuffled the papers on his desk and looked impatiently toward the door. "Do you wish to go and find Mrs. Smith, Ambrose?"

"There is no need." Mrs. Smith's pleasant voice came through the open door. "I was talking to Lieutenant St. Clare in the kitchen."

Christian stood as Mrs. Smith came into the room. She wore the plain blue gown that was too big for her and had a thick shawl wrapped around her shoulders. Her long hair was tightly braided into a complex coronet on the top of her head. He remembered how soft her hair felt against his skin when she bent her head and . . .

"Good morning, Mrs. Smith. You are fifteen minutes late."

She curtsied to him, her expression calm. "I apologize, Mr. Delornay. It is quite difficult to stop Lieutenant St. Clare when he is in a talkative mood. He was telling me about your sister."

"Which sister? I have several." Christian gestured to a chair in front of his desk beside Ambrose and then sat down again.

"Your twin, Lisette, who I understand is married to the lieutenant's best friend."

Christian grunted. "I'm surprised Paul didn't insist on accompanying you to this meeting. He seems to be here more than I am these days." He tapped his pen on the paper. "Now, may we proceed? I told my mother I would offer her some suggestions as to the improvement of the pleasure house."

"Actually, Paul might have some good suggestions of his own." Ambrose crossed his legs. "Are you sure you don't want me to fetch him?"

"Let's see what we come up with between ourselves first, and then we can ask everyone else for their ideas." Christian pointed his quill at Elizabeth. "Let's start with you."

"I have several ideas, Mr. Delornay."

He met her calm smile with one of his own. "I'm sure you do, Mrs. Smith. Perhaps you would care to share them."

"You will not be offended?"

"At this point, I am beyond taking offense at anything you might say. My mother has humbled me far too often."

"Then might I suggest you offer some more structured entertainment?"

"What do you mean by that?"

She sat forward, her hands clasped together in her lap. "You offer the occasional 'show' in the main salons, but I think you should offer such entertainment more regularly and involve the guests more intimately."

"Go on," Christian said.

"For example, perhaps you could organize games such as hide-and-seek or Simon says, childish games, but with a more wicked and adult purpose? These games might even appear to begin spontaneously, but would, of course, be carefully instigated by your staff."

Christian caught Ambrose's eye. "That sounds like an excellent idea. What do you think, Ambrose?"

"I think it would work very well on both of the main floors. We would have to train our staff, of course, but that wouldn't be an issue. They would probably enjoy it."

Christian wrote the bones of the idea down on his piece of parchment and continued to write as the ideas began to flow. Ambrose became quite animated, and even Mrs. Smith looked flushed. By the time the clock struck eleven, Christian had quite a list in front of him.

"There is one more thing," Christian said. Ambrose and Mrs. Smith looked expectantly at him. "The room of hidden desires."

Ambrose frowned. "Is that still in use? I haven't directed anyone toward it all year."

"Exactly, but I believe it will reintroduce an element of forbidden erotic excitement that has been missing at the house."

"What exactly is the room for?" Mrs. Smith asked.

Christian met her interested gaze. "It is a room where guests can express their most private and illicit sexual desires, and they will be provided within the shortest time available."

"But surely everything is openly available here?"

"But not everyone wants to be seen participating publicly by their peers. And some people truly do believe that what they desire is so shocking that they can barely acknowledge it to themselves." He of all people knew that. "The room is very strictly monitored and controlled so that no mention of what goes on in there ever gets out."

He fixed his gaze on Mrs. Smith. "I would expect both you and Ambrose to participate in the fulfillment of these special sexual desires."

Ambrose nodded. "I assumed you would ask me. I'd also suggest Paul as a candidate. He's always willing to try new things."

Christian groaned. "Paul again? I'm not sure why I don't simply cancel his membership and employ him permanently."

"Perhaps because he is officially still employed by the army—if only on half-pay." Ambrose stood and nodded to Mrs. Smith. "And I suspect his family would be horrified if they knew he would be paid a wage like a tradesman for having sex."

Christian smiled. "I suspect you are right. Despite his ragged appearance, he has the most lofty connections." He sighed. "Ask him if you like. At least I know he'll keep quiet about it."

Ambrose left, closing the door behind him, and Christian turned his attention to Mrs. Smith, who remained quietly in her chair.

"Would you be willing to participate in the sexual fantasies of the room of desires?"

She raised her eyebrows. "I thought you'd already decided that I was."

"And then I thought better of it." Christian put down his pen. "From what little you've told me about your life, I have to suspect that sex might not always be a pleasure for you."

"In truth, it became far more pleasurable when my husband was unable to bed me."

"Because you were left alone?"

"Because my husband shared me with other men."

Christian barely managed to hide his surprise at her bald statement. "I find it difficult to believe you were so sanguine about it at the time." He abandoned his desk and went to take the seat next to Mrs. Smith that Ambrose had vacated.

"Why?" She held his gaze, wry amusement in hers. "Are women not supposed to enjoy themselves with men other than their husbands?"

"If that were true, the entire British aristocracy would be miserable as sin."

"Exactly."

Christian tried again. "But you did not make a choice, did you?"

She folded her hands together in her lap and stared down at them. "I was eighteen when my husband first started to have problems in my bed. At first he blamed me and beat me for my supposed failings. Eventually he preferred to let others fuck me while he watched. He seemed to derive satisfaction from the sight, and I was simply relieved not to be beaten."

"You make it sound so simple."

She raised her head to meet his skeptical gaze. "It was simple. What would you prefer me to say? None of the men he brought to me were vicious or depraved. Some of them were very drunk, and it wasn't as if I was left alone with them to fend for myself."

Christian had a sense that she was hiding something important from her calm recital, but he couldn't yet pinpoint exactly what it was.

"Then why run away?" There it was, the hint of fear in her gaze. "Why, if everything was to your liking, did you run?"

"Because my husband died, and his family . . ." She stopped speaking.

"And his family did not approve of what he had made you?"

"They . . ." She paused. "They wanted certain things from me, certain guarantees that I was unable to give them."

"Such as?"

She smiled. "My husband also had a mistress living with us who hated me ever since my marriage. She used her considerable influence with his family to make sure the conditions they wished to impose upon me were intolerable."

"Don't change the subject."

"I am not," she protested.

Christian frowned at her. "Are you saying that the family considered you more of an embarrassment than your husband's mistress?"

"It was quite complicated. The lady was also sleeping with my husband's cousin and he—"

"And he wanted you to stay." Christian nodded. "I begin to see how it all fits together."

"Then you will also understand why I had to leave."

"I'm sure you had your reasons, although I'm not sure if you have explained them to my satisfaction."

"But surely my reasons have nothing to do with your original question as to whether I was happy to engage in the more intimate sexual games of the room of desires?"

She opened her eyes wide, and he fought a smile. It was almost a pleasure sparring with a mind that was as devious as his. He was also becoming aware that her apparent openness about her past life was yet another device to shield the complete truth.

"Touché, Mrs. Smith."

"Indeed, sir."

He rose to his feet and held out his hand. "I need to work on this paper for my mother. Perhaps you might take the time to familiarize yourself with the rooms on the second floor and speak to Marie-Claude?"

"I will do that, sir."

He lightly kissed her knuckles. "And I have arranged for a local modiste to visit you at six this evening. She will meet us in your room."

She drew her hand away. "Meet *us?*"

He shrugged. "I have some ideas as to how I wish you to be dressed."

For the first time, her gray eyes flashed fire. "And as you have obviously decided to pay for my garments, you feel you have the right to dictate what I wear?"

"Dictate? Surely not, but a second opinion is always valuable."

She exhaled and favored him with her usual calm smile. "Of course, sir. And perhaps my opinion could be taken into account, seeing as I intend to pay you back for everything."

He patted her cheek. "Don't worry. I intended to deduct the cost from your wages anyway."

She went up on tiptoe and kissed him. "Oh, thank you, sir."

Her smile was quite beautiful to behold, and for a moment he was almost taken in, until he noticed it didn't quite reach her eyes. He kissed her back. "You are quite welcome, Mrs. Smith."

He watched her leave and returned to his desk. The thought of watching her undress for the modiste was already exciting him. The thought of what he intended to do to her after the modiste left made him impatient for the day to end. Mrs. Smith would not be able to resist his lovemaking for a second night in a row.

Elizabeth took herself back down to the kitchen and lovingly imagined Mr. Delornay's head on a platter with an apple in his mouth, being served for supper. He was as difficult to argue with as a French lawyer. Yet it was also quite exciting to bait him. She shook her head at her own stupidity. She was not here to speculate about her employer. She was here to provide him with the sexual services he required and receive a wage in return. She must not forget that she needed all the money she could gather to fight against her husband's family.

In the kitchen, Ambrose was talking to Paul, who was for

once dressed smartly in his uniform, as if he'd either just arrived or was leaving. They both looked up as she entered and smiled. Despite her wariness, she couldn't help but smile back at them.

Paul put on his hat and bowed. "I have to go and report in to my commanding officer, Lieutenant Colonel Constantine Delinsky. I'll be back for dinner."

"Delinsky?" Ambrose frowned. "He's a member, isn't he?"

"Indeed he is, but for some reason he prefers not to conduct military business here." Paul winked at Elizabeth. "It would make my life a lot easier if he did, as I find him remarkably appealing." He headed for the door and then paused. "From what Ambrose just told me, it seems as if I might be enjoying more of your company after all, Mrs. Smith."

"So I understand, Lieutenant."

He bowed. "I look forward to it."

Ambrose waited until Paul had left and then turned to Elizabeth. "He is quite harmless, really."

"Lieutenant St. Clare?" Elizabeth took a seat at the kitchen table. "I'm not sure about that."

"Despite his joking, he would never force himself on anyone."

"I know." Elizabeth accepted the mug of coffee Ambrose offered her and waited until he sat opposite her at the table. "He told me that he has been encouraged to explore all types of sex at the pleasure house."

Ambrose rubbed a hand through his cropped hair. "When he first came here, he was still enamored of Gabriel Swanfield, and we were all concerned about how he would react to Gabriel's marriage."

"And how did he react?"

"Rather better than anyone expected. He seemed genuinely pleased that Gabriel had found someone to love him. But with Paul it is hard to know exactly what he is thinking."

"I noticed that." Elizabeth sipped at her coffee. "He pretends that everything is a great lark, but beneath the surface I suspect he is not at peace with himself."

Ambrose nodded. "I thought you would understand."

She looked up at him. "I am at peace with myself."

"I can scarcely comment on that, can I?" His smile was warm. "But I know from my own experiences that trying to pretend that everything is fine takes a huge toll on a person."

"What do you mean?" He hesitated and she continued. "I should imagine your life experiences have been very different from my own. I would be honored if you would share your story with me—if it does not pain you to speak of it."

He settled himself more comfortably on the bench and rested his chin on his fist. "As a child, I was taken from my home and brought over on a slave ship from the West Indies. I cried the entire time and received more than a few beatings on the long voyage.

"When I arrived in London, I was sold to a very aristocratic family as a page boy. It was all the rage twenty years ago. My mistress liked to dress me in costly silks and velvet, with a turban on my head and a gold collar studded with rubies around my neck. I thought I was in heaven. I was pampered like a lapdog, petted and adored. I thought of those people as my family."

Elizabeth waited as his expression darkened. "Of course, I kept growing and suddenly I was a young man and unable to sit on anyone's lap anymore. They still wanted to touch me, but not in a childish way. I loved my mistress and I was willing to do anything she told me to, so when her husband discovered me in her bed, he had me beaten and thrown out of the house without a character."

"That is terrible." Elizabeth reached across and took his hand. "How did they expect you to survive?"

"I'm not sure they cared." His quick smile flashed out. "I almost died that first year and probably would've done that last winter, if Mr. Delornay hadn't come across me and offered me a job here."

"How did you meet?"

"I tried to pick his pocket." Ambrose met her gaze, his brown eyes full of memories. "I almost succeeded, but despite those good looks, he's a dangerous bastard when cornered."

"And he brought you here."

"Aye, he did, but not to work. I could barely read or write, and he insisted that I receive an education before he would allow me to become a part of the pleasure house."

"And Mr. Delornay paid for this?"

Ambrose chuckled. "You sound so skeptical. I told you—he is a good man."

Elizabeth wasn't quite as sure about that and hastened to change the subject. She didn't want to think about Christian Delornay being a good man. He was simply her employer and her temporary lover.

"Do you think Madame Helene will agree to the changes he suggests to her this afternoon?"

"I hope she will, or I am afraid Mr. Delornay will follow through on his threats and leave the business."

"But where would he go? This is also his home, is it not?"

"He owns an unentailed property in Hertfordshire that his father gave him. I suppose he could go there." Ambrose frowned. "Although, what he would do with himself as a gentleman farmer I'm not quite sure."

"I cannot quite imagine that," Elizabeth replied.

"I wish he would find another outlet for his talents, though. The pleasure house has started to consume his life, and he doesn't even own shares in it."

"It still belongs to his mother?"

"And to his father. I believe they bought out all the other shareholders several years ago."

"Then one wonders why Mr. Delornay stays."

Ambrose's smile was wry. "That is indeed the question, Elizabeth, and one that I do not have the answer for. I suspect things are coming to a head, though, and that Mr. Delornay will soon have to choose between his need for independence and his devotion to his mother's creation."

6

"I think your ideas are very promising, Christian." His mother clapped her hands and smiled down at him. "Very promising, indeed. And I'm certain that I detect the hand of Mrs. Smith in several of them."

"You would be right, *Maman*. Mrs. Smith proved to be most helpful." Christian poured them both some more coffee and felt himself start to relax for the first time in days.

Helene took her cup, added cream, and sipped at the fragrant brew. "Then you admit that I was right, Christian? You did need some help after all."

Christian clinked his cup against his mother's. "Indeed you were, *Maman*, as always."

Helene's warm laughter meant he had to smile back at her.

"Ah, you are just like your father, *mon cher*. So stubborn."

"And not like you at all."

Helene sighed. "I have been told that I, too, can be stubborn, but I cannot accept it." She leaned forward and placed her hand over her heart. "It is just that I *know* when I am right, and I am quite prepared to fight for it."

Christian hid a smile and finished his coffee. In truth, his parents were equally hotheaded on occasion, a trait he had tried hard to suppress in his own dealings with his family. Controlling his emotions had served him very well.

"I hear you are sharing a bed with Elizabeth Smith."

"That is correct."

Helene nodded, her blue gaze considering. "She is an interesting woman."

Christian glanced up at her. "Speaking of Mrs. Smith, do you think you could find out more about her?"

Helene put down her cup and slid off her perch on the edge of Christian's desk. "I have already made some inquiries on your behalf, although it is difficult to get information out of France since the downfall of that rat Napoléon."

"I appreciate your help, *Maman*. I've never been one to like a mystery."

"Yet you've taken her to your bed."

"Do you object?"

Helene shrugged. "It is not my place to tell you how to conduct your love life."

"Really? You were quick enough to come to me with your concerns last year."

"Because I was afraid for you." Helene hesitated. "Those clubs can be . . . dangerous."

Christian met her worried gaze head-on. "I know that. Why do you think I frequent them?"

"I . . . I could tell you why, but I don't think you would wish to hear what I have to say. And we are getting along so nicely today that I don't want to spoil it."

Christian managed a smile. "Then perhaps we should talk about something else." He gathered up his papers again. "I hear that Lisette and Gabriel are about to travel up north to their property there. Do you plan on visiting them this Christmas?"

"Philip and I are considering it. I believe Marguerite and Anthony will join us after they return from France. I should imagine Lisette would wish you to come too." Helene looked over her shoulder at him. "Would you come with us?"

"And leave this place to run itself?"

"Perhaps Ambrose and Mrs. Smith could manage it without you."

Christian realized his smile was becoming forced. It was always like this with his mother. Somewhere inside him, he resented her for making familial demands on him, demands he still felt she had no right to make considering her long absence from his childhood.

A knock at the door saved him from answering.

"Come in."

The man who entered the room was about his height and age and eerily familiar. Helene made a small choked sound, and Christian moved from behind his desk to stand in front of his mother.

"May I help you?"

The stranger bowed. "I certainly hope so. Am I addressing Mr. Christian Delornay?"

"Indeed you are." Christian indicated his mother, who had recovered her composure and looked as serene as ever. "And this is my mother, Lady Philip Knowles." Despite the fact that it was something of a secret, he deliberately used his mother's full title, anticipating the effect it would have on their unexpected visitor.

"A pleasure, my lady." The man inclined his head a stark inch. "You must be my stepmother. I'm Richard Ross."

Helene studied him, her head angled to one side. "I have no doubt of that. You are the image of your father." She moved past Christian and held out her hand. "It really is a pleasure to finally meet you."

Richard Ross smiled and brought her hand to his lips. "And

it is a pleasure to meet you, too, and to find you are nothing like the woman I had imagined."

Christian raised his eyebrows. "What exactly were you expecting to see—some raddled old whore?"

"Christian!" Helene frowned at him, but Richard seemed unperturbed by Christian's pointed comment.

"Hardly that. Reports of Madame Helene's beauty have reached all over Europe." He gazed at Helene appreciatively. "And obviously were not exaggerated at all."

Christian was used to men ogling his mother, but something about Richard Ross set his hackles rising. He deliberately placed himself between his mother and his half brother and indicated they should all sit down beside the fire.

"Are you looking for Philip, Mr. Ross? I believe he had business with his solicitor this morning."

Richard sat down and crossed one booted foot over the other. "Actually, that's where I found him earlier. He was kind enough to give me the address of this establishment so that I could come and pay my respects to you all."

"Your respects?" Christian sat forward. "Rumor has it that you have never accepted your father's second marriage or the revelation that he already had children. Is that not so?"

Richard sighed. "I must admit that in my youth, I did publicly air my grievances about my father's behavior, but I am older and wiser now." He glanced at Helene. "I was hoping we could settle our differences."

Christian shrugged. "We have no differences to settle with you."

Richard went to speak and then hesitated. "Can we not be friends? I understand that my sister Emily is already welcome here."

"She is welcome in our family home and the kitchens here, but not upstairs," Helene said firmly. "We have great hopes for her social success."

"She is indeed a treasure," Richard said, his smile wider and far more genuine. "I hope to further my acquaintance with her now that I am home for good."

Christian regarded his half brother through narrowed eyes. Despite everything Richard was saying, *he* wasn't convinced the reasons for Richard's return were that simple or that easy. He hadn't failed to notice that Richard was expending all his energy on captivating Helene rather than facing his slightly older and definitely illegitimate brother. Not that Christian blamed him, but he sensed there would have to be an honest exchange of views between them at some point in the future if they were truly to exist in the same family.

Richard rose to his feet. "I'm sure you are both far too busy to sit and chat with me all day. I just wanted to make myself known to you and assure you of my goodwill."

Helene held out her hand, and Richard took it and brought it to his lips. "A pleasure to finally meet you, Madame Helene."

Christian wondered if Helene was about to suggest he might call her *Mother* and realized the notion annoyed him.

Richard finally turned to him and nodded. "A pleasure to make your acquaintance, too, Delornay." Richard paused. "Do you not use the Ross name? My father said that he had legally given you his family name."

"I choose not to advertise the relationship too widely, Mr. Ross."

Christian didn't bother to explain exactly what he meant and waited to see if Richard would have the balls to ask why. His half brother chose to nod as if he perfectly understood Christian's position and walked with Helene out into the hallway.

Christian contemplated joining them and then heard his mother's airy laugh and Richard's answering chuckle. It seemed his mother didn't need his protection after all, and she was, in truth, perfectly capable of defending herself from any man alive.

Christian sat on the edge of his desk and tried to examine his response to Richard's sudden appearance. He felt . . . threatened, and that was nonsensical. He'd always known in the back of his mind that Richard would return one day and reclaim his position as Philip's heir. Bastards, even acknowledged bastards like Christian, were unable to inherit a title, even if their parents later married. He'd always known that and understood it, so why was he feeling so unsettled?

He contemplated the open doorway. Nuns in an orphanage had raised him. Perhaps it would have been better if he'd studied his Bible more carefully. He hadn't expected his mother and father to be quite so welcoming to this particular prodigal son.

As she approached her bedroom, Elizabeth heard voices, which indicated that both Christian and the anticipated modiste were already awaiting her appearance. She straightened her shoulders and fixed a polite smile on her face. Christian was sitting by the fire chatting to an elderly dour-faced woman who seemed remarkably unaffected by his charm.

When he saw her, Christian rose and bowed. "Mrs. Smith, may I make you known to Madame Wallace?"

"A pleasure, madame." Elizabeth curtsied and received a sharp nod in reply. "I am in sore need of some new clothes."

"I can see that."

Madame Wallace's blunt reply in an accent that held little hint of France and much of Northern England made Elizabeth want to laugh.

"I need to take your measurements first, Mrs. Smith, and then create a muslin toile my girls can work from at my establishment." She advanced upon Elizabeth with her tape measure. "You will, however, have to report to my workroom regularly for fittings. I do not usually make house calls."

"I understand, madame," Elizabeth replied as the modiste stepped behind her and began to loosen her gown. Christian settled back into his seat by the fire, his hazel gaze fixed on the gradual reveal of her skin.

"I would like Mrs. Smith to have one of the newer, lighter pairs of stays," Christian stated.

Madame Wallace looked up from her measuring and nodded. "I assumed you would want something more fancy. Using the measurements you sent me yesterday, I've already set my best girl on it."

Elizabeth raised her eyebrows at Christian. "You guessed my size?"

He shrugged, the motion hardly wrinkling the exquisite lines of his coat. "You aren't the first woman I've chosen a wardrobe for."

Elizabeth raised her chin. "I thought we had already discussed this. I was not aware that you were choosing this one."

Madame Wallace made a huffing sound. "I don't care who pays for the clothes as long as you both stop talking and let me do my work."

Elizabeth obediently raised her arms and allowed Madame to remove her stays completely. She was now clad only in her thin shift and the stockings that she had borrowed from Marie-Claude. She stood quietly while Madame made notes in her book and continued to take her measurements, aware all the time of Christian's gaze on her and the anticipation in his narrowed eyes.

Of course he wouldn't be able to leave it be; he was a man, after all. He would have to prove he was the best lover she had ever had and make her climax. He wasn't the first man who had attempted it, and if she had her way, he wouldn't be the last.

Eventually, she and Madame settled into a discussion about the number of gowns she needed, their purpose, and the fabrics and trimmings that would adorn them. Elizabeth found herself enjoying the experience. It had been quite a while since she had worn anything new, let alone ordered so many new garments. Her husband had been remarkably frugal with his money, and his taste had been old-fashioned and veered toward the puritan.

Christian occasionally added his comments, but for the most part he allowed Elizabeth to choose what she liked. Their only disagreement came over the number of gowns he considered necessary, which was far more than Elizabeth calculated she could ever afford.

By the time Madame left with a stern admonishment for Elizabeth to present herself at the modiste's shop in one week, Elizabeth was feeling quite in charity with her employer. She moved across to the bed where Madame had left a simple green muslin gown for her to wear and admired the braided piping on the edge of the bodice.

"Don't bother putting the dress on, Mrs. Smith." She jumped when Christian murmured in her ear. "I'd just have to take it off you again."

His arms came around her waist from behind, bunching the thin muslin of her shift against her skin. She waited, her breathing slow and even as one of his hands eased upward to cup her breast. His thumb settled over her nipple and she sighed. He always surprised her. When she expected him to be demanding, he coaxed a response from her with far greater skill and sensitivity than she wanted.

He lowered his head and his lips brushed her ear and moved downward, sampling her flesh, nipping and biting at her earlobe until she trembled. He tightened his grip around her hips, drawing her against his already-erect cock. She found herself struggling to maintain her composure and deliberately pushed her hips back and rubbed herself against him.

He spun her around, his expression cool. "You do not need

to use whores' tricks on me. Watching you dress and undress for half an hour was quite arousing enough. I don't need any more stimulation and you know it."

Elizabeth glanced down at his pantaloons, which amply displayed the evidence of his lust. She reached forward and ran her finger down the length of his satin-covered shaft.

"I thought you might wish to climax quickly. Most men do."

"And I'm not most men." He stepped away from her. "Don't try and distract me, Mrs. Smith. We are here to seek out your pleasure, not mine."

Elizabeth swallowed hard and smiled into his eyes. "My pleasure is in satisfying you, Mr. Delornay. Is that not enough?"

"We've already had this conversation." He stripped off his coat, cravat, and waistcoat and tossed them over a nearby chair. "My pleasure can only be enhanced by yours. Sit on the edge of the bed."

Elizabeth caught the note of implacability in his request and slowly turned toward the bed. Her heart was beating far too erratically as Christian followed her over, his cool gaze on her body, assessing her, much as she was used to doing with men. She realized she didn't like it, that she wanted to run from the room and hide in a dark corner somewhere until he forgot about her.

"Is something wrong?"

And by all that was holy, he was far too perceptive. In the candlelight his hair gleamed like a wheat field in the sun. His shirt fell open at the neck to reveal the fair hair on his muscled chest. Without his coat, she could plainly see the strength of his legs and tight buttocks. An angel, a devil, she couldn't make up her mind.

Elizabeth forced a smile. "What do you wish of me?"

"Take off your shift."

Although she'd expected the request, she still found it re-

markably difficult to bare her body completely to him—a body
that he'd already seen, caressed, entered . . .

"Touch yourself."

"What?" Elizabeth brought her startled gaze back to his
face.

He shrugged. "If you will not allow a man to bring you to a
climax, perhaps you can manage it for yourself."

"While you watch?"

He smiled. "Are you suggesting that no man has ever
watched you climax before?"

She held his gaze and saw no hint of leniency in his hazel
eyes, only a calm certainty that she would refuse and that he
would be the victor if she did. And she wanted to refuse,
wanted to slap his face and . . . and what? She had nowhere else
to go and she needed money.

She brought her hands up to cup her breasts and pinched her
nipples between her finger and thumb until they were hard
points. Christian continued to watch her, one shoulder against
the upright corner post of the bed, one hand casually unbuttoning his pantaloons. She closed her eyes and allowed her right
hand to drop between her thighs to play with her sex.

Of course she wasn't wet and the friction of her finger only
made it worse, but she pretended all was well.

"Open your eyes and look at me."

She obediently did as she was told and continued to touch
herself, writhing a little more, allowing gasps of "pleasure" to
escape her.

"Oh for God's sake."

Elizabeth froze in place as Christian headed for the door. He
didn't leave as she had anticipated but opened the top drawer of
her bedside table and withdrew a glass bottle. He uncorked the
bottle and returned to her side, bringing the pleasant scent of
flowers with him.

He coated two of his fingers with the oil and knelt in front of her, sliding his fingers in alongside hers, easing her work. She moaned as he lowered his head and licked at her clit, threaded his fingers between hers, and probed her now-slick entrance.

She felt herself grow tense until the ache and the need threatened to overcome her, until she wanted to scream out her frustration. Christian didn't stop, his mouth an incessant presence against her most tender flesh, his fingers driving into her as she ground against him.

She wanted this, oh God she wanted this. She grasped his shoulder, her nails digging into his shirt, desperate to anchor herself against the gathering tension low in her belly.

"Stop, Mr. Delornay, I can't . . ."

With a sob, she shoved him away from her and tried to scramble off the bed. But he was too quick and she was soon under him again, her face pressed into the mattress as she struggled to be free of his weight.

He made no attempt to stop her fighting him, but he refused to let her go. After a while, she gave up and just lay still, awaiting his judgment and his likely contempt. But he said nothing and continued to hold her, one arm locked around her waist, his face buried in the crook of her neck. He was murmuring to her, a litany of soothing, meaningless words in French that made her want to cry.

She realized she had to speak, had to try and regain some control of the situation.

"I'm sorry. I just *can't* . . ."

He remained silent, and she squeezed her eyes tightly shut. She gasped when he moved and rolled her over onto her back. His smile was the last thing she had expected to see.

"Congratulations, Mrs. Smith. I think that's the first honest thing you've ever said to me in bed."

* * *

Christian stared down into Elizabeth's startled gray eyes. At least he hoped she was being honest. One could never be entirely sure with a woman. The scent of the oil drifted up to him, and he realized his cock was still hard and pushing through the confines of his unbuttoned pantaloons. But there were more important things to deal with than a little sexual discomfort.

"In the spirit of continuing our honest discussion, have you ever climaxed?"

She swallowed hard. "I wanted to climax for you."

"So you can make a choice?"

"I thought I could, but it seems I have denied myself for so long that I have lost the ability."

"I doubt that."

She moved restlessly against the sheets, drawing his gaze to the lush curve of her breasts and her tight nipples. "I tried, Christian."

"I know, but I'm not willing to leave it there. I'm sure we will find a way to make you climax again."

She grabbed for his arm. "Please, don't bother."

He smiled at her and closed his fingers around her wrist, repositioning her hand on his cock.

"Perhaps I might ask a favor of you before we discuss this matter more thoroughly."

She bit her lip. "Surely there is nothing more to be said?"

"I'm sure you would prefer it if we didn't speak of it ever again." He shoved down his underthings. "But you will have to indulge me a little further."

She contemplated his cock. "Do you wish to fuck me?"

"As if I would subject you to that after what you have just said."

Despite his words, his shaft jerked at the thought. Her attempt to get away from him had excited him more than she could possibly imagine. But it was not the time to share that unwelcome revelation. At the moment, he was still selfish enough to need relief, relief he would take at his own hand if she balked. He sat back against the headboard, releasing her completely, allowing her to come to him—if she wanted to.

"I would appreciate the pleasure of your talented hands and mouth on me."

She regarded him carefully, her knees now drawn up to her chin, her arms wrapped around them. "And you will be satisfied?"

"For now." He stroked his cock, pulling down the foreskin to expose the sensitive gleaming head where he was already wet. "But I'll give you fair warning. Probably not forever."

7

Elizabeth was sitting in the kitchen drinking her morning cup of coffee and chatting in French with Madame Durand when Ambrose came in with the latest newspapers. As was her custom, Elizabeth immediately went to the back of each paper and checked the personal announcements. She had no idea if the Saint-Brieuc family would attempt to contact her but reckoned the advertisements were the only way they could possibly hope to reach her.

She wanted to write and find out if everything was well, but there was no one left at the château she trusted not to betray her to Armand. She paused, one finger on the tiny print, and stared blindly at the jumble of letters. Were any messages being conveyed to France in these still-troubled times?

"Is everything all right, Elizabeth?"

She looked up to see that Ambrose had taken the seat opposite hers. Would he help her? Could he? But Christian controlled the staff at the pleasure house just as completely as Armand Saint-Brieuc controlled his, albeit with less violence. She shuddered at the thought of confronting Armand again. It might have to be done, but she hoped subterfuge would work instead. When she had enough money, she would employ people to help get her back across the English Channel and break into the château.

"Everything is fine, Ambrose."

He raised an eyebrow. "Pardon my continuing curiosity, but it looks as if you are searching for something in the newspaper. Did you contact your family in England after all?"

Elizabeth sighed and put down the paper. "The trouble with letting my guard down with you, Ambrose, is that now I feel obliged to explain myself."

He chuckled. "That is indeed the price of friendship." His smile died. "Do you believe I would betray you?"

"You work for Mr. Delornay—we both do. I wouldn't feel right confiding in you and then expecting you to keep my secrets from him."

He grimaced. "I see your point." He hesitated. "Are you sure you don't want to tell Mr. Delornay anyway, and then we both can help you?"

"I wish I could," Elizabeth said. "But I fear I will have to keep my secrets and strive to deal with the problem on my own."

Ambrose stood up and bowed. "If you change your mind, you can always ask for my help."

Elizabeth smiled up at him. "I know that and I appreciate it more than I can say." She rose to her feet as well and smoothed out the skirts of her new green gown. It was imperative that they move away from this all-too-painful discussion and concentrate on the here and now.

"I was wondering if you could take me to see the room of desire. Mr. Delornay said it probably needed refurbishing."

Ambrose offered her his arm. "Of course, Elizabeth."

The room was situated at the end of a long hallway on the second floor, right next to the servants' stairway. Ambrose unlocked the door and they both went in. As the door swung shut, darkness engulfed them, and Elizabeth grabbed Ambrose's arm.

"Why aren't the curtains open?"

"They've always remained closed to maintain an air of privacy. Wait a moment and I'll light a candle or two."

Elizabeth reluctantly released her grip on his coat sleeve and tried to get her bearings. She had no idea how large a space she was in. There was no sound from the street or from the rest of the pleasure house.

"There, that's better."

Ambrose returned to her side, a candelabra blazing with light held above his head. Elizabeth realized she was in a small circular space that contained little more than a chair and a card table. At least five doors opened off the space, and all of them were closed, which at least accounted for the silence.

"The guest waits here until someone asks him or her what they desire," Ambrose said.

"And how does anyone know a guest is here?"

"When the main door is opened, a bell rings in Christian's office and in the kitchen. There is another entrance into this room directly off the back stairs."

Elizabeth examined the walls and frowned as her fingertips encountered a thick layer of dust on the wainscoting. "It definitely needs to be cleaned and at least painted."

"I agree." Ambrose opened the nearest door and angled the light through the doorway. "I suspect all the rooms need to be redone as well."

Elizabeth looked past Ambrose. There was nothing of interest in this particular room except a bed, which was not even made up.

"The rooms vary in size. They are all quite plainly decorated, as we tend to bring the necessary props from other rooms in the pleasure house."

"Because you never know what someone will ask for." Elizabeth nodded and walked back toward the door. "Well, we should definitely tell Mr. Delornay about the state of the place. I believe he wishes to start using these rooms as quickly as possible."

"So I understand."

Ambrose blew out the candles and followed Elizabeth out into the main hallway. "Are you still willing to play your part in the sexual games?"

"Of course I am." Elizabeth forced a laugh. Why would Ambrose suddenly ask her that? Surely Christian would not have mentioned to Ambrose what happened between them?

He paused to look down at her. "I only ask because some people would be reluctant to touch a man of color."

Elizabeth stood on tiptoe and kissed him deliberately on the mouth. "Obviously, I am not one of them."

He kissed her back, his lips firm and warm. "Thank you."

She cupped his cheek in a brief caress before continuing on down the stairs, still chatting about the necessary improvements. She proceeded into the kitchen and found Christian ensconced at the table drinking coffee and scowling at the newspaper. Elizabeth gathered her courage and approached him.

"Good morning, Mr. Delornay."

"Good morning, Mrs. Smith." He briefly looked up at her before returning his gaze to the newspaper. Elizabeth took a seat at the table and contemplated his averted profile. It was not often that she got a chance to observe him. He was usually far too aware of her and she of him.

Ambrose poured some coffee for Elizabeth and himself and took up position beside her. "Mr. Delornay, the room of desires needs to be painted, dusted, and cleaned."

"See to it, then. I don't want to leave those rooms idle for much longer."

"I will, sir."

Christian suddenly looked up, his gaze directly on Elizabeth. "Perhaps Mrs. Smith might advise you about the choice of color and furnishings. Expense is no object."

For a moment Elizabeth pondered the idea of double-crossing Mr. Delornay by claiming huge expenses while stealing the money for herself. Unfortunately, she suspected he was an excellent bookkeeper and would spot any discrepancies immediately.

"Mrs. Smith, there is a very calculating look in your eyes."

Elizabeth tried not to look guilty. "Only because you said no expense spared. Every woman dreams of those words."

"And every man," added Ambrose, making Elizabeth laugh out loud.

Christian studied them both and then smiled. "It is nice to see you laughing, Mrs. Smith." He stood up and held out his hand. "May I speak to you in my office?"

Elizabeth followed him out, her stomach filled with dread. Despite his words in front of Ambrose, was Christian planning to dismiss her after all?

She took a seat by the fire and he joined her, his expression pensive.

"I wanted to make sure that you still wish to participate in the sexual games we will be playing in the room of desire."

Elizabeth smiled brightly. She was becoming quite tired of answering this particular question. Did all the men at the pleasure house think she was so fragile? "Of course I will, Mr. Delornay. Why ever would you doubt me?"

He studied her, his hazel eyes skeptical. "Are you absolutely sure?"

"Do you think that just because I can't climax I can't enjoy sex?" Elizabeth asked, a deliberate challenge in her voice.

"Well I wouldn't enjoy sex if I couldn't come."

Elizabeth looked down at her hands and realized she was twisting her fingers together into a knot. "You are the only man who has ever noticed that I fail to climax. I can assure you that no one else will ever know I'm not enjoying myself *immensely.*"

He frowned and she kept speaking. "Mr. Delornay, I need this job and I need the money. Please don't let your soft heart deprive you of my excellent services."

"My soft heart?" He blinked at her. "I've never heard myself described thusly before. I am, however, concerned about you."

"Then, please, don't be. If you no longer wish to bed me, I understand, but don't make a poor business decision because of that."

Christian rose and bowed to her. "I rarely make poor decisions, Mrs. Smith, either in or out of bed. I'll continue to fuck you, and if you insist that you wish to participate in our sexual activities, I'm not going to stop you."

"Thank you." Elizabeth kept smiling as he went to open the door for her. "You will not regret your decision."

His expression clouded. "I hope I won't, Mrs. Smith. You make me feel far too much as it is."

On that cryptic note, he ushered her out of his office and firmly closed the door behind her. For a long moment, Elizabeth stayed where she was, simply allowing her breathing to calm down. She had to stop baiting Mr. Delornay and concentrate on earning her keep. Eventually she headed up to the second floor, where she was due to meet Marie-Claude. Her feet slowed on the stairs. What had Christian meant about her making him feel too much already? She hadn't noticed any outpouring of emotion on his part. All the excessive sentiments had been hers.

Marie-Claude awaited her in the smallest salon, which was closed off to the guests. She was unpacking a large straw-filled crate and beckoned Elizabeth over to view the contents.

"One of our longtime clients, Mr. Peter Howard, has a friend, Mr. Fan, who resides in Southampton and imports interesting artifacts from the Orient. When Mr. Howard is in

Southampton, he always visits Mr. Fan and sends a couple of boxes of unusual items for us to use at the pleasure house."

Elizabeth peered doubtfully at the newspaper-wrapped package. "Unusual in what way?"

Marie-Claude removed the paper to reveal a jade phallus. "The kind of things that most Christian civilizations would consider sinful."

Elizabeth stared at the intricately carved dildo. "Oh."

She settled beside Marie-Claude and began to unwrap one of the packages and found another shorter carved phallus, this time in red stone. As she worked, Elizabeth tried to gather the courage to ask Marie-Claude a question, but years of not confiding in anyone were harder to overcome than she had imagined.

After a while, Marie-Claude glanced up at her. "Is there something wrong? You seem a little quiet. Mr. Delornay is not being his usually impossible self, is he?"

"Mr. Delornay is"—Elizabeth sighed—"being remarkably understanding."

"Now that is something to ponder." Marie-Claude chuckled. "I would be worried too."

Elizabeth looked into Marie-Claude's warm brown eyes. "There is something I would like to ask you."

"Ask me anything you like about that man. I've known him since he arrived here as a sulky, disruptive eighteen-year-old hell-bent on disapproving of everything his mother had created here."

It was tempting to allow Marie-Claude to change the direction of the conversation, but Elizabeth had a sense that if she didn't continue, she'd never find the courage again.

"It's not actually about Mr. Delornay. It's about me."

Marie-Claude took her hand and patted it. "Are you breeding?"

"No, thank God," Elizabeth said. "It's something far more

personal. I don't even know if I can explain it to you. I feel so unnatural."

Marie-Claude squeezed her fingers hard. "Elizabeth, I am almost forty years of age, and I have worked here for half my life. I truly believe that apart from Madame Helene, I have seen more people fucking in more peculiar ways than almost any other woman on Earth. You can tell me anything and I doubt I will be shocked."

Elizabeth stared down at their clasped hands and took a deep breath. "I can't climax anymore."

"Have you ever been able to?"

"When I was first married I could."

"Why did you stop, then?"

"I stopped because I didn't want to climax for the other men my husband introduced into my bed."

"Ah."

"I learned how to pretend. It amused me to see them imagine themselves to be such great lovers."

"And I assume Mr. Delornay wasn't fooled."

Elizabeth swallowed hard. "No, he wasn't."

"Do you want to climax for him?"

Elizabeth thought about that. "No, I want to do it for myself."

Marie-Claude laughed and patted her hand. "That is the answer I was hoping for. There are many ways to help you. In fact, I have one just here."

She sat back and retrieved an unwrapped package from the table. It appeared to be a small silk bag. Marie-Claude held it out to Elizabeth.

"Open it."

Elizabeth loosened the silk ties around the mouth of the bag and tipped the contents out onto her palm. Three metal balls emerged and chimed softly as they rolled together.

"What exactly are they?" Elizabeth asked.

"According to Mr. Fan, they are called 'the celestial globes of passion.' "

"They don't appear to be very passionate, and they look too big to be swallowed. What am I supposed to do with them?"

"You put them inside yourself," Marie-Claude said serenely.

"All of them?"

"All of them. They are supposed to stimulate you and make you more able to climax."

"Why?"

Marie-Claude shrugged. "I have no idea, but I have heard that they work. The other thing you might consider is having Mr. Delornay touch you and make love to you more frequently."

Elizabeth thought about that and shivered not unpleasantly. "I suppose that makes sense. Familiarity might make me worry less about climaxing."

Marie-Claude patted her hand. "Try the celestial globes first and let me know how you find them. Some women cannot get used to the sensation. Others find the stimulation quite exquisite. See if you can make yourself climax if you don't wish to bother Mr. Delornay."

Elizabeth put the chiming globes back into their bag and hid them in the pocket of her skirt. "Thank you, Marie-Claude."

"Thank me if they work. I will think of some other ways to satisfy you as well." She moved back across the crate. "Now come and help me finish the unpacking."

Christian glanced up at the clock in his office and groaned. He was still behind in his work, but he had promised to visit his mother before she left on a visit to Philip's country seat. She would be most displeased if he didn't show up, and he needed all her good will at the moment.

A tap on the door drew his attention, and he got up from his desk to open the door. Marie-Claude stood there, her smile bright.

"Are you going out, sir?"

"I have to be at my mother's house within the next half hour, but I can always spare a moment for you. Is anything wrong?"

Marie-Claude stepped into the room and closed the door firmly behind her.

"Nothing is wrong, but I wanted to offer you some advice about Mrs. Smith."

Christian frowned. "Does she know you are telling tales on her?"

"In this case, she will be glad that I did. Now let me explain what you need to do . . ."

By the time Christian arrived at his parents' town house, he was still mulling over Marie-Claude's explicit instructions about how he should deal with Elizabeth. The thoughts she had inspired in his mind made it difficult for him to contemplate a sedate half hour sitting with his parents. All he wanted to do was turn around, go back to the pleasure house, and strip Mrs. Smith naked.

He forced that salacious image away and managed to smile at Philip's butler.

"Good afternoon, Sutton. Are they home?"

"Her ladyship is upstairs packing, and his lordship is in his study." Sutton let Christian through the door. "I will let her ladyship know that you have arrived."

"Thank you. I'll take myself to the study."

As Christian approached Philip's study, he heard the rising murmur of angry voices, a sound that he remembered very well from his own more brattish, wilder days. For a second, he contemplated being the better son and retreating to the drawing room to wait for his mother, but he'd never been that well behaved.

He barely bothered to knock and kept on walking straight into the study where Philip stood confronting Richard over his desk.

"Good afternoon, Philip, Mr. Ross."

Richard answered him without taking his gaze from their father. "You may call me Richard. We *are* family, as my father has just been reminding me."

"Christian," Philip said tightly. "Perhaps you might care to join your mother until Richard and I have finished our conversation."

"And miss this?" Christian took a seat by the fire and glanced expectantly at his father. "It reminds me of the old days."

Richard raised his eyebrows. "You fought with my father too?"

"He abandoned me, my sisters, and my mother for eighteen years. Of course I fought with him."

Richard frowned. "He didn't exactly abandon you. As far as I understand it, he didn't know you existed."

Christian crossed one leg over the other. "He didn't want to know. Any man who beds a woman must surely realize the risks."

"Christian, this is not helpful," Philip snapped.

"I didn't intend it to be. I'm just sharing a few truths with my newly returned half brother. How can you object to that? I can't imagine what he has to argue with you about, though."

"Surely that is none of your concern?" Richard asked.

Christian met his gaze. "Didn't you just say that we were family, Richard? Don't families share their problems?"

"Very well, then. Our esteemed father has been telling me what an excellent son you are. His intention, of course, is to make me ashamed of my lack of filial duty."

"That is not the case. I—" Philip said.

Richard continued speaking. "I am sick and tired of hearing what a paragon you are, Mr. Delornay."

"Me? You are sadly mistaken." Christian started to laugh. "I almost drove Philip into an early grave when he first married my mother."

"And yet you took on the challenge of the pleasure house and have settled down."

"Have I?" Christian glanced at Philip, who was standing quite still, his expression grim. "Perhaps you should talk to my mother about that before you make such pronouncements, Philip."

He rose and nodded to both men. "And now I really must go and make my bow to my mother. Perhaps you and Father will join us when you are ready?"

He sauntered back out into the hall, his smile disappearing as he headed toward the drawing room. How ironic that Philip was holding him up as an example to Richard when he'd always known that Richard had his father's heart.

His mother was already dressed for traveling in a dark green pelisse and sat by the fire deep in thought. Christian went over to kiss her hand.

"Are you all ready for your trip? Is Philip excited about showing Richard his new inheritance?"

Helene sighed. "Richard insists that he doesn't wish to accompany us, and Philip is not very happy with him."

Christian sat beside his mother. "I gathered that. They appear to be having a frank exchange of views in the study."

"Oh, dear," Helene said. "I hoped Philip would allow Richard more time to adjust himself to London life and to his family, not start lecturing him about his new responsibilities within a few days of his arrival."

"Apparently Philip is telling Richard he should be more like me, which is quite amusing."

Helene raised her eyebrows. "Why is it amusing? You have proved your worth a thousand times over."

"That is very kind of you, *Maman,* but I have no choice but to earn a living. Richard, on the other hand, has a perfect right to swan around society and live off the sweat and rents of his father's tenants."

"Philip doesn't want that."

"Why not?"

"You'll have to ask him."

Christian grimaced; sometimes his mother's loyalty to Philip still annoyed him. He heard Richard's voice in the hallway and nodded at the doorway. "It seems as if they have finished arguing—for now at least."

He smiled as Philip came through the door. "Ah, there you are, Father. Are you looking forward to the peace of the countryside?"

Philip glared at him. "Actually I am. Sometimes my children still have the capacity to disappoint me."

"Are you talking about Richard or me?"

Philip sat down opposite Helene. "I believe I'm referring to both of you."

"I thought I was a paragon."

"Hardly that." Philip gestured at Richard. "Ring the bell and then take a seat. You might as well join in the conversation."

Richard complied. "I intend to. I'm finding this whole family togetherness quite fascinating."

"We do tend to be a little frank," Christian noted. "We find it clears the air."

"I'd noticed that."

Richard sat back as the butler brought in a tea tray and a selection of cakes and placed them on a small table between them. Without asking for their preferences, Helene began to dispense tea. Christian would have preferred a brandy, but the look on his mother's face was enough to dissuade him from making that mistake.

Richard accepted his tea with far better grace than Christian and sipped at it without even a grimace. Eventually he turned to Christian.

"It has been quite a while since I have visited London. Perhaps I might ask your advice as to the latest pleasures to be found here."

"What kind of pleasures do you have in mind?" Christian inquired, all too aware that Philip was struggling to keep his temper. "There are so many."

"As I have already offered to show you around town, Richard," Philip said shortly, "I'm not quite sure why you are asking Christian."

Helene patted his hand. "Christian and Richard are of a similar age, and their interests may well be more compatible."

"Christian's interests are hardly likely to attract Richard," Philip snapped.

Christian felt himself bristle. "How do you know? We are both your sons. We might share more than you think."

Richard met his gaze and nodded. For one moment it seemed that they were united against a common enemy—their poor father.

"That is true."

Christian put down his cup. "If you like, we can go to my club and discuss the matter further." He kissed his mother on the cheek and bowed to Philip. "Have a good trip. I'll keep Richard entertained."

"I'm sure you will." Philip didn't look any happier. "We'll see you in a week."

"I'll try not to ruin either the business or my brother's reputation before I see you again." Christian winked at his mother, who didn't smile.

He nodded at Richard, who had also risen and was busy

kissing Helene's hand. "If you don't mind the cold, we can walk to my club from here."

It took less than half an hour for Christian to find himself sitting opposite Richard in the quiet confines of his club. There were very few people about, but those who saw them tended to look quite hard at his half brother, as if trying to make the connection between them. Some even stopped to make conversation or ask for an introduction, which Christian was quite happy to give them.

As yet another acquaintance wandered off, Richard caught his eye.

"Are we creating gossip?"

Christian shrugged. "I'm used to it. My family has been a source of constant excitement to the *ton* for years."

"Which is why I went abroad in the first place." Richard grimaced.

"Because of us?"

"Partly, but even before that scandal emerged, there were some unpleasant rumors flying around about my father's treatment of my mother."

"I must confess that I know very little about your mother. It is not a subject that comes up very often."

"Of course not. That's because my father is probably too ashamed of his behavior to speak of it."

Christian frowned. "If you are suggesting that my mother had anything to do with your mother's unhappiness, I'll not take it well. As far as I understand it, your mother was dead before my parents met again, and *that* was purely a matter of chance."

Richard studied him over the rim of his glass. "I'm not suggesting your mother seduced him away from mine."

"I'm glad to hear it."

"But you have to understand that I grew up with a mother

who seemed permanently unhappy and unwell." Richard paused. "And it wasn't difficult to see why she was like that. Whenever my father was near her, she became far worse."

"So you believe the rumors that he perhaps caused her death?"

"Believe them? My mother told me herself that he was killing her."

Christian stared at Richard. "And you believed her?"

"I . . . used to but then as I grew older, I realized I had never really asked my father for his side of the story and that perhaps I had been unjust to him."

"What brought that about?"

"My change of heart?" Richard's smile was just like Philip's at his most sardonic. "I started corresponding with Emily, and even though she is younger than I am, she reminded me that our father was not always the villain I had painted him."

"And so you came back."

"I did. Only to find that my father seems disinclined to talk to me about anything apart from my new responsibilities and how perfect my half siblings are."

Christian stared at Richard and debated how far he wished to involve himself in family politics. He'd always tried to keep away from the emotions, preferring to stir things up and cause problems rather than solve them, but for some reason he was feeling a strange urge to defend his father.

"If I may be so bold, Philip has missed you immensely. I think if you stay in London, he will begin to trust you again."

"I'm not so sure about that." Richard glanced away from Christian. "I fear I have left it too late."

"Oh, no. Remember that Lisette and I have an immense capacity to disrupt Philip's peace of mind. One of us will undoubtedly do something to incur his wrath soon, and you will be back in favor."

Richard smiled. "I do intend to stay. I've grown weary of wandering."

"Then remain in London, visit your inheritance with Philip, and learn the things you will need to know to become an accomplished peer of the realm." Christian raised his glass to his half brother. "I wish you all the luck in the world."

"You don't wish it was you?"

Christian felt as if he had been avoiding that particular question his whole life, but Richard of all people had a right to know the truth. "You'll probably not believe me, but I think you have to be born into such a duty." He shuddered. "The thought of all those obligations horrifies me."

Richard looked unconvinced, but Christian knew that was exactly why Richard was the right man for the job and he was not. He signaled to the waiter to bring them another brandy.

"You might care to consider making this your club, unless you wish Philip to sponsor you into his?"

Richard shuddered. "That will have to happen eventually, but I'd prefer to put it off for a while. Do you have any influence with the principals of this place?"

"As it happens, I do." Christian had already noticed another gentleman hovering at his elbow. "Good morning, Lord Ralston."

"Ah, good morning, Mr. Delornay." Lord Ralston's interested gaze slid toward Richard, who looked resigned.

Christian made the introductions. "May I present you to Mr. Richard Ross, my lord? He is my half brother and heir to all my father's titles and wealth."

"Oh, I . . . I say," Lord Ralston stuttered. "A pleasure, what?"

"Actually, Ralston, I would ask a favor of you," Christian continued. "My half brother would like to be considered for membership of this club. As one of the founding members, would you be willing to propose him for admittance if I second the motion?"

"Absolutely happy to oblige you, Mr. Delornay." Ralston nodded at them both. "Shall we go and see to the paperwork?"

Christian rose from his seat. "Stay and finish your brandy, Richard, while Lord Ralston and I work out the finer details. I'll be back in a moment."

"Don't worry, I'll stay put," Richard replied, his amused gaze on Christian. "I'll keep myself busy counting my titles and wealth."

Christian fought a smile as he followed Ralston to the rear of the house where the offices were situated. Despite his misgivings, it appeared as if Richard might be a worthy addition to the Delornay-Ross menagerie. He certainly had a sense of humor, and that was a necessity.

It took but a few moments to alert the club secretary to Lord Ralston's request and to fill out the nomination form that would be put before the committee on the last day of the month.

As they left the secretary's office, Ralston swung around and blocked Christian's path.

"There is something I wish to ask you."

"What is it, my lord?"

Christian waited, his gaze fixed on the other man's face.

"Are you coming back to the Demon Club soon?"

"I'm not sure. Why do you ask?"

Ralston swallowed hard and then looked down at the floor. "I . . . miss seeing you there."

A snake of lust unfurled itself deep in Christian's gut, and he pushed Ralston up against the wall. "I'm sure there are plenty of others who can take care of your needs."

"No one like you, Mr. Delornay." Ralston grabbed Christian's hand and brought it to his groin. "Even thinking about watching you makes me hard."

Christian squeezed Ralston's cock until he groaned and then let go. "I'll think about it, Ralston."

"Thank you, sir," Ralston gasped.

Christian turned on his heel and went back to find Richard. His cock was half-erect now, and he was more eager than ever to get back to Mrs. Smith. What would she think if she'd just seen him? Would she think him a sadistic bully, or would she offer him her usual bland smile and not care at all? He hadn't even fucked Ralston. Sometimes he wished it were as simple as that, but the reality was far more complex.

He rejoined Richard with a smile and indicated that they should leave. Outside, it had just started to rain, and he hailed a hackney cab.

"Let's go back to the pleasure house. I wish to introduce you to Marie-Claude. She will make sure that you are offered everything a man could desire."

8

"Mr. Delornay asks if you will do him the pleasure of meeting him in his bedchamber."

"He has returned from his parents' house?" Elizabeth paused on the stairs and looked back at Ambrose. "I thought I was supposed to be making myself pleasant on the second level this evening."

"Apparently your plans have changed." Ambrose smiled at her. "Don't worry. Marie-Claude has offered to take your shift. I believe she is about to show Mr. Ross around the pleasure house, and she is quite excited about it."

"Mr. Ross?"

"Mr. Delornay's half brother, Richard."

Elizabeth nodded. "Ah, Emily's brother."

"That's right. He has returned to London and seems determined to make all well with the Delornay branch of the family."

"There was friction in the past?"

Ambrose gave an exaggerated shudder. "Ask Mr. Delornay to tell you about it. It is a long story."

"I will."

Not that she intended to stay long enough to ask Mr. Delornay anything of a personal nature. Elizabeth resumed her ascent and walked back to the private apartments. She always liked letting herself through the locked door into the quieter areas of the house. She felt like an actor who was finally able to shed her stage persona and be herself. But she couldn't let down her guard completely. She still had her secrets, and there was always Christian to contend with.

She knocked on the door to his suite and waited until he asked her to enter. He sat by the fire reading a book, his coat and waistcoat discarded, his fair hair damp from either the rain or a recent bath. Elizabeth walked over to him and inhaled his warm scent. A bath, then, and he hadn't bothered to get dressed because he was expecting her company.

"Good evening, Mr. Delornay."

She curtsied and he looked up, his appreciative gaze taking in her cream gown with the low bodice edged with seed pearls.

"Good evening, Mrs. Smith. You look very fine in that gown."

"Thank you." She smiled and waited to see what he wanted her to do next.

"I have decided that if you are to pretend to be lovers in the room of desires, you need to become more familiar with Paul and Ambrose." He angled his head to one side to study her more closely. "Does that offend you?"

"Not at all, Mr. Delornay. In truth, I think it is a good idea."

"Then I shall be asking them to join us." Christian stood and moved behind Elizabeth to start unlacing her gown. His businesslike tone was surprisingly reassuring. "Unfortunately, they can't stay all night, as we have a business to run, but I've asked them to make time for us in their schedules."

"Paul doesn't work here."

His chuckle stirred the soft curls at the back of her neck.

"He might as well. I treat him like an employee more often than not these days, and he seems to thrive on it."

He continued to undress her until she was quite naked and then took her hand and led her over to his bed. Before she could scramble up, he picked her up and tossed her into the center of the bed and came after her. His gaze wandered over her body and her nipples hardened.

He made an appreciative sound and bent his head to lick one taut peak, nipping and nuzzling until she squirmed. He didn't stop, his fingers busy on her other nipple, pinching and shaping it until she was panting at the extreme sensations. His fingers slid over her hip and inward to her sex, and he cupped her mound in his palm. She wondered if he could detect the orbs of pleasure she had inside her, and what he would do when he discovered them.

He returned his mouth to hers and began kissing her, his chest rubbing against her tight nipples, his hand still resting possessively between her legs. He kissed like a god, and Elizabeth found herself lifting her hips against the pressure of his hand, as if seeking her pleasure.

"Wait," he murmured, moving off her and reaching behind him. Elizabeth lay still until he came over her again. "Have you ever tried these?"

He showed her two small jewel-like objects and she shook her head. "What are they?"

He pinched her nipple hard, making her jump. "They go here."

Elizabeth licked her lips. "Won't they hurt?"

"That depends."

She narrowed her gaze at him. "What exactly does that mean?"

He regarded her steadily, one hand cupping her breast. "I believe it will enhance your pleasure. Do you trust me?"

"I don't trust anyone."

He smiled at that. "And if I insisted?"

A lick of excitement curled through Elizabeth's stomach, and she saw him respond to it, his hand tightening on her breast. "I am yours to command, Mr. Delornay. You know that."

"Good," he said, and bent his head to suck her nipple into his mouth. She caught her breath as he used his teeth on her, and she writhed against him.

"Now." He lifted his mouth and caught her nipple between his finger and thumb, elongating it until she whimpered. He fitted the jeweled clamp and slowly tightened it, watching her face, reacting to every shiver of pleasure and pain that she couldn't control.

"Don't hold your breath," he commanded. "Breathe out slowly."

She struggled to obey him as he prepared her to receive the other clamp. The strange tightening pressure made her feel restless, and a taut heat gathered low in her stomach.

"Breathe, Elizabeth. Stop fighting it."

He licked her trapped nipple, and the shock of it made her gasp. He murmured her name and kissed her between her breasts before heading lower to her sex. She lay still and bit her lip as her heart beat so rapidly she thought she might pass out.

The first touch of his tongue on her clit made her moan his name. His second made her arch upward toward his mouth. His teeth grazed her thigh, and she reached down to slide her fingers into his hair, desperate for some anchor against all the unfamiliar assaults on her body. His finger slid inside her and she tensed.

A second later he looked up at her, his beautiful, sensual mouth wet with her juices. "What do you have in here?"

His finger probed more deeply, and she heard the faint chiming sound of the balls rubbing against each other.

"Marie-Claude gave them to me."

"You asked her advice?"

"Yes. Why do you sound so surprised?"

His smile was wry. "Because you don't exactly share much of yourself with anyone, do you?"

"I share my body with you."

"But not yourself."

She held his gaze. "I thought we agreed our affair would be about the physical and not the emotional. That's why I talked to Marie-Claude about my *physical* limitations."

He stared at her. "Neither of us is willing to trust anyone, are we?" He looked down at her sex and licked his lips. "Now where was I?"

Elizabeth closed her eyes, glad of her reprieve. She hated it when he held her to account. He really was the most difficult man she had ever bedded. His tongue circled her clit, and she forgot about thinking and concentrated on what he was doing to her instead. She gasped when he slid his finger back inside her, and she felt him stirring the globes around, creating the most unexpected sensations in her sex.

As he continued to torment her with his mouth and fingers, she grabbed his shoulder and held on, her nails digging into his flesh. Didn't he understand by now that she was unlikely to climax?

A knock at the door made her jump and made Christian lift his head.

"Come in."

Paul appeared, his smile widening as he took in their positions on the bed.

"Good evening, Mrs. Smith, Mr. Delornay. How can I help you?"

"Come and sit on the bed, Paul. I want you to lick her breasts while I use my mouth on her sex."

Christian sat up and took off his shirt, leaving his breeches unbuttoned but still on. He gazed down at Elizabeth's flushed face, and his cock kicked against the confines of his underclothes. She looked beautiful with her hair spread out on the pillows, although he still wanted to banish the anxiety from her eyes.

"A pleasure." Paul bowed and started on the buttons of his coat. "Do you want me to undress fully or just down to my pantaloons?"

"Down to your pantaloons."

Christian glanced back at Elizabeth, but she didn't seem overly alarmed, her body still tense under his, her alluring scent making him want to forget Paul and the lessons and just fuck her the way he wanted to. He'd sensed her response to his commands and the pain-pleasure of the clamps, and he wanted to explore her needs, to give her exactly what he increasingly suspected she needed.

"Kneel on her left side and be very gentle. I don't want her to come yet."

He caught Elizabeth's startled expression and wondered whether she thought he'd told Ambrose and Paul about her inability to climax. He wasn't quite that much of a bastard, and if he was honest, he wanted to claim that victory solely for himself.

Paul climbed up on the bed, smiled at Elizabeth, and kissed her gently on the mouth.

"Mrs. Smith, an honor."

Before Christian lowered his head to Elizabeth's sex, he watched as Paul began to delicately lick his way around Elizabeth's breast, heading for her clamped nipple. His own cock thickened at the sight of Paul's tongue, and he cupped his shaft and balls, thinking of all the exciting permutations of having more than one willing body in his bed.

He slid two fingers into Elizabeth and played with the orbs, sliding them over his fingers and against her flesh. Her clit was already a hard, hot bud against his tongue. He wanted to bite her, but that would never do at this point in time.

With a sigh, he pulled his mouth away from her luscious flesh. Keeping his fingers embedded inside her, he watched Paul's exploration of her breasts and the way Elizabeth responded to their dual caresses.

He kissed her mouth and murmured, "Did your husband let two men have you at once like this?"

"No," she whispered. "He would not permit—" She gasped as he kissed her again, harder now, cutting off her words.

He took her clenched fist and brought it to his mouth to kiss. "I want you to kneel and suck Paul's cock."

Paul sat back and Christian moved behind Elizabeth, giving her space to kneel in front of Paul. He waited as she carefully released Paul's cock from his pantaloons.

"Now suck him."

He knelt behind her, his erect shaft wedged against her soft buttocks, one hand cupping her left breast, the other between her legs. While she sucked, he just played with her, gentle strokes and touches designed to build anticipation, to make her ache and become ready for the full penetration of his cock.

She pushed back at him with her hips, and he wondered again whether Marie-Claude's suggestion that more than one man touching her at a time would stop her focusing too much on climaxing and set her free. The desire to fuck her intensified and he knew he would have to do something.

He reached over to get some oil and applied it liberally to his fingers before sliding two of them deep into Elizabeth's arse. With his other hand, he could feel the orbs in her cunt and massaged them as he widened her for his cock. Paul was groaning now, his hips slamming into Elizabeth's mouth as she took every inch of his shaft.

"Don't come yet, Paul," Christian said. "And, Elizabeth, I want you to release his cock."

"What next?" Paul asked breathlessly, and raised an eyebrow at Christian.

"Sit with your back to the headboard." Paul complied and Christian slathered some of the oil onto Paul's erect shaft, making Paul groan. "Now slide your cock into Elizabeth's arse." He glanced at Elizabeth. "You've had a man like this before, haven't you?"

"Yes," she whispered.

While Christian watched, Paul drew Elizabeth back against him and, holding the base of his shaft with one hand, gradually eased her down over him. Both of them gasped as she settled against him, his thighs bracketing hers, his hands around her hips.

Christian crawled in front of them and pushed Elizabeth's knees even wider so that he could see where Paul filled her arse and the delights of her wet and swollen sex. The urge to just slam himself into her resurfaced and he fought it down.

Instead he fingered her swollen bud, marveling at how hard it was, intent on making her even needier. He reached over to the bedside table, picked up another jeweled clamp, and showed it to Elizabeth.

"This one goes on your clit."

Elizabeth's startled gray eyes met his, and he wanted to smile. Her composure was definitely disturbed, if not quite shattered yet. And he wanted her to shatter; he wanted that more than anything. He fixed the clamp and gradually tightened it, watched her gaze cloud with lust and something more visceral that tightened his balls and made him want to loose the devil that lurked inside him.

"Paul, cup her breasts and play with them," Christian murmured as he bent to lick her clit and felt her shudder and try to move away from him. But surely she must know there was no escape with Paul behind her impaling her on his cock and Christian ready to do the same to her cunt?

He worked her sex and then gently hooked a finger around the orbs inside her and drew all three of them out.

"I'd like to fuck you with these still in there, but that can wait until another time. Two cocks at once are enough excitement for tonight."

Her gray eyes widened, but she made no attempt to speak. Christian took off his pantaloons and underthings, releasing his aching cock. He was wet and as hard as iron. He ran a hand over his flesh, pulling the foreskin back to reveal the thick, swollen crown.

Paul sighed. "Let me lick you, Christian. Just for a moment."

Christian glanced at Elizabeth. "Would you object if he tasted me?"

She shook her head, and he smiled before moving to her right. "Paul, you can lick me and fuck Elizabeth at the same time."

Paul responded with a groan and began to lift Elizabeth up and down over his shaft. Christian held his cock ready, and Paul closed his lips around the crown and sucked him. Christian knew he wouldn't last long and soon pulled free and knelt between Elizabeth's thighs again.

He was beyond being careful now and pushed himself deep and hard into Elizabeth, loving her gasp and Paul's as he slid inward, aware of both Paul's pumping cock and Elizabeth's tightness. He took over the fast rhythm, making Paul follow his thrusts in counterpart. He slid his hand between their bodies, found Elizabeth's clit, and pushed hard with his thumb. He wanted to roar in triumph as she screamed his name, and he felt her cunt tighten around him like a vise and continue to pulse. Then he forgot anything else except the force of his own climax and the fact that Paul was joining them.

When he could finally breathe again, he realized he was slumped over both Elizabeth and Paul. He eased himself out of Elizabeth and drew her off Paul. She immediately curled up on the sheets away from them.

Paul whistled and grinned at Christian. "Thank you both. I should really be getting back downstairs. Shall I send Ambrose up?"

Keeping his gaze half on Elizabeth, Christian managed to smile at Paul. "Thank you, yes, but tell him not to come right away."

Paul dropped a kiss on Elizabeth's shoulder and climbed off the bed, pausing only to pick up his discarded clothes.

Elizabeth kept her face pressed into the pillows as Paul departed. She felt . . . How did she feel? Manipulated? She wasn't sure if that was the right word. Having two men to deal with had definitely prevented her from obsessing over whether she could climax or not.

"Elizabeth."

She tensed as Christian touched her ankle. In an instant, he rolled her onto her back and straddled her, leaving her with no escape.

"Are you all right?"

She licked her lips and stared up into his eyes. There were signs of triumph there, along with the remains of satisfied lust. Anger coiled low in her gut and only seemed to intensify the currents of desire that still shuddered through her sex.

"Am I supposed to thank you now?" To her relief, she sounded a lot less shaken than she felt.

"Thank me for what?"

"For making me climax."

He studied her for a long moment. "Didn't you enjoy it?"

"I . . ." She stopped speaking and just glared at him.

His smile made her want to slap his beautiful face. "I hope you did, because I'm going to do it again."

His mouth descended over hers and he kissed her, his tongue deep and possessive, his long fingers already touching her aching breasts and relighting the embers of her passion. His cock sought entrance to her wet and swollen sex, but he didn't push himself deep, just teased her with the thick crown until she wanted to scream at him to either finish it or stop.

Her gaze flew to his face, and she found he was watching her intently, almost as if he could read her thoughts. Her frustration boiled over and she reached between them to grab his shaft. His reaction was too quick and he pulled away, grabbing her wrist. She tried to wrench her hand away, but he held it fast.

"No whores' tricks, Mrs. Smith."

"Let me go."

"Why? You were going to interfere with my lovemaking."

She twisted her hand in his grasp until she could dig her nails into his flesh and he winced.

"Don't do that."

"Then let me go!"

"Only if you promise to behave yourself."

She glared up at him. "What do you want me to do? Lie still and let you huff and puff over me?"

"I'm not an old man like your husband, and of course I don't expect you to lie still." His grip tightened. "I expect you to participate fully." His gaze slid over her body. "But I don't appreciate it when you seek to control me."

Sudden rage filled her and she kicked out, only to find herself flattened beneath him once more.

"Stop it, Elizabeth."

She struggled to gain control of her anger and finally succeeded. "You said I could participate. I am sorry if I displeased you."

He sighed. "Oh for God's sake, we're back to that, are we?"

"To what, sir?"

"To the role of dutiful, unshockable doormat."

She closed her eyes against the bite of his words. "What do you want from me?"

"I want . . ." He moved off her. "Let me take those clamps off you. They must be hurting."

"I thought that was the idea," Elizabeth forced herself to reply.

He looked down at her. "There are many ways of hurting someone, but pain can also be very pleasurable." He carefully unscrewed the clamp on her clit. "You should understand that now." He kissed her mound and moved to examine her breasts.

"Ah . . ." She sucked in her breath as he cupped her breast and released her right nipple from the restraint. He bent his head and drew her breast into his mouth, his tongue a wet, warm bath against the heat of her aching nipple. She shivered as he quickly dispensed with the other clamp and then drew her into his arms and held her tight against his shoulder.

She couldn't stop shuddering, and he seemed to know that, drawing the covers up over them and just continuing to hold her. She found herself cuddling into his warm, muscular body, her mouth pressed against his chest, his fingers tangled in her hair. How long had it been since someone had held her after sex? Or simply held her?

"It's all right. You will be fine."

Tears pricked at her eyelids. What did he know about anything? She'd given him the last thing she had—her pleasure. Couldn't he see that meant she'd learned nothing? She knew him well enough by now to understand he wouldn't be content with a single victory, that he would expect—no, *demand*—that she came for him as often as he wanted.

After a long while, she managed to pull away from him and smile. He smiled back but there was a watchfulness about his gaze that didn't bode well.

"Are you feeling better now, Elizabeth?" he asked.

"Never better, sir." Elizabeth sat up and looked brightly toward the door. "Aren't we expecting Ambrose?"

9

In a futile effort to get more comfortable, Elizabeth shifted her position on the hard wooden bench. Apparently being penetrated simultaneously by two men meant one would suffer the next morning. Not that she regretted the occasion. It had been surprisingly erotic in its way.

After she'd expressed her feigned interest in bedding Ambrose, Christian had abruptly picked her up and dumped her back in her own bedroom. He'd told her very politely that Ambrose would be quite happy to wait for another night. Elizabeth sighed. He'd sounded civil but she knew he wasn't happy with her at all.

She picked up the first of the newspapers and turned her attention to the personal advertisements. Apart from Madame Durand, the kitchen was almost deserted at this early hour. She was glad of that. Christian Delornay was far too formidable to face before she had come to terms with her surprising reactions to the events of the previous evening.

She started reading through the columns of announcements of births, marriages, and deaths followed by society gossip and social events. Christian had made her angry, and that was unacceptable. Elizabeth raised her head and stared at the kitchen door. She'd decided years ago that there was no point in anger. Why couldn't he be like all the other men she'd encountered and be happy for her to be a mute, smiling doll?

Her gaze caught on her first name. She held her breath and placed her trembling finger under the two lines of text and read the message through twice.

Who was RR? She desperately tried to think of anyone she knew with those initials and could recall no one. But did it matter? She had no real choice. Whatever the dangers, and she was well aware that it was probably a trap, she would have to meet with this person.

She carefully refolded the paper and put it back in the middle of the pile. Her possessions . . . what an odd way of putting it.

"Good morning, Elizabeth."

She looked up to see Christian coming through the door and tried to compose herself. He was dressed immaculately in dark gray and, unlike her, looked as if he had slept well.

His faint smile died. "What's wrong?"

"Nothing is wrong, sir. I'm just contemplating all the things I need to accomplish today."

He walked over to the stove, nodded to Madame Durand, and helped himself to coffee. "I wish you wouldn't lie to me, Mrs. Smith."

She forced herself to hold his gaze. "If you really want to know, I am a little sore!" she hissed.

"I'm not surprised." His half-smile didn't comfort her. "And you're not embarrassed to see me at all?"

"Why would I be embarrassed, sir?"

He contemplated her over the rim of his coffee until she feared she might be blushing and then sat down at the table. "Because you like to portray a certain image and I undermine you. Naturally you don't like it." He cradled his earthenware mug in his hands. "I wouldn't like it either."

"When have I ever succeeded in undermining you?"

His enchanting smile flashed out. "You'd be surprised, Mrs. Smith. You inspire certain . . . emotions in me that I thought to expunge from my memories."

Elizabeth clasped her hands to her bosom. "Are you suggesting that you are in *love* with me, Mr. Delornay?"

His warm laughter flowed over her, and she couldn't help but smile back. Pleased that she had diverted his attention away from her, she curtsied and hurried toward the door.

"I must speak to Marie-Claude. I will see you later, Mr. Delornay."

He half rose and she fled the kitchen before she said anything to make matters worse.

Christian's smile died as he finished his coffee.

"Madame Durand, what was Mrs. Smith doing just before I came in?"

Madame didn't bother to turn around and speak to him directly but continued stirring her pots. "She was reading the newspaper, Mr. Delornay."

"Thank you."

Christian stared at the pile of newspapers on the table. Was Elizabeth simply keeping up with current events, or was her purpose more complicated?

"Good morning, Mr. Delornay."

He looked up to find Ambrose smiling down at him.

"Good morning." Christian drew the stack of newspapers toward him. "Does Mrs. Smith always read the papers in the morning?"

Ambrose sighed. "Yes, she does."

"Would you say that she looks for anything in particular?"

"Yes, I would, and before you ask, she wouldn't tell me

what she was looking for, because she didn't trust me not to tell you."

"That doesn't surprise me at all." Even though Ambrose wasn't revealing anything unexpected, Christian still didn't like it.

"I assured her that we could help, but she didn't believe me."

"I don't think Mrs. Smith is the trusting kind, do you?"

Ambrose sat down and smoothed a hand over his short hair. "Considering that she ended up on the streets, she has no reason to trust anyone, does she?"

"You trust me."

"But it took me several years to do so." Ambrose separated out the papers and handed half to Christian. "She only reads the announcements and advertisements."

Christian turned the first newspaper over and began scanning the tightly printed text. Madame Durand placed a plate of eggs, ham, and a croissant at his elbow and he thanked her before resuming his search.

After a while, Ambrose cleared his throat. "This might be it: 'Elizabeth S-B lately of France. Re your possessions. Contact the above office, yours RR.' "

He looked up at Christian. "It certainly sounds promising. I wonder what the *S-B* stands for?"

"Certainly not *Smith*." Christian took the proffered newspaper and read the message again. "The question is, what do we do about it? Do we wait and see if Mrs. Smith asks for our help, or do we take that decision out of her hands and simply follow her when she visits the newspaper offices?"

"You think she'll go, then?"

"If she's been obsessively reading the papers ever since she arrived here, of course she'll go." Christian frowned. "I wonder what possessions are being referred to. Perhaps it is a well-wisher who has retrieved her belongings from France and wants to pass them on to her."

Even as he said it, he didn't like the thought of someone else stepping in to help Elizabeth. He wanted her to ask for *his* help and confide in him. And when exactly had that happened? When had he started feeling so possessive about another human being? He was famous for his detachment from his lovers.

He tossed the newspaper back onto the table. "I'll leave you to handle the details, Ambrose. If she does confide in you, I'd appreciate it if you tell me what she says."

Ambrose carefully refolded the newspaper and slid it back into the pile. "I doubt she'll tell me anything. But if she does, she already knows I'll share that information with you. I made that quite clear."

For some reason that didn't make Christian feel any better. He got up and Ambrose rose as well.

"I'll be out this afternoon," Christian said.

"Then I'll let you know of any developments when you return," Ambrose replied. He followed Christian back to his office. "In the meantime, I must find Mrs. Smith and consult with her about the finishing touches for the room of desires."

"Is it nearly done, then?" Christian asked, unreasonably glad for the change of subject.

"It is, and I think you will be very pleased with it."

"Excellent." Christian headed for his desk and paused, his back to Ambrose. "And if you and Mrs. Smith wish to *experiment* in the new setting, that would be helpful."

"Are you suggesting I fuck her?" Ambrose asked quietly.

Christian sat down and faced his friend. "That was the idea, wasn't it?"

"Without you being there?"

Christian shrugged. "My presence isn't necessary. You just need to become accustomed to each other."

Ambrose just looked at him, and Christian raised his eyebrows. "What is it?"

"You are her lover. Paul and I are just . . . acting."

"I'm not sure what you are implying."

Ambrose leaned against the door frame and crossed his arms. "You really wouldn't mind?"

"Not at all." Christian busied himself selecting a pen and opening his inkwell. "I might be her lover, but I certainly don't own her, nor would I wish to."

"She is very beautiful."

"Beauty is easy to find, my friend."

"And she is strong, intelligent, and likable . . ."

Christian forced a smile. "She certainly can portray all those attributes."

"You think her false?"

"How can I not? She doesn't even use her own name, for God's sake. Why would any man trust a woman like that?"

Ambrose studied him carefully. "Sometimes a man has no choice in the matter."

Christian realized he was glaring. "If you feel that strongly about Mrs. Smith, I'll stop fucking her and hand her over to you. To her, one man is as good as any other."

"I doubt that. And she isn't a possession to be handed around." There was an edge of anger to Ambrose's reply that Christian couldn't mistake, but for once he didn't give a damn about his friend's feelings about ownership.

He took out a piece of paper and slammed the drawer shut. "May I suggest you keep your opinions to yourself?"

"I'll—" Ambrose suddenly straightened and looked out into the hallway. "Good morning, Mrs. Smith. I didn't see you there."

Christian watched as Elizabeth swept past Ambrose and came to a halt in front of his desk. She curtsied to him, her smile bright and her gray eyes completely guileless. He concentrated on keeping his expression just as bland.

"Mr. Delornay."

"How much did you hear?" Christian asked bluntly.

"Of your conversation? Most of it."

"Well you should know that eavesdroppers never hear good about themselves."

Her eyes widened. "I heard nothing that offended me, Mr. Delornay."

"Good." He realized that he was glaring at her. "Then enjoy your afternoon with Ambrose."

"I intend to, sir." She turned away from him and smiled sweetly at Ambrose. "Are you ready to go up to the room of desires with me?"

"Indeed I am, Elizabeth." Ambrose bowed low, which made Christian grind his teeth. "I'll speak to you later this evening, Mr. Delornay."

Christian was left sitting at his desk as the happy pair disappeared down the corridor, laughing and talking to each other as if they had not a care in the world. He looked down at the letter he was attempting to write, screwed the paper up into a ball, and threw it toward the fireplace.

"Damn their merry souls to hell," he muttered. "I think it's time I visited the Demon Club again."

As they rounded the corner and Christian's office disappeared from view, Elizabeth let out her breath and Ambrose patted her hand.

"I'm sorry, Elizabeth."

"For what?"

"For discussing you in those terms."

She smiled up at him. "You have nothing to apologize for. In truth, you were very flattering."

"Thank you for the compliment. I wish I deserved it. But I was deliberately goading Mr. Delornay."

"Goading him?"

Ambrose held the door open for her, and she started to climb the stairs. "Most people believe Mr. Delornay is a cold-blooded, amoral man."

"I can see why."

"He is much more than that," Ambrose said softly. "I occasionally have to remind him that he is allowed to show he cares about people."

Elizabeth swallowed as she recalled Christian's dismissive words about her person and his casual insistence that Ambrose should hurry up and fuck her. It hurt more than she had anticipated. Perhaps she should see it as the warning it was and harden her heart against everyone and everything at the pleasure house.

"Mr. Delornay didn't say anything that wasn't true. I am here under false pretenses, and I am willing to participate in the sexual games."

Ambrose produced the key to the room of desires and unlocked the door. "Elizabeth, you are almost as bad as Mr. Delornay about sharing your feelings. No one likes to hear themselves spoken of like that."

"Perhaps I'm used to it," Elizabeth replied lightly.

Ambrose cupped her face with his fingers. "No one should have to get used to that."

She moved away from him, toward the new pale gold drapes, and turned to survey the room. "It looks so much better in here, doesn't it?"

"Yes, it does. You have an excellent eye for color. The gold and brown palette work very well together. It looks warm and welcoming but also quite mysterious."

Elizabeth nodded. "And painting each room a different

color should help determine the best space for each particular client request."

Ambrose opened the nearest door to reveal blue walls and gray silk furnishings. He went in and Elizabeth followed him.

"Do you wish to fuck me, then?" she asked.

He spun around to grin at her. "Right now, when you are still hurt by the conversation you overheard? I don't think that would be a good idea, do you?"

"I'm not sure. I have a strange desire to thumb my nose at Mr. Delornay."

"That's because despite what you said, he hurt your feelings."

She raised her chin at him. "He did not."

Ambrose just smiled at her and she turned away to smooth the bed linen.

"Ambrose . . ."

"Yes, Elizabeth?"

"There *is* something I would appreciate your help with."

"What is that?"

"I have to go out this afternoon. I would like someone to accompany me."

Ambrose straightened. "I'd be delighted to oblige you. Where do you need to go?"

Elizabeth headed back into the main room and Ambrose followed her. "When I say *accompany me,* I mean that perhaps someone might follow me at a distance and make sure I return from the place I intend to visit."

She felt her cheeks heat as he studied her.

"I don't quite understand."

"Let me put it this way. I'm aware that I might be walking into a trap. I'd rather someone know what happens to me in case I disappear again."

"I see, but surely for that to work, the person or persons

you are meeting need to see you are accompanied so that they will not try anything?"

Elizabeth frowned. "That's a good point. But they might be reluctant to approach me if I am obviously guarded."

"If they really wish to contact you, they'll try again. I'd rather you were safe, Elizabeth, wouldn't you?"

"I suppose so." She half smiled at him. "I suppose you think I should just tell you exactly what is going on and have done with it."

Ambrose chuckled. "Well, that would be nice. If I knew what the threat was, I would be better able to protect you from it."

He held the main door open, and Elizabeth went to walk past him and hesitated. "I would tell you if I could, but I fear I am not the only person involved."

His expression gentled. "I'm glad you told me something. There are many people here who would miss you if you suddenly disappeared."

She fought against the desire to believe him. She didn't want to be liked, did she? If the staff at the pleasure house knew what she had done, they would denounce her as easily as her husband's family had. She hoped to God that there was a way out of this tangle, but she already feared that the price was too high and that too many people might get hurt.

"Would two o'clock be convenient?" Elizabeth asked abruptly.

"It would."

Christian knocked on the very discreet door of the Demon Club and then stepped back so that the man who guarded the entranceway could see him through the peephole. The door opened and Christian walked through with a quiet word of thanks. The hallway was now deserted, so he left his hat and gloves on the table and made his way to the back of the house.

As he approached the double doors, he could hear the sound of voices and he smiled.

There weren't many people present in the far-from-elegant room. He recognized Lord Kelveston, one of the club's original founders, at one of the gaming tables and walked across to pay his respects. Kelveston was in his early thirties but was already beginning to go bald. He looked up briefly to acknowledge Christian.

"Delornay. Care to take a hand?"

"Not today, thank you, my lord. I'd prefer to watch."

Kelveston gave a bark of laughter. "That's not like you."

"I know." Christian took a seat on the couch. "But I had a long night." It had just occurred to him that after his absence, he needed a reason for visiting the club that wouldn't offend his host. "I just wish to ask you about something. I'm happy to wait until you have finished your game."

His gaze wandered to the three other players. One of them he knew slightly; the other two were quite unknown to him.

"I believe you know Cole, but have you met the Pattersons, Delornay?" Lord Kelveston asked.

"I don't believe I have." Christian nodded at the man and the woman. "It is a pleasure."

They both nodded at him, and the woman held his gaze, her blue eyes widening as she stared at his torso. Christian let her stare. She was a luscious armful, and if she was here, she obviously understood the rules of the club. To Christian's dismay, the expected kick of lust didn't materialize and his cock remained unimpressed.

When she looked back at her cards, Christian beckoned one of the footmen over. While he waited for his brandy to arrive, he studied the occupants of the large, gilded gold cage by the fire. There were three people sitting on the floor, one woman and two men; all of them looked anxious and he wasn't surprised.

The smell of sex and expensive perfume wafted over him, and he stiffened as two thin arms wrapped around him from behind.

"Christian, my *darling*. Wherever have you been?"

"Melinda."

He put his hands up to grip her wrists, but she wouldn't let go. He increased the pressure until he felt her bones grind together, and she moaned into his ear and released him.

To his annoyance, she merely flounced around the chair and plonked herself down on his lap. She wore stockings, garters, a muslin shift, and her stays but no gown. He inhaled her sickly perfume and unwashed body odor and wanted to gag.

"Where have you been?" she demanded again.

"Busy."

She pouted, catching her lower lip in her teeth. "But I missed you. We all missed you." Her outflung hand indicated not only the Pattersons, but also her husband, Lord Kelveston, who was frowning down at his cards. She nipped at Christian's earlobe. "I needed you."

Christian accepted a glass of brandy from the footman and brought it to his lips, his gaze fixed on the card game.

"Christian . . ."

There was a pleading edge to Melinda's softly spoken word that made him want to shove her off his lap and head for the door. He didn't like easy conquests. He never had. And once he dominated someone, they lost their allure. Would he feel that way about Elizabeth? He was no longer sure, and that was unacceptable.

"Damnation!" Lord Kelveston threw down his cards and pushed his chair away from the table. "You win, Mrs. Patterson." He looked over at the gilded cage. "Which one do you want?"

Christian watched as Mrs. Patterson walked over to the occupants of the cage and subjected them to her intense scrutiny.

"I want the black-haired man," she announced loudly.

Lord Kelveston beckoned one of the footmen forward to unlock the cage. "You may have him for the rest of the day and then his debt is paid."

"May my husband join us this time?"

"Since this is your third win, he may if you wish, but you must not damage the goods. I've heard Mr. Patterson can be a little rough with the merchandise."

The black-haired man blanched and his gaze darted around the room as if seeking assistance. Christian could only feel sorry for him. There would be no kind heart to help him here. Lord Kelveston and his cronies had very specific payment terms for those who gambled and lost at the Demon Club. The man must have known that, but like most young fools, he'd obviously assumed he was a better cardplayer than he actually was.

"I'd not bed him. He looks far too weak to me," Melinda whispered, wiggling provocatively on his lap. His cock still failed to respond. "I must ask my dear Kelvy if he's better than he looks."

"He isn't worth it, my dear," Kelveston replied. "You need a strong hand. Now, what did you wish to ask me, Delornay?"

Melinda shivered and Christian kept his expression bland. "I wanted to ask you when the next card tournament is scheduled for." It was as good an excuse as any.

"I believe it is in a month or less. Do you want me to send you an invite?"

"I'd appreciate that." Christian stood up, letting Melinda fall from his lap and find her own feet. "May I bring a guest?"

"Of course." Kelveston nodded.

Other than to annoy Melinda, Christian had no idea why he'd said that. But the thought of seeing how Elizabeth dealt with these less-than-salubrious surroundings appealed to him.

If anything could shock her out of her sexual complacency, it would be one of the Demon Club's wild nights.

"Thank you, I'll look forward to it."

Lord Kelveston turned in his seat to survey Christian and his wife.

"Are you sure you won't take a hand, Delornay? There's a new woman in the cage today, and I'd like her to see us at our best."

With some difficulty, Christian looked past Melinda and back at the occupants of the cage. There was only one woman there. Christian frowned. She looked far too young to be selling herself at the Demon Club.

"What did she do?" Christian asked idly.

"She didn't do anything. The debt is her stepfather's." Kelveston licked his lips. "When I saw the girl, I was quite willing to accept her instead of her stepfather. If you don't want her, Delornay, I'll try her out myself."

"Ooh!" Melinda squealed. "Can I play, too, my lord?"

"If you wish, my dear. Perhaps you can show her some new tricks." His laugh was unpleasant. "She'll certainly need them for her new trade after we ruin her."

Christian studied the bowed head of the young woman. "I'll play a hand for her. You know how I enjoy a challenge."

Kelveston pulled out the chair Mrs. Patterson had vacated. "Come and sit here, Melly, and make up the four. If you win, we'll have her. If Delornay wins, he gets the privilege of breaking her in."

Christian took a seat and focused on his cards, ignoring both Melinda's whispers and her attempts to stroke his cock beneath the table. Gambling came naturally to him, and he had no doubt that he could easily beat the other three players. The skill was in not letting them know that.

After a while he sat back and allowed himself a small smile. "My game, I believe?"

Lord Kelveston smiled back and rose to his feet. "You have the devil's own luck. I'll get the girl for you. I want her to realize exactly who you are and why she should start pleading now."

Christian got up, too, and followed Kelveston, leaving Melinda pouting at the table.

Kelveston opened the cage and grabbed the girl's arm to drag her out. In the dim light, Christian could see the fear in her blue eyes and the way she bit her lip to stop it from trembling.

Kelveston chuckled. "Your debt is almost paid, my dear Miss Retton. Make your curtsy to Mr. Delornay, one of the most respected members of the Demon Club. He will make sure that you remember this day for the rest of your life."

"But the debt isn't mine, sir," she whispered.

Kelveston's face hardened and he shoved the woman toward Christian. "Be silent. Your stepfather sent you in his stead, and the debt must be paid in any way I wish it."

"That isn't fair. I—"

Christian covered the woman's mouth with his hand and wrapped his other arm around her waist. "May I suggest you do as Lord Kelveston says and remain silent? I would hate to have to punish you right here in front of everyone. Or is that what you secretly wish?"

She fought him for a desperate second and then seemed to go limp in his arms. He kissed the top of her head and looked across at Kelveston.

"I'll manage from here, my lord. Which room is free?"

"Take the third one at the end of the corridor," Kelveston said. "Are you sure you wouldn't like Melly and me to join you?"

"Not this time, my lord. I think I'd like to savor her . . . surrender all by myself."

For a moment Kelveston looked wistful. "There's nothing

like that moment when they realize they aren't going to get away and that you intend to extract every penny of their debt from their flesh, is there?"

As Christian agreed with Lord Kelveston, the woman in his arms gave a convulsive shiver and he tightened his grip on her. This was not the place to show weakness. If she swooned, she'd wake up on the floor with every man in the room on top of her trying to fuck her.

"Come, my dear." He manhandled her toward the doorway and down the hall to the room at the end. He passed the Pattersons, who were pressing the black-haired man against the wall. Mrs. Patterson's hand was delving inside the man's breeches, and from his muffled cries, he wasn't enjoying himself.

Christian opened the door, pushed the woman inside, and locked it, even though locks meant nothing here. There were more peepholes and mirrors in each room of the Demon Club than there were at the pleasure house. Christian had never liked being spied on unless he wished it. He took his time drawing the curtains and moving certain pieces of furniture until the room lay in darkness and was as protected as he could make it.

He turned back to the woman, who had retreated as far away from him as she possibly could. He had to assume that he was still being watched.

"Miss Retton, isn't it?" She simply stared at him. "If you wish to get through this, may I suggest you do exactly as I say?"

She still didn't speak, her eyes widening as he walked toward her. He put one hand under her chin and made her look at him. "Take off your clothes."

A single tear appeared on her cheek, and Christian stifled a sigh. "Take them off, Miss Retton, or would you prefer me to call Lord Kelveston?"

Her hands went to the bodice of her simple muslin gown,

and she started to undo the buttons, her fingers shaking as she tried not to cry.

"Please, sir, do not make me do this. I've done nothing wrong, I swear it."

Christian put his finger against her lips. "I'm not interested, Miss Retton. All I want is you naked and under me. Now be quiet or do I have to gag you as well?"

A year ago, such a display might have excited him—the thought of the struggle ahead, his eventual victory, but not anymore. Now it was merely a matter of surviving his disgust at the antics of the Demon Club. Hot tears fell down her cheeks and he wiped them away.

"Get on the bed and I'll explain exactly what I expect from you."

By the time he closed the door and left a sobbing, grateful Miss Retton behind him, Christian was exhausted. He reached the vestibule and reclaimed his hat and gloves. Melinda appeared between him and the exit, her bosom heaving and her mouth trembling.

"Who are you bringing to the party?"

"That's hardly any of your business, my lady," Christian replied.

She held up her hand. "But I'll be here! You don't need anyone else!"

He sighed. "Melinda . . ."

Her expression changed and she came at him, her fingers arched into claws. "You bastard!"

He winced as she caught his cheek with her nails, scoring a line down to his throat. With a snarl, he caught her hands. "Stop it."

She gazed up at him, her eyes swimming with tears. "I'll do anything you want, I swear it! Just tell me what it is and I'll do it . . . please!"

"There is nothing you can do." He tried to say it gently. "We had an enjoyable time together and now it is over, and we can explore new possibilities."

"But I still want you!"

He held her gaze. "And I don't want you. I'm sorry, but that is the truth."

She swallowed hard. "What does she do for you that I didn't? Tell me what she does and I swear I'll do it better."

"She . . ." Christian stopped speaking. He couldn't even begin to compare the two women. Melinda was available to any man who could offer her the dark excitement she craved, and Elizabeth? She made herself available to no one.

He released Melinda's hands and stepped back. "I have to go."

She didn't try to stop him this time, and for that small mercy he was profoundly grateful. He hailed a hackney cab and climbed in. In truth, he felt like the bastard Melinda thought he was, but he couldn't lie. No woman or man had ever held his sexual interest for more than a night or two. He'd told Melinda that before starting their affair, and she'd chosen to forget it.

With a sigh, Christian sat back and watched the London scenery pass by. It didn't make him feel any better. He now regretted his impulse to visit the Demon Club. His confused thoughts about Elizabeth had sent him there. To make matters worse, he'd invited himself to one of their more notorious sexual events and reactivated Melinda's obsessive interest in him. He was indeed a complete fool.

10

Elizabeth tied the ribbons of her bonnet and lowered the veil. Despite her protests that she would never need them, Christian had chosen both the black bonnet and the matching pelisse, and now she was glad of it. She checked the clock in her room and hurried down to the kitchen.

Ambrose was in deep conversation with Paul, and at first neither of them noticed her. It was strange that despite having shared a bed with Paul, she felt none of the confusion at seeing him that she felt with Christian.

Ambrose looked up and saw her. "Elizabeth. Are you ready to go?"

"Indeed, I am."

She put on her gloves and picked up her reticule. Inside, along with all her money, she had a serviceable sharp knife purloined from the kitchen and the address of the newspaper office.

Paul put his hand on Ambrose's arm. "I think I should accompany Mrs. Smith."

Elizabeth frowned. "Why?"

Ambrose shrugged. "Paul thinks I am too well known and that it would be easy for anyone to trace you back to the pleasure house. Unfortunately, he might have a point, but I'd rather leave the decision up to you."

"I hadn't thought of that . . . ," Elizabeth said hesitantly.

Paul moved to stand beside her. "Then let me come with you. Men in uniform are ten a penny on the streets these days. I'm a nonentity compared to Ambrose, here, but I can defend you. I have no compunction in killing."

Elizabeth met Ambrose's worried gaze. "Would you mind if I went with Paul? I don't want anyone following me back here."

"I don't mind at all, although what Mr. Delornay will say is another matter."

"Mr. Delornay isn't here," Elizabeth said sweetly. "He obviously had far more important things to do than worry about me."

She still wasn't sure if she was glad or hurt by his casual dismissal. But it was better not to care. At least she knew that.

Paul offered her his arm. "Then, shall we go?"

"We should." She smiled at Ambrose. "I won't be long."

"You'd better not be. We have our first clients for the new room of desires, and I'll need you both back to prepare."

Elizabeth followed Paul out into the square and waited as he hailed a hackney cab and helped her inside.

She consulted the address. "We could have walked, Paul."

"I know but this is safer." He patted her knee. "We can take a more circuitous route back as well."

Elizabeth tried to laugh. "I feel quite foolish asking for protection."

He studied her intently. "Why? Whoever you are afraid of made you leave everything behind. No one runs away for fun."

"Thank you," Elizabeth murmured. "I had no choice. At least I thought I didn't . . ."

Paul leaned forward and touched his finger to her lips. "Don't tell me any more. I have no wish to keep secrets from Christian and Ambrose." He grimaced. "In fact, if they offered me certain sexual favors, I'd probably offer them up quite willingly."

"You underestimate yourself," Elizabeth said.

"No, I don't. I just know what a coward I am."

She frowned at him. "From all reports, that is not true. I hear you acted quite heroically in the war."

"Only to impress Major Lord Gabriel Swanfield."

Elizabeth fixed him with her most severe stare. "You might choose to undervalue your achievements, but I do not believe a word of it."

His smile was beautiful and yet tinged with sadness. "You are an angel."

"Hardly." Elizabeth shivered as she thought of what she might find out today.

"Now who is belittling themselves?" Paul chided her.

The cab pulled up, and Elizabeth braced her gloved hand against the door. She waited until Paul came around to help her down the steps.

He pointed down the long roadway. "This is Fleet Street. The newspaper offices are about halfway down on the left, opposite Somerset House. You walk ahead and I'll follow discreetly behind."

Gathering her courage, Elizabeth lowered her veil and set off in the direction Paul had shown her. It was a cloudy day, and a few spots of rain already dampened the stone slabs of pavement. Elizabeth kept her gaze fixed resolutely ahead. If anyone wanted to kidnap her, they'd have a fight on their hands.

She opened the door into the main lobby of the newspaper offices and found herself in what appeared to be the general office. Several men sat at desks behind a high counter. Three older men were serving various customers, and Elizabeth joined one of the lines and patiently waited for her turn.

When she reached the front of the queue, she produced the clipped advertisement and passed it across to the clerk.

"Do you have any information for me about this? I believe I am the woman the advertiser is trying to contact."

The man glanced at the clipping and frowned. "Now this here is a tricky one, ma'am, seeing as I don't know if you are who you say you are. The best thing I can do is send a boy out to the person who placed the advertisement and give him your details."

"But I'd prefer to meet him here," Elizabeth said as pleasantly as she could. She should have anticipated his response. Now she felt like a fool. "Would that be possible?"

"Yes, ma'am. Perhaps you'd like to write a note suggesting a time, and I can send it with the messenger."

"That's an excellent idea," Elizabeth replied.

The man offered her both paper and a pen, and she stood to one side composing a brief note to the mysterious RR. She handed the man the message and a small coin for his trouble and turned to leave, her reticule clutched firmly in her hand, her anxiety still high.

Outside the office, she took in a deep breath of the damp air and started to walk back toward where she had agreed to meet Paul. She had a strange sensation that she was being watched and found herself wanting to walk quickly. It was highly possible that Armand had somebody watching the newspaper offices. Her earlier fears suddenly seemed real, and she scanned the crowds for a glance of Paul.

A hackney cab pulled up alongside her, and she looked up into Paul's familiar face. He extended his hand, and before the cab fully stopped, he brought her inside, his strength surprising. She took a seat and he continued to look out the window, a frown on his pleasant face.

"I think there was a man following you. Did anyone try and speak to you?"

"No, they didn't." Elizabeth fought for her usual composure. "The clerk at the office took a message from me to the person who placed the advertisement. I have asked to meet him tomorrow at three."

"You believe it is a man?"

Elizabeth cursed her unruly tongue. "It's possible."

Paul turned to look at her. "Your husband?"

"My husband is dead."

"Are you sure about that?"

"I saw him being laid to rest in his family tomb."

"Your lover, then?"

Elizabeth raised her chin. "Which one? There were so many."

"They weren't your lovers." Paul regarded her steadily. "From what I understand, they were not of your choosing."

"My customers, then, although I scarcely got paid."

Paul reached for her hand. "I'm sorry, Elizabeth. My curiosity sometimes overwhelms me. I didn't mean to upset you."

She glared at him. "I'm not upset."

He continued to hold her hand between both of his, and she stared down at her lap. It was ridiculous to be upset. Paul had only asked the questions that Christian and Ambrose would expect him to. She gathered her thoughts.

"I didn't recognize anyone in the office or on the street. If someone was following me, I didn't know them."

"They'll be more ready for you tomorrow. They'll have a time and a place to go on."

"I didn't know what else to do."

He squeezed her fingers. "Have you considered whether you really want to make this contact?"

"I have no choice."

"Ah." He went quiet for so long that she thought he'd forgotten her. "Whatever it is must be important to you."

"It is." Elizabeth closed her lips firmly.

"And you are certain that we can't help you? Madame Helene has an enormous amount of influence in all circles of the aristocracy. You might be surprised at what she can help you with."

"I don't believe Madame Helene would be able to help me," Elizabeth said. "I'm responsible for this mess, and it is up to me to fix it."

Paul released her hands and sat back. "I think you're wrong, but I doubt I'll be able to convince you otherwise." He winked at her. "I'll still offer my companionship to you for tomorrow, though."

"Thank you."

Elizabeth managed a smile and then spent the rest of the journey back to the pleasure house staring out the window to ensure Paul would not try to converse with her again.

After one of the maids released her from the black gown, petticoats, and stays, Elizabeth sat at her dressing table to brush out her damp hair. Her fear had subsided, leaving her feeling curiously shaken. Would it be better just to give up, to go back to Armand and continue the charade, as he wanted? She had to consider that even if the very thought made her stomach turn.

Her door opened and in the mirror she saw Christian. She briefly closed her eyes. She was in no state for one of his interrogations.

"Good evening, Mrs. Smith."

"Good evening, Mr. Delornay."

Elizabeth continued brushing her hair and met his gaze only in the mirror. He came up right behind her, took the brush out of her hand, and started to comb her hair. The smell of expensive perfume wafted over her and she stiffened.

"Did you enjoy your afternoon, Mrs. Smith?"

"Not particularly. I'm sure that Paul has already given you

all the details." She glanced over her shoulder and saw three red parallel scratches that marred the perfection of his cheek. "Did you enjoy your afternoon, sir?"

"Not particularly. The Demon Club lacked a certain something today."

She tried to stand up, but he pressed a hand onto her shoulder. "I haven't finished brushing your hair yet."

"But I need to get ready."

She twisted out of his grasp and faced him, searching his expression for the lazy, satiated look of satisfied lust she had come to know and found instead a coldness that startled her.

Unbidden, her hand rose to his damaged cheek and he went still.

"Does it hurt?"

He shrugged. "A little. It is of no importance."

His voice held as much expression as if they were discussing a broken fingernail. She tried to match his disinterested tone.

"Did she also douse you in the contents of her perfume bottle?"

"No, she just draped herself all over me." His nostrils wrinkled. "I suspect she bathes in the foul substance."

"You should pick your mistresses more carefully."

"I do." He caught hold of her chin. "You always smell very pleasant, especially when I've made you wet."

"I meant your other mistresses."

"Are you jealous?" he asked softly.

"Do you want me to be?"

He kissed her mouth, his teeth nipping at her lower lip. "Always so polite and accommodating. Wouldn't you fight for me?"

"If you wanted someone who throws tantrums and screams, I fear you chose the wrong person." She met his gaze. "I've learned that when a man wants something, there is very little that a woman can do about it."

"And I want you right now." His hand slid around her hips, drawing her close until she could feel the hot press of his cock against her stomach. He backed her toward the bed and came down on top of her, his mouth devouring hers, his hands busy rucking up her shift.

She grabbed a handful of his hair and pulled hard, almost relieved to have something physical to fight about to get rid of her fear.

"I have to get ready!"

"By God, I'll get you ready."

His mouth descended again and he kissed her, leaving her the choice of fighting him or letting him have his way. She tried to push at his chest, and he grabbed her wrists, bringing her arms over her head and holding them there, locked within his grasp.

His mouth moved lower and closed over her breast, his tongue flicked her nipple, and then he nuzzled it, sending streaks of pure lust straight to her sex. Her back arched as he drew on her, his other hand now between her legs cupping her, his thumb circling her clit.

"I'm not yet . . . prepared," she managed to gasp.

He looked up at her, his eyes narrowed, his fingers still working inside her. "For sex or for an orgasm? I'll just use my mouth on you, then, and you can use your mouth on me. But I'll make you come, I swear it."

He released her hands and moved down between her legs, his fingers stabbing into her as his tongue flicked and played with her clit. She reached down to his head again, desperate for something to hold on to.

"Touch your nipples. Pinch them hard."

She obeyed him and moaned as he increased his efforts between her legs, her sex now wet both from his mouth and her excitement, his fingers sliding easily inside her.

"Wait."

Elizabeth moved her hands from her breasts as Christian reversed his position until his cock and balls hung temptingly over her mouth. "Suck my cock while I suck you."

She willingly opened her mouth, and he slid deep and she started to suck him. He responded by diving back into her already-sensitive sex, his mouth everywhere, the rasp of his stubble an added torment on her suddenly sensitive bud. He pumped his hips harder, taking control of his cock, making her keep to his tempo, and she let him, her thoughts divided between the fullness of him in her mouth and what he was doing to her.

He groaned against her flesh and she shuddered as his cock kicked in her mouth, growing even bigger. He started to come, and she concentrated on relaxing and letting him spill his hot seed deep down her throat. But even as she responded to him, his teeth settled over her clit and he bit her, the pain-pleasure of it sending her into a climax of her own that went on and on until she was struggling to breathe.

He remained on top of her, his body heavy, his breathing as erratic as her own. It was only when she opened her eyes that she realized he'd only unbuttoned his breeches to release his cock and still wore his boots.

When he moved away, she watched him set himself to rights, his motions fluid and unhurried. Her sex throbbed now from his rough treatment but she didn't mind. At least he made her feel *something*.

"I'll send up some hot water for you," Christian said. "And I'll tell Ambrose to expect you in half an hour."

"Yes, Mr. Delornay."

He walked back over to the bed and kissed her on the mouth. "I'll be watching in the room of desires, so don't imagine that you are unprotected."

"Thank you, sir."

His gaze drifted down between her legs. "Are you sore?"
"Yes."

He nodded and bent his head, his tongue flicking over her clit until she gasped. She wanted him to keep touching her; she wanted him to give her that exquisitely painful sensation again.

He looked up at her. "I'm still going to fuck you later."

"Yes."

His smile surprised her, but he turned to go before she could ask him what it meant. As she contemplated the closed door, she realized something else. Either Christian had bathed before coming to her, or his cock hadn't come into contact with that other woman. He'd tasted only of himself.

She rolled onto her front and buried her face in the pillows. Or he'd worn a French letter to avoid the pox, or withdrawn, or cleaned up earlier . . . She of all people knew there were many ways for a man to deceive a woman. And what did it matter anyway? She swallowed hard and tasted him all over again. And Christian wasn't her husband—he was only her lover.

11

Elizabeth found Ambrose on the back stairs, close to the door of the room of desires. He unlocked the door that led directly into the room from the stairs and beckoned her inside.

"The clients aren't here yet, so we have time to prepare."

"Clients?" Elizabeth looked around the lobby.

"A married couple, apparently," Ambrose replied, and led the way into the smallest of the anterooms, which was decorated in rich red and gold.

"And where is Paul?"

"He was called away to attend to some family business. I will be standing in for him."

"That will be pleasant," Elizabeth said as Ambrose lit the fire and set light to several branches of candelabra illuminating all of the small space. "Do you have our instructions?"

"We are to put on masks and await their arrival here. After that, they will be issuing all the instructions we need."

"But someone must have agreed to their desires?"

"I believe Christian did, so we have nothing much to worry about."

Elizabeth raised her eyebrows. "Are you sure about that?"

To her surprise, Ambrose didn't immediately reassure her and she tensed, her thoughts drifting to Christian's earlier behavior and the rough way he'd taken her mouth and her sex. . . .

"Christian is very careful of the reputation of the pleasure house. He will allow nothing here that would offend his mother," Ambrose finally said.

"But what about outside the pleasure house?" Elizabeth asked, and Ambrose looked away from her. "Does Mr. Delornay take his pleasure elsewhere?"

"You'll have to ask him about that." Ambrose moved over to the chest of drawers set against the wall. "Now come and choose a mask."

Elizabeth followed him over, her thoughts in a whirl. Had the woman who'd marked Christian's face been at the pleasure house? But Christian had said he was going out and had mentioned the Demon Club. . . .

Ambrose helped Elizabeth tie on her mask, and they turned in unison as the door opened and a masked couple entered the intimate room. They didn't seem particularly young, or drunk, or even excited.

The man bowed. "Good evening. I want you to fetch two chairs and place them back-to-back in the center of the room."

Ambrose brought two chairs from the wall and placed them where the man had directed.

"Now I wish you to undress each other. And do it slowly so that my wife, Maude, and I can watch."

Elizabeth faced Ambrose and waited until he shrugged out of his coat before unbuttoning his waistcoat and unpinning his simply tied cravat. His face was impassive, his eyes difficult to read through the mask. The thought that Christian was watching made Elizabeth's clit throb in time to her heartbeat.

Ambrose touched her shoulder, and she presented him with

her back and stood quietly while he unhooked the bodice of her gown and unlaced her stays.

"Wait," Maude said. Elizabeth grabbed hold of the front of her gown to stop everything falling down and glanced across at her. She remained still as Maude reached forward and tugged at Elizabeth's bodice, baring her down to her thin shift.

She cupped Elizabeth's breasts with both hands and then bent her head. Elizabeth shivered as she felt the flick of a tongue over her already-sensitized nipples.

"Very nice. You will enjoy touching her, St. John."

"I'm sure I will."

When Maude stepped back, Elizabeth undid Ambrose's breeches and untucked his shirt, and he allowed her to pull it over his head. He was already aroused, his thick cock pushing against the linen of his underthings.

"Take off his boots," St. John instructed her.

Elizabeth turned around, straddled Ambrose's leg, and pulled his boot off and then did the same for his other foot. The buckskin of his breeches abraded her already-wet sex, and the hand he placed on her buttock to help her ease the second boot off didn't help matters at all. Silently she cursed Christian's earlier intervention. She couldn't seem to summon her usual detachment, and that was unacceptable.

Eventually they were both naked and faced each other again, the other couple circling them and making admiring comments as to the size of Ambrose's cock and the fullness of Elizabeth's breasts. Elizabeth felt rather like how she imagined a slave might feel and wondered how Ambrose was taking it. He seemed unperturbed, his breathing relaxed and his hands hanging by his sides.

Maude touched Elizabeth's shoulder. "Sit in the chair facing the wall, and you, sir, sit in the other chair with your back to her. Then hold hands."

Elizabeth sat down and waited for Ambrose to do the same. She had a good view of Maude rummaging in the drawers of the chest. She turned, brandishing a set of long red silk scarves and Elizabeth tensed.

St. John took one end of each scarf and helped his wife wrap the long lengths of fabric around both the chairs and Elizabeth's and Ambrose's upper torsos. Ambrose gripped her hand and squeezed hard in a reassuring manner.

"Now we must blindfold you both."

Elizabeth almost protested, but she managed to stop herself. She had never liked losing her sight. It made it impossible to judge the mood of her opponent. She submitted to the blindfold and forced herself to breathe evenly.

A hand insinuated itself between her knees and she relaxed her thighs.

"Thank you," Maude murmured. "I'm going to tie your ankles to the chair as well, so don't be afraid."

Elizabeth felt the silk against her skin and then the press of the carved chair leg as her ankle was immobilized. From what she could hear, Ambrose was receiving the same treatment from St. John.

Silence fell and then she heard Maude and St. John whispering together. A moment later someone kissed her and she realized it was St. John. Her nerves were steadier now. She knew how to do this. She didn't stop him opening her mouth and delving deep with his tongue. He smelled faintly of peppercorns and smoking fires, not scents she needed to be afraid of at all.

He kissed her throat and then her breasts, his lips fastening around her nipple and sucking hard. She heard Ambrose groan and wondered if he was being suckled too. A waft of air and St. John was gone and his companion replaced him, the pull of her mouth on Elizabeth's breast far gentler.

Ambrose's grip on her hand tightened, and she knew he was experiencing the more masculine touch of St. John. This time she definitely heard him cry out.

Another shift and St. John was in front of her now, his mouth on her inner thigh, working its way toward her wet core. His tongue flicked out over her clit and she bit back a moan. He did it again, circling her swollen bud and delving deep inside her. Sucking sounds indicated that Maude was working Ambrose's cock with equal vigor.

Elizabeth realized that she was panting and that Ambrose's grip was almost painful on her hand. Maude touched her now, her tongue quicker and her fingers adding to Elizabeth's excitement level. She was almost ready to climax, almost there, almost . . .

Maude's mouth left her and Elizabeth gasped and Ambrose did too. The sounds and smells of fucking filled the room as Maude and St. John fell on each other, leaving Elizabeth feeling bereft and slightly indignant.

After a while, the noise diminished into softer sighs and moans. The next thing Elizabeth heard was the sound of the door closing swiftly followed by Ambrose cursing in an unknown language.

"Did they leave us?" she whispered.

"They did," Ambrose answered.

"Tied up?"

"Yes." Ambrose tried to extract his hand from Elizabeth's grasp but with no success. "Christian!"

Within seconds, she became aware that the door had opened again and that someone else had entered the room.

"Well, well, well, we are in a pickle, aren't we?" Christian asked.

"Mr. Delornay, sir, just get us out of here."

Ambrose sounded as desperate as Elizabeth felt.

"I'm not sure I want to."

Elizabeth tensed as her nipple was pinched hard.

"Mr. Delornay." Ambrose sighed. "Don't . . ." His sigh turned into a gasp, and Elizabeth recognized the sound of a man's cock being worked. "Oh, God . . ."

Ambrose's whole body jerked and she smelled the scent of his seed being pumped from his cock.

"Now sit quietly while I attend to Mrs. Smith."

Elizabeth tensed as Christian moved around to stand in front of her. He brushed his thumb against her lower lip and she tasted Ambrose's come.

"Do you want to climax, too, Elizabeth?"

She didn't say anything to him, and he pinched her nipple hard enough to make her jump.

"I asked you a question. Do you want to come?"

She licked her lips. "I will do whatever you want me to do, Mr. Delornay."

His fingers closed on her other nipple, and he pulled on both until she thought she would have to lean forward to relieve the pressure or beg him to stop.

"That's not a good enough answer. What do you want, Elizabeth?"

Even though she still wore the blindfold, she closed her eyes very tightly. "Whatever you want, sir."

One of his hands dropped to her sex and he touched her clit. "Elizabeth . . ."

There was a clear warning in his voice. She felt Ambrose stir behind her.

"Mr. Delornay, perhaps you might release me. I'd be more than happy to take care of Elizabeth's needs—whatever they may be."

"Are you afraid I'll hurt her, Ambrose?" Christian laughed. "Trust me, she is made of sterner stuff than that." He backed away from her. "But I'll release you both from your bonds."

Elizabeth waited as Christian used some kind of blade to

saw through the scarves. As soon as her arms were free, she ripped off her blindfold and rubbed at her eyes. Ambrose drew her into his arms and bent his head.

"If you want me to assist you, I will," he whispered. "I don't like the mood Mr. Delornay is in."

Before Elizabeth could reply, Christian was there, his arms around both of them. "Ambrose, go to bed." He stared at Elizabeth. "Tell him he may leave."

For a moment Elizabeth debated telling Christian that she wanted to go with Ambrose, but it wouldn't be the truth. Ambrose deserved better than being used in her and Christian's sexual games.

She touched Ambrose's cheek. "I'll be fine. Thank you for offering, but Mr. Delornay is right. You should go to bed."

Ambrose ignored Christian and concentrated his gaze on Elizabeth's face. "Are you certain?"

"Yes, I am," Elizabeth answered.

"Then I'll leave you two alone." Ambrose gathered his clothes and stepped into his breeches. "Good night."

"Good night," Elizabeth echoed softly as he turned and left, although not all the worry was erased from his face.

Christian watched Ambrose leave and then gave his full attention back to Elizabeth. Watching her being touched by Maude and St. John had aroused Christian to the point of pain, and he intended to enjoy every moment of it. Elizabeth's nipples were already hard, elongated points and her cunt was wet and ready to be fucked. He wanted nothing more than to bring her down to the floor and just fuck her as hard as he could until she was screaming and begging and . . .

His attention was caught by her moving away from him and gathering up her clothes.

"I didn't tell you to get dressed."

She went still and her expression formed into that smiling, compliant mask he'd begun to hate.

"Of course, Mr. Delornay. What can I do for you?"

"Put those things on the chair and take your hair down."

She reached for the pins and began to do as he had told her. He waited as her glorious hair cascaded down her back, his cock throbbing, his breathing ragged.

"Come here."

She walked back toward him, her gaze lowered to his booted feet, her breasts swaying as she moved. He put his hand under her chin so that she had to look up at him.

"Did you like that woman touching you?"

She shrugged. "I've been touched by a woman before—it is no different from being touched by a man."

"Yet you almost came and I thought you said you couldn't usually do that."

"Yes, but you . . ."

Something flashed across her face and he tightened his grip on her chin. "I did what?"

"You touched me earlier."

"So it was my fault."

"I didn't say that."

"You wouldn't, would you, because that would imply you had an opinion about something or that you were angry about my treatment of you and that would never do, would it?"

She tried to avoid his gaze. "I'm not sure what you want me to say."

"Dammit, I want you to tell me the truth!" He wasn't sure why he was so insistent. He knew that women couldn't be trusted. It wasn't like him, but something about her made him quite irrational. "It makes you angry, doesn't it? Being forced to have sex with people. Why not admit it?"

"Because it isn't true!"

He kissed her hard, his teeth grating against hers as she fought him. "You like this, then, being fucked, being used, being treated like nothing?"

She shoved at his chest and broke away from him. "I do not wish to have this conversation with you."

He came after her and grabbed her hand. "But I do. I want to hear you admit that you hate this."

"I don't!" She pulled out of his grasp, her eyes narrowed and her chest heaving. "You just enjoy confusing me. I am used to this!" She flung her arms wide to encompass the room. "It is the only thing that marriage prepared me for!"

He smiled at her. "And you're not even very good at it, are you?" He paused deliberately until he was sure he had her complete attention. "Who wants a woman who can't come?"

She came at him then, her arm raised to slap his face, and he caught her wrist as excitement roared through his veins. But her resistance crumbled and she didn't even try to fight against his grip.

"I don't want this, Christian," she whispered. "Not today, not now."

"What don't you want? A fight? A fuck?"

She shook her head, her hair covering her face. "I'm tired. May I be excused, please?"

He released her wrists, aware that she was hiding from him again. Frustration rose in his throat. Why wouldn't she fight him? He was giving her every opportunity to share her problems, and yet she resisted him at every turn. Every other woman of his acquaintance would be crying and sharing her woes with him by now. But damnation, he liked the fight in her as well, gloried in it and wanted that fury directed at him.

He watched as she gathered up her clothes again and put on her shift.

"Do you think yourself too good for us?"

She stared at him. "What?"

"Do you think we are your social inferiors?"

"Of course not! I'm the one who is inferior. You took me in off the streets."

"And yet you feel no loyalty to me or my family because of that?"

She sighed. "What exactly do you want, Mr. Delornay?"

He shrugged. "Your trust?"

She simply turned her back on him and walked to the door that led out to the servants' stairwell. He followed her out and up the stairs.

"Don't walk away from me." His voice echoed in the bleak stairwell.

She turned to look down at him. "I'm too tired for this. It has been a very difficult day."

"Because you've had to lie so much?"

"Because"—she swallowed hard—"because I've realized just how alone I am and how much I am to blame for this mess."

"Then confide in me!"

"I cannot!"

He came up the stairs after her. "Why not?"

She suddenly turned and met his gaze, her gray eyes flashing fire. "Because trust has to be earned, Mr. Delornay, and you trust no one. How could I ever expect you to understand *anything*?"

He took a step backward, and she ran away from him, her bare feet soundless on the stairs, her hair flowing out behind her like a banner.

Christian stayed where he was, her final words ringing in his head. He glared after her retreating form. How dare she criticize *him* when she was the one deceiving everyone? He was perfectly justified in his decision not to trust every single person who crossed his path. What fool would do that? And he of all people had no reason to believe in anyone. He sank down onto the nearest step and rested his head in his hands.

Lisette trusted him and so did Ambrose. The staff of the pleasure house trusted him to keep them in employment and to keep the business solvent. Dammit, even Philip and his mother knew he'd do that! He raised his head and stared out into the dimly lit stairwell. Then why did Elizabeth's words still hurt?

12

Elizabeth didn't see Christian at all the next morning, and she was profoundly grateful. She spent the time working on the second floor with Marie-Claude and consulting Ambrose about the schedule for the room of desires, which, as word spread, had started to fill up. But even all that activity didn't stop her from thinking. What exactly did Christian want from her? Her total submission, or was it something more complex?

She wasn't sure if he knew himself. She sensed at some level that he simply disliked meeting someone who was as good at hiding emotions as he was. She represented a challenge. But what did she really know about him? He was at odds with his parents but was obviously much beloved by the staff of the pleasure house. He seemed to be loyal to those he loved and would never understand why she had decided to risk everything she loved and leave France.

In truth, she no longer understood her reasons for leaving anymore either. It was humiliating to discover that blind panic had reduced her to acting like an imbecile. She should have stayed and fought for what she wanted.

"Elizabeth?"

She looked up and found Paul in front of her and held out her hand. "Oh, good, I was wondering where you were."

He kissed her fingers with easy familiarity. "I'm sorry I wasn't available last night. I had to make a call on my cousin. It was her birthday and I was shamed into staying for dinner and then accompanying her to a ball."

"Shamed?"

"That's hardly fair of me, is it?" He winced. "Lucky does not deserve that. She is a good friend of mine. The shame was all mine for having neglected her."

Elizabeth patted his arm. "I'm sure she had a delightful evening with you by her side."

He still looked glum. "I believe she did. She was certainly in fine form." He stuck a finger down the inside of his collar. "But I feel the weight of familial expectation tightening every time I see her."

Elizabeth linked her arm through his and drew him down the main staircase toward the private part of the house. "Your family wishes you to marry her?"

"I believe they do. Through some bizarre and remote family connections, I'm the closest male heir to her father's title. My own parents died when I was a child, and Lucky's family brought me up. I've always called her parents *uncle* and *aunt.*"

"And now they wish to make the connection more permanent." Elizabeth glanced up at Paul's unsmiling face. "Do they know that you . . . ?"

"I'm fairly sure they've heard the rumors. I presume they are choosing to ignore them and are hoping for the best."

He held the door open for Elizabeth and she thanked him. "And what about Lucky? Does she know?"

"I doubt it. She's only one and twenty and very sheltered." He sighed. "It's so damn difficult. She truly is a very sweet girl and she deserves better."

SIMPLY CARNAL / 143

"Better than you?" Elizabeth picked up her black bonnet and pelisse and turned back to Paul, who had remained by the door. "I hardly think that."

Paul bowed. "Kind words, but in this case I have to disagree with you. I'd make her a terrible husband and you know it." He gestured at her coat. "May I help you put that on? I believe it is quite windy."

She allowed him to assist her and to change the subject to something more practical. Unlike Christian, she knew when to stop probing and prying.

Twenty minutes later, they were back on Fleet Street and she was ascending the steps of the newspaper offices once again. It took another ten minutes for her to be attended to, by which time she had already taken notice of the man sitting in the waiting area. He looked rather pleasant and also slightly familiar. When the clerk went to consult with his superior, she studied the young man surreptitiously through her veil. He looked like a gentleman, but appearances could be deceptive.

The clerk reappeared and led her toward the man who immediately got to his feet.

"Good afternoon, ma'am. I'm RR."

Elizabeth curtsied. "Sir?"

He looked at the door. "Would you care to walk down to the river with me? We might be more private."

"No, sir. I'd prefer to stay here where everyone can see us."

He frowned. "I mean you no harm." He switched into perfect French. "I'm merely acting as a go-between for your family in France."

"I have no family in France."

"That is not what I've been told." He hesitated. "I can understand your reluctance to trust me, ma'am, but how are we to proceed if we cannot even converse?"

Elizabeth stared at him. "I am conversing with you. Tell me what you have to say and then you can leave."

He studied her for a long moment, and she sought desperately to think of where she had seen him before. Could he be one of the men she'd bedded in France? She didn't think so and yet there was something so familiar about his face. . . .

"The message is quite simple, ma'am. Your cousin Armand wishes you to return home and take your rightful place at his side."

Elizabeth shuddered. "Rightful place?"

"That is the message, ma'am. He also says to tell you that no one will mention your precipitous and impetuous flight or condemn you at all."

"That is very generous of him."

"He also asked me to give you these as a token of his sincerity."

The man handed her a heavy leather pouch, and Elizabeth quickly stowed the purse inside the pocket of her pelisse.

"I believe that is the jewelry you own outright from your marriage and inherited from your family."

"I know what it is. The question is, why is Armand returning the jewelry to me now?" Elizabeth took a deep breath. "Have you met my cousin?"

"Indeed I have. His concern for you seems quite genuine."

"His concern is all for himself and his financial status. You can tell him I do not wish to return."

The man nodded. "He said you might react with anger. He also said to remind you that he holds the power of life and death over every inhabitant of the château until you return."

"And you did not think that remark at all threatening?"

"I assumed he meant that he must make decisions if you are not there and that he would prefer you to return and make them with him."

"And that just confirms my suspicions that you know *nothing* about this situation at all."

"So your answer is still no?"

Elizabeth drew herself up. "You may tell him I will return on *my* terms, not his, and that he had better be very careful in exercising his *powers* because I will be watching him very carefully indeed."

"And what exactly are your terms, ma'am?"

"He knows what they are. He knew them before I left. Nothing has changed. He is just being greedy."

"Surely you would fare better if you went back to France and took him to court there?"

"The court system has not recovered from the war and is in disarray. Do you really think that a man like Armand wouldn't be able to bribe his way to victory?"

For the first time the man looked thoughtful. "I must agree you have a point. But surely you cannot achieve anything by running away?"

"A strategic retreat is not the same as a rout, sir. Ask the Duke of Wellington."

He smiled and Elizabeth almost smiled back.

"Point taken, ma'am. I'll take your message to your cousin." He hesitated. "Do you have an address where I may contact you more directly if there is a reply?"

"You may contact me through the newspaper office. That seemed to work perfectly well."

"If that is what you prefer." He bowed. "I'll wish you a good day, ma'am."

Elizabeth inclined her head and waited until he walked out of the office. She found it necessary to sit down and stare aimlessly at the paneled walls for a minute to gather her wits. Familiar and yet not familiar . . . The turn of his head, his smile, and his eyes all reminded her of someone. But she also knew she'd never met RR before in person, and she had no idea how connected he was to Armand. He'd seemed far too amiable and amenable to be working for her husband's dastardly relative.

With a sigh, Elizabeth got to her feet, thanked the clerk, and headed out into the street. Paul had told her to meet him in the courtyard of Somerset House, so she turned the other way and hesitated before she crossed the road. Several large wagons filled with beer barrels were making their way along the street, raising a cloud of dust and dried mud in their wake. For once, Elizabeth was glad of the veil that partially obscured her vision because it kept out the worst of the filth.

She made her way across the street and was just stepping up onto the pavement when someone trod on the back of her boot, making her stumble. As she went down, she fought for balance and found herself pulled into someone's arms and held tightly.

"Thank you, sir," she gasped, and then looked up into an all-too-familiar face. "Gaston!" she whispered.

He ripped off her veil and smiled down at her. "*Oui, Madame la Comtesse.*"

Elizabeth kicked her husband's valet hard in the shin, but his grip on her upper arm tightened and he started to drag her in the opposite direction of Somerset House. She continued to resist him, hoping desperately that someone would help her. No one seemed to notice or care that she was being abducted in broad daylight. Gaston drew her into the shadows and slammed her face-first against a brick wall. She cried out as he tried to manhandle her hands behind her back.

"Let her go."

Even though she couldn't see him, Elizabeth almost wept as she heard Paul's calm voice. Gaston cursed and his grip began to loosen. She took full advantage of it, wrenching away from him and digging into her reticule for the knife she had secreted there.

Paul already had a pistol to Gaston's head. His expression was so lethal that even Elizabeth quailed.

"Do you want me to kill him?" Paul asked, and Gaston began pleading in French.

"No. Send him back to his new master where he belongs,"

Elizabeth replied. "He isn't worth a bullet or the stain on your conscience."

"Oh, I wouldn't feel guilty about killing scum like this," Paul said. "I've killed far more honorable men without a thought."

Gaston started to pray loudly, and Paul gave him a contemptuous push until he fell to his knees and stayed there babbling.

"Shall we go, ma'am? I have a hackney waiting."

Elizabeth took his remarkably steady hand and walked back with him to Somerset House, where their transportation awaited them. Her face hurt and she had an absurd desire to laugh that she attributed to the shock of her near abduction. Paul continued to hold her hand throughout the journey home, his keen gaze never leaving her face.

He helped her down from the hackney, and they entered the pleasure house through the kitchen door in the basement. Unfortunately, the kitchen was full of people who immediately stopped what they were doing and stared at Elizabeth.

Paul led her to a seat beside the fire and turned to say something to Madame Durand. Elizabeth concentrated on untying the ribbons of her bonnet, unbuttoning her pelisse, and avoiding all the questions raining down on her.

"Here." She jumped as Paul crouched on the floor in front of her and handed her a large glass of what she took to be brandy. "Drink this."

She heard Ambrose's concerned voice, and then Marie-Claude was patting at her face with a wet cloth and murmuring under her breath.

"Everyone get out," Christian said.

There at last—the voice Elizabeth had been hoping for and dreading at the same time. The chattering stopped and Christian's familiar face replaced Marie-Claude's. He gently touched her cheekbone and then swore softly and eloquently in French.

Elizabeth gasped as he leaned forward, swept her into his arms, and headed for the door.

"Paul, come with us, please."

Paul hastened to pick up her brandy glass and ran ahead of them, opening the doors until they reached her chamber and Christian was able to deposit her on the bed. He gently removed her reticule from her grasp. His hazel eyes were narrowed and full of rage.

"Where are you hurt?"

She tried to sound calm. "My arm is aching where he grabbed me, as is my ankle from when I stumbled. My face you can already see."

He ran his hands over her shoulders and down her arms and legs. She winced at least twice when he encountered some newly developing bruise. She would be sore in the morning, and heavens knew what her face would look like. Eventually Christian stepped back and swung around to glare at Paul.

"Why the hell didn't you take better care of her?"

Elizabeth tried to sit up. "He saved my life. Don't shout at him!"

The glance Christian threw her was chilling. "Please lie down and don't interfere, Mrs. Smith."

"I have a perfect right to interfere. I am the one who was nearly kidnapped, after all!"

Christian's gaze slid back to Paul. "Do you think it was a kidnapping attempt?"

"I assume so. The man had plenty of time to kill her before I reached them. He had a knife."

"He could have slit her throat."

"Exactly, but he didn't use it. I found it tucked in his belt when I had him cornered."

"Did he threaten you with the knife, Elizabeth?"

"No. He didn't need to. When he grabbed me, I had no chance to do anything, even scream." Elizabeth shook her head and then felt dizzy. She reluctantly lay back on the pillows. "He was trying to tie my hands when Paul caught him."

There was a gentle tap on the door and Ambrose appeared with a tray containing a bottle, a spoon, and a small glass of water. "I have some laudanum for Elizabeth. It will help her sleep."

Christian sighed. "You might as well stay, Ambrose, and save me having to repeat everything to you later."

Ambrose glanced at Elizabeth. "If that is all right with you?"

She waved a hand at him. "Perfectly."

Her face was starting to throb as if she had a toothache, and she really wanted to be alone. She knew Christian was unlikely to leave until he had extracted every detail from her and Paul. Which begged the question, how much did she want to tell him? Her close encounter with the obnoxious Gaston had shaken her more than she would have imagined.

Ambrose opened the laudanum bottle and measured out a dose into the glass of water. "Drink this, Elizabeth."

"Thank you, Ambrose." Elizabeth shuddered at the bitter taste but knew she had no choice but to drink. It was like most of her choices at the moment, bitter but unfortunately necessary.

Christian waited impatiently until Elizabeth swallowed the dose of laudanum Ambrose offered her. The right side of her face was scratched and bloodied, and he feared she would have a black eye in the morning. A cold rage settled over him as he contemplated what he would have done if he'd been the one to catch her attacker.

But he hadn't been there, had he? He'd delegated the task to his companions because he feared he was becoming too involved with his newest employee. And much good it had done him. Now he was even more enraged and still involved.

He brought one of the chairs over from beside the fire and placed it with a deliberate thump by the bed. Elizabeth lay against the pillows, her eyes closed, her hands clasped tightly on top of the covers like a marble effigy on a tomb.

"Elizabeth, if we are to stand any chance of helping you, I need to know exactly what happened."

She opened her gray eyes to look down at him. "I understand that." She sighed. "I will do my best."

"Thank you."

Christian didn't like the hint of reserve in her voice, but he knew her well enough to accept that a partial victory was better than nothing. He reached out and took her hand, uncurled her shaking fingers, and interlaced them with his own.

"So tell me exactly what happened from the beginning," Christian commanded.

"I met with the man who placed the advertisement in the newspaper and spoke to him for a few minutes."

"His name?" Christian demanded.

"He didn't give it to me. I only know him by the initials RR he used in the advertisement."

"Was this RR the one who followed and attacked you?"

She frowned. "No, the man in the office was a perfect English gentleman, although he spoke French very well."

"And what did he want?"

"He said he had a message from a member of my deceased husband's family and that they wanted me to return to France. I told him I had no intention of returning on their terms."

"And did he become enraged?"

"No, he took the news very calmly. He told me he would take my answer back to the family and that he would contact me again if necessary."

"Did he not seem angry at all?"

She started to shake her head and then winced. "No, which was why I was so surprised when I was attacked."

Christian contemplated their joined hands as he thought through the issues. "Did you see RR, Paul?"

"I didn't. Once I was certain that Mrs. Smith was in the newspaper offices, I set about organizing our transportation home. I knew she wouldn't be foolish enough to leave with anyone, so I assumed she would be safe for a moment." Paul groaned. "Of course, it took longer than I anticipated to get the hackney and now I feel like a fool."

Christian agreed with that sentiment, but he didn't want to arouse Elizabeth's wrath again by mentioning it to Paul. "What happened next, Elizabeth?"

"The man left, and I waited a few minutes in the office before I left as well. Paul asked me to meet him at Somerset House, so I turned in that direction." She hesitated and Christian squeezed her hand. "I crossed the street, and just as I stepped up onto the pavement, someone caught my heel and I almost fell. When I tried to straighten up, I realized I was trapped against . . . against a man I recognized."

"What man?"

She bit down on her already-bruised lip. "My deceased husband's valet."

"What is his name?" Christian asked.

Another tiny hesitation. "Gaston."

He thought back over the scraps of information she had let fall about her marriage. "The same Gaston who would beat you when your husband became too frail to do so?"

She swallowed hard. "Yes."

"Why do they want you back so badly, Elizabeth?" She tried to pull her hand out of his grasp but he held on. "Elizabeth . . ."

"Because there are some legal matters that I control, and the family wants to control them instead."

"What kind of legal matters?" Christian persisted despite the stiffening of her expression.

"Matters concerning the finances of the estate."

"Why weren't these matters settled before you left France?"

"Because their 'demands' were not beneficial to my health."

"You were in fear of your life?"

Elizabeth still failed to meet his gaze. "That is the only reason why I would have left."

Somehow he knew there was more to the story than she was sharing, but at least he had the bones of it.

He released her hands. "I shall speak to my mother about finding you the most knowledgeable French lawyer available. Until then, you are not to leave the house without an escort. Do you understand me?"

"I am quite prepared to accept an escort, but I do not want you to involve your mother in any of this."

Christian met her gaze head-on. "You are employed by my mother. If she chooses to defend you, I believe that is her prerogative."

"I do not need her to defend me or to interfere."

"Why not?" Christian paused as he finally recognized what lay behind her defiance. "What are you afraid of?"

"Mr. Delornay, it is not that simple," Elizabeth whispered. "It never is."

"Then tell me what the real problem is, and let me help you."

Elizabeth closed her eyes and lay back against the pillows. Apart from the livid red marks on her cheek, her skin was the color of palest porcelain. Christian stared down at her as he sensed her deliberately shutting him out.

"Do you wish to live your life like this, Mrs. Smith? Always hiding in the shadows, afraid to use your real name or venture out in case you are kidnapped again? What kind of an existence is that?"

She turned her head away from him, and he stood up and took a sudden violent step toward the bed. He halted as he noticed the tears sliding down her cheeks. Something inside him twisted and his hand dropped to his side. Ambrose touched his shoulder and brought his finger to his lips.

"Let her sleep, Mr. Delornay. Perhaps she will have more answers for us in the morning."

Christian reluctantly allowed Ambrose to usher him out of Elizabeth's bedchamber and down to his study where Paul handed them both large brandies. Christian swallowed the entire glass in one gulp and held it out for a refill.

"I don't care what she says. We are going to help her."

"Hear, hear," Paul replied, holding up his brandy glass.

Ambrose said nothing, his gaze fixed on the swirling brandy, his expression thoughtful.

"I will talk to my mother tomorrow," Christian said, and then groaned. "Damn, I'll have to write to her. I believe she and Philip are still traveling."

Ambrose looked up. "I'm not sure what we can do."

"There must be something!"

"I'm sure there is, but we don't have a lot to go on." He paused. "Why are you so anxious to help Elizabeth, Mr. Delornay? Shouldn't you just turn the whole matter over to your mother?"

"I know Elizabeth far better than my mother does," Christian said. "I have an obligation to help her."

"But she refuses to trust you with her problems."

"She refuses to trust anyone." Christian glared at Ambrose. "I am hardly the one at fault here. If you think you can do any better, please go ahead!"

Ambrose raised his eyebrows. "Perhaps I will."

Christian pulled a piece of paper from his desk and got out his pen. "I have to write to my mother. Please make sure that someone checks on Mrs. Smith during the rest of the night to make certain she is well."

Ambrose put down his untouched brandy and rose to his

feet. "I'll take care of that, Mr. Delornay. Marie-Claude has already offered to sit with her."

"Good." Christian didn't look up. His patience with his old friend was wearing terribly thin, and he was reluctant to see the condemnation on Ambrose's face. He stared down at the blank piece of paper and saw instead Elizabeth's bloodied face.

"Christian?"

He reluctantly looked up and saw that Paul had lingered by the fire. "What?"

"I'm sorry about what happened to Elizabeth while she was in my care."

Christian put down his pen. "You saved her in the end. That is really all that matters."

Paul's hands clenched into fists. "But that was only by chance. I was lucky enough to see him take her. I had to fight my way through the crowds to get to them. I could so easily have been too late."

"But you weren't."

"And yet you are still angry with me."

Christian sighed. "No, I'm angry at myself for misjudging the severity of the situation and not taking proper care of Mrs. Smith."

"She's hardly made it easy for you, has she?"

"That is true."

Paul straightened and turned for the door. "If it is any help to you, I suspect Elizabeth's family come from Sussex."

"Why do you think that?"

"Because that's where my family came from originally, and I can hear it in her speech. She also seems familiar with some of the landmarks I've mentioned in conversation."

"Well, it's a start," Christian said.

"I'll write to my great-aunt Agatha," Paul said. "She knows all the gossip in Sussex for the last fifty years—she started most of it herself, actually, and she might know of Elizabeth's family."

"Thank you, Paul." This time Christian met Paul's brown gaze without rancor. "I'd appreciate that."

"Good night, then."

Paul half saluted and left Christian sitting by himself with far too many questions still unanswered and the safety of the woman he'd reluctantly become involved with preying on his mind.

13

Early the next morning, Christian was back at his desk reading the morning mail when Ambrose came in and shut the door.

"Mr. Delornay, there is something I need to show you." Ambrose laid the black pelisse Christian had chosen for Elizabeth on the desk. "This is the coat Elizabeth wore yesterday." It was muddied to the knees and the wool was badly creased.

"What of it?"

"I was going to send it to be laundered, so I checked the pockets."

Christian sat forward. "You found something?"

"I found this." Ambrose placed a surprisingly heavy leather pouch into Christian's outstretched hand. "I suspect it is jewelry of some sort."

"I wonder if this came from the mysterious RR?"

"One would assume so. The advertisement did mention possessions."

"Did you open it?" Christian asked.

"Of course not!"

"I assume you want me to do it instead."

"Despite my past as a pickpocket, you have always been far less scrupulous than me, Mr. Delornay."

"That is true." Christian searched Ambrose's face. "If you hate the idea of violating Elizabeth's privacy so much, why didn't you just give it back to her and not tell me about it?"

Ambrose grimaced. "Because I suspect this is the only way we might find out something useful about her. And I truly believe she needs our help whether she wants it or not."

Christian weighed the purse in his hand. "I'll open it. If she's angry, I'll willingly take the blame. She might not realize that jewelry can be traced back to its maker and thus to its owner."

"Why would she know?" Ambrose said. "Only thieves, gamblers, and pawnbrokers need that information."

"And proprietors of upper-class houses of pleasure. How many pieces of jewelry have we discreetly traced and returned to their grateful owners after a night of drunken revelry here?"

"Several," Ambrose replied. "It's amazing what people will forget or misplace in the heat of passion."

"Or in a writhing mass of naked bodies." Christian opened the drawstring and tipped the contents of the bag out onto his blotter. "Jewelry, it is." He carefully spread the jewels out. "A mixture of new and old." He looked up at Ambrose. "How likely is it that Elizabeth had time to catalog exactly what was in here?"

"Very unlikely I'd say."

"Well that could play to our advantage. If we find anything of note, we can probably remove it temporarily. She'll assume RR didn't bring everything with him or that he helped himself to some choice pieces."

He stared down at the precious gems and gold and stirred them with his finger. Most of the newer pieces appeared too large and gaudy to suit Elizabeth's beauty. He reckoned someone else must have chosen them. He paused to admire a string of perfectly matched pearls and then spotted something completely suited to their purpose.

"There's a locket here, Ambrose."

He picked it up, disentangling the thin gold chain from a diamond and ruby hair clip. The locket was oval and appeared to have a worn family crest engraved on the front. Christian tried to open the locket but met with no success. He passed it over to Ambrose, who couldn't open it either.

"I'll take it to Mr. William Neate, the jeweler on Cornhill. Send him a note, Ambrose, and ask when it will be convenient for me to see him," Christian said. "I'm sure he'll be able to find out who made the locket and reveal what's inside."

Ambrose sat back. "I still don't like this."

"This may surprise you, but I don't like it either," Christian replied. He got out his handkerchief and laid the locket in the center before placing it back in his pocket. "I've been harping on about being honest to Mrs. Smith for weeks and now I'm stealing her jewelry."

"I suppose it is for a good reason." Ambrose sighed. "Is there anything else there that might help us?"

Christian perused the rest of the jewelry. "There's a silver bracelet that might yield a hallmark and a maker's name. I think I'll keep that in reserve." He removed the bracelet, put it in the top drawer of his desk, and locked it. "I suggest you delay returning this jewelry to Elizabeth until she thinks to ask for it. With any luck, I might be able to get the locket back into her possession before she even realizes I've borrowed it."

"That would probably be for the best." Ambrose stood up. "But if she asks for the bag, I will give it to her."

"Fair enough, my friend." Christian gathered up the remaining items and put them back in the soft leather pouch. "Here you are."

Ambrose took the bag and put it in his coat pocket. "I dispatched your letter to your mother this morning."

"Excellent." Christian rose too. "Let's hope she has some answers for us as well."

Ambrose went along to the kitchen and Christian turned toward the stairs. When he reached Elizabeth's room, he knocked softly on the door and was surprised when she asked him to enter. He halted inside the room, his gaze drawn to the empty bed.

"Why aren't you still in bed?"

"There is no reason for me to be there," Elizabeth answered him far too lightly. "I am feeling much better."

"Are you sure?"

She was busy drawing the curtains to let in the weak sunlight. She was fully dressed in a gray muslin morning gown with a paisley pattern. She looked over her shoulder at him and he saw that she did indeed have the makings of a black eye.

"I'm a little stiff and sore, but that's all."

Christian leaned against the bedpost and regarded her. Her dogged independence continued to both impress and alarm him. "I haven't scheduled you to work today."

"Why not?" She lifted her chin.

"Because you'd frighten all the guests."

"Oh . . ." Her hand flew to her cheek and she blushed. "I could easily cover the bruises."

He walked across the room and took her hands in his. "You don't need to."

"Then what am I supposed to do all day?"

"You can help me with the accounts?"

She looked dubious and he raised her hands to his lips and kissed her fingertips. She looked up, her cool gaze guarded.

"Why are you being so pleasant?" Elizabeth asked.

"How did you expect me to be?"

"Angry, and busy pestering me with a thousand more questions."

"I assume you told me everything there was to tell." He paused. "Was I mistaken?"

"I told you everything I could."

"That's not the same and you know it."

"But it is more than you knew before."

He watched her carefully. "Did you think I would still be angry with you?"

"Of course I did. You hate my unbecoming independence."

"That's not quite true," Christian said. "In some ways you remind me of my mother."

She shivered. "Don't say that. I'll wager you would have preferred it if I'd turned up here, cried buckets of tears, and flung myself on your mercy. You probably imagine you could have solved all my problems by now."

"No, because I would still have underestimated the severity of the threat against you."

She sighed. "I'd forgotten that money is a powerful motivator."

"You obviously inherited something they want."

A shadow passed across her exquisite face. "I suppose I did."

"If you could relinquish those rights, would you do so?"

"Some of them, yes. I even offered to . . ." She closed her mouth and looked away from him. "I cannot relinquish them all. It's not that simple."

"You keep saying that, and it is beginning to annoy me."

"*Beginning* to?" She opened her gray eyes wide. "You hate the fact that you don't know everything about me and that I keep secrets."

"I suppose I do," he said slowly. "I'm not used to being denied anything." He studied her grazed cheek and the swollen cut on her lower lip. "But I want to find the man who did this to you and beat him to a bloody pulp."

"That is very noble of you. I doubt it would help."

"I disagree. He frightened you, didn't he?"

Her expression stilled. "Why do you say that?"

"Because you finally told us more about the threat to your person."

She sighed. "He did frighten me. Even when my husband was alive I never liked Gaston."

"Did he do more than beat you?"

Her answering smile was perfect. "Yes, he did. I don't believe he was supposed to touch me, but he found plenty of opportunities."

Christian's longing to find Gaston increased tenfold, and he dwelt lovingly on an image of hanging the damned Frenchman by his testicles and leaving him like that to die.

"Despite your concerns, I'm still going to ask my mother to help you."

"There is no need." She hesitated. "I'm hoping this will be the last we hear of them."

Christian snorted. "Elizabeth, if your husband's family is prepared to chase you across the English Channel and abduct you in broad daylight, a slight setback like this is hardly going to put them off."

She moved away from him and started pacing the room, her hands clasped together at her waist. "Then perhaps we could set a trap and force them out into the open."

"With you as bait? Do you really think I would agree to that?"

"It is not your decision to make."

He watched her carefully as his suspicions deepened. "I suspect you are planning something else entirely." He paused and she went still, her calm gaze fixed on his. "Something that involves only you."

She turned away from him. "I did think to give myself up and go back."

He frowned at her averted face. "Like a meek little lamb? Do you really believe I'd fall for that? You are just trying to draw me away from your true purpose."

She walked away from him toward the door. "I might have no choice. Even you said that running away from everything was foolish."

"And running straight back is any better?" She opened her door and Christian started after her. "I don't believe you are that foolish."

He also hoped to God he could find out something about her life before she attempted to solve all her problems herself and ended up in danger.

"I'm not foolish, just practical." She glanced up at him, her gaze clear and steady. "I've brought you nothing but trouble, Mr. Delornay, and I regret that immensely."

He wanted to tell her that wasn't true, but the words stuck in his throat. Her arrival *had* changed everything, and he still wasn't sure if he liked it. She simultaneously intrigued and delighted him, made him crave her sexually and worry about her safety—all the softer emotions he'd striven to control or eradicate from his personal life.

"I don't regret meeting you, Mrs. Smith."

But it was too late and too little. She'd already retreated behind her smiling mask, and he'd lost the opportunity to reassure her that she was valued and safe with him. Part of him regretted that; the rest of him was simply too relieved that he hadn't made a terrible mistake. He of all people knew that showing how you felt was never a good idea.

Christian left Elizabeth with Marie-Claude and went down to the kitchen. Paul arrived through the back door, his blond hair damp and curling from the drizzle. His boots left muddy tracks on the flagstone floor, which Madame Durand was sure to notice and complain about.

Paul held up a bundle of papers. "I have some post for you. Shall I put it in your office?"

Christian patted the tabletop. "You might as well give it to me here."

"And how is Mrs. Smith this morning?"

"She seems quite well," Christian said, his attention caught by a letter that bore his mother's unmistakable handwriting. It was too soon for a reply to his message, so he assumed she had some news of her own to share. "Mrs. Smith is upstairs talking to Marie-Claude if you want to see for yourself."

"I'll do that, thank you."

Paul disappeared while still being scolded by Madame for the state of his boots. Christian slit the seal on the letter. It was closely written in dark ink and seemed to contain a great deal of exclamation marks, which was fairly typical of his mother's style.

He frowned as he read. His mother had consulted with her many acquaintances in the shipping world and obtained a list of passengers who had crossed from France to England in the past year. She had narrowed down the list of possibilities to three women who might be Elizabeth. All three had crossed from Calais to Dover and had traveled alone.

She went on to say that she had information coming as to where each of the three women had traveled from in France to reach the port of Calais. Christian paused briefly to admire both his mother's methods and her thoroughness. It hadn't occurred to him to try and trace Elizabeth back to France from her port of entry. He read the letter again and then took it into his study and locked it away in his desk.

It seemed that Elizabeth's attempts to hide her past would come to naught. Once he knew exactly who she was running from, he could form a plan to help her. He thought back over the tiny snippets of information she'd let fall. Hadn't she mentioned that the current heir was enamored of her and that there was a mistress involved somewhere? He'd have to see if he could prise anything else out of her.

There was one more thing to arrange before he got down to the serious business of balancing the books. Even though Elizabeth would be unaware of it, he intended to place an advertisement in the newspaper that would draw her assailants into a trap of his own devising. He flexed his fingers. The thought of meeting up with the mysterious RR and the French valet and showing them how he felt about men who preyed on defenseless women gave him immense pleasure.

He stilled. Why was he so damned interested in helping a woman he hardly knew? Getting involved with a woman like her went against everything he believed in, everything he'd fought so hard to achieve over the years since he'd found out his mother owned a pleasure house and had lied to him for his entire childhood. Perhaps that was why Elizabeth affected him. She was as independent as his mother and obviously equally adept at lying to him. Surely that should make her obnoxious in his eyes—or did he secretly crave a challenge?

If so, he was a fool. His gaze fell on his open diary and he noted that the room of desires was booked for the evening. He scanned the requested scenario and realized that Elizabeth's attendance, or a replacement for her, was not required. It seemed that the lady who had reserved the room wanted all male attention. He pondered his options and smiled as he realized that Elizabeth could help after all and that she might even enjoy the role he planned for her.

Elizabeth woke up from her nap with the suggestion of a headache and pressed a careful hand to her brow. Despite her best intentions to appear unaffected by her ordeal, Christian and Marie-Claude had insisted she take a nap in the middle of the day to conserve her energy. She'd only capitulated because Christian had suggested that he needed her assistance during the evening shift. She was too proud to admit that she had begun to doubt her ability to make it through the day.

She lit a candle and glanced at the clock on the mantelpiece. Her body still ached a little, although she was definitely feeling a lot better. Christian had asked her to meet him in the room of desires at eight o'clock, and it wasn't yet seven. She had time to go down to the kitchen and have something to eat. As if in support of that idea, her stomach growled and she pressed her hand to it.

She wanted to show Christian that she was unaffected by her ordeal, and presenting herself ready to work should lessen his concern. As she descended the stairs, she pondered his insistence on involving his mother in her dilemma. From what she'd been told, Madame Helene was surely one of the few people alive who might understand why Elizabeth had acted as she had. But could she risk asking Helene directly for help without involving Christian, who already saw too much of his mother in her for her comfort? She didn't think so.

Ambrose was in the kitchen and he rose and bowed to her. Her attention was caught by her black pelisse, which lay over the back of one of the kitchen chairs.

"It was covered in mud," Ambrose said. "I had it cleaned and brushed for you, Elizabeth. I hope that was all right?"

"I . . ." Elizabeth dived for the coat and thrust her hand into the single pocket. It was empty. She turned to Ambrose, her mouth dry. Had she lost the pouch during the struggle, or had Gaston deliberately been sent to take it back? "Was there anything in the pocket?"

"Yes, there was." Ambrose held up the leather bag. "Is this what you are looking for?"

"Thank you." Elizabeth took the pouch and realized that her hands were shaking. "I thought . . ." She shook her head. "I thought I must have lost it."

Ambrose sat back down at the table and poured her some milk from the big earthenware jar. "You should eat something. Madame just made some buns."

"That sounds delightful."

Elizabeth reached for the milk and concentrated on sipping it until her nausea subsided. She was surprised Ambrose hadn't asked her any questions about the pouch until it occurred to her that he had probably checked the contents anyway. But as far as she knew, there was nothing that could help identify her, nothing with her real name or rank, anyway.

Madame Durand put a plate with two warm buttered buns, slices of soft cheese, and a peeled pear in front of her, and Elizabeth resolved to eat. By the time she finished, she was feeling much better and Paul had arrived. Despite the fact that he wasn't in uniform, he saluted Elizabeth, took off his hat, and sat beside her. He then proceeded to steal half of her bun and the remainder of her pear from her plate. Elizabeth had never met a man who always seemed so hungry.

When the kitchen clock chimed the quarter hour, Ambrose stood up and turned to Elizabeth and Paul. "Shall we go upstairs to the room of desires?"

"You are going there too?" Elizabeth looked at them both.

"Yes," Paul said, and placed her hand on his arm. "Didn't Christian tell you?"

"He just told me to meet him there just before eight." Elizabeth followed Ambrose up the stairs and waited as he unlocked the door. "I'm not quite sure what he wants me to do, seeing as he says my appearance will frighten the guests."

Paul kissed her nose. "You look adorable."

"I look as if I have been brawling in the street."

"Well, you have." Paul stood back for her to precede him through the door. "Maybe Christian has a different role for you to play tonight."

"Indeed, I do."

Elizabeth looked up to see Christian waiting for them in the center of the waiting area. He'd taken off his coat, cravat, and waistcoat, and his shirt had fallen open to display the elegant lines of his throat. He held aloft a candelabra, which illuminated the guinea gold of his hair.

"Elizabeth, you will wait in here." He gestured at the first door and opened it. "Ambrose and Paul, get undressed. Our client will be here shortly."

Elizabeth walked over to him, and he bowed as she went past him into the smallest of the rooms. Instead of shutting the door, Christian pulled black drapes across the opening. Within, a single chair awaited her, and a gold curtain covered a large section of one of the walls.

"I assume you wish me to greet the guest, let Ambrose know that she has arrived, and watch what happens from here," Elizabeth said.

"Very good," Christian replied. "When she enters the room next door, you may pull back the curtain and observe. If she seems to be hurting anyone, or they signal you, feel free to intervene."

"And how will I do that without making things worse?"

"Run down to the kitchen and find one of the Kelly lads. They are big enough to frighten anyone." He nodded and turned back to the door.

"Where will you be?" Elizabeth asked.

He raised his eyebrows. "In there, of course."

He disappeared before she could form a reply, and she settled down to wait for the appearance of the guest. The chime of the bell when the exterior door opened had her rising and walking across to the thick black curtain. She could vaguely see the shape of a woman on the other side of the curtain silhouetted against the candlelight.

"Good evening, madame, and welcome to the room of desires," Elizabeth said. "Please enter through the door marked with a one and all your requests will be met."

The woman didn't say anything, but she obediently headed for the right door, and Elizabeth ran to open the gold curtain and knocked on the mirror. She remembered when Ambrose had first shown her the clever trick, how from the other room it looked just like a normal reflective mirror, but from her side it was as clear as looking through glass.

Elizabeth swallowed hard at the glorious sight that appeared. Paul, Ambrose, and Christian were naked, apart from masks, and were lined up in the center of the room awaiting the woman's appraisal. All three men were much of a height, but there the similarities ended. Paul was as slender as a greyhound, Ambrose more richly muscled, but it was Christian who drew her gaze. He seemed as perfectly formed as a Greek statue. Elizabeth sank down onto the solitary chair and prepared to enjoy herself.

14

Christian studied the woman who had arranged this little sexual scenario with keen appreciation. She was a mature lady, probably in her early forties, with a voluptuous figure. She wore a wedding ring but was now apparently a widow. She had been quite specific about her demands. She wanted three men at the same time in whatever sexual combinations she desired. The men were not to speak to her; they were just to obey her commands. That was one of the reasons why Christian had decided to participate. It had been a long time since anyone had told him what to do in bed, or out of it, and it was good to remember how it felt to be dominated.

And to be perfectly honest, he wanted Elizabeth to see him like this. He suspected she would get more enjoyment out of watching him submit than the woman who was fucking him.

"Gentlemen, you may call me Mistress. You may only speak if I address you, and then only to say yes or no." She raised her eyebrows. "Do you all understand?"

"Yes, Mistress," they all replied, and she smiled.

"Excellent. Clasp your hands behind your backs. I'm sure

you realize that you may not touch me unless I specifically say so."

She came closer and began a leisurely stroll along the line, touching and stroking each of them, tweaking nipples and cupping buttocks. Christian's cock started to swell, and he noticed that Ambrose and Paul were similarly affected. She stopped beside Paul.

"You, go and get me some collars and leashes."

Christian had already laid them out on the silk counterpane of the bed, so Paul had no difficulty finding them. He presented them to the woman and stepped back into line.

"Thank you. Now all of you kneel down."

Christian waited until she buckled the leather collar around his neck and attached the leash. The leather leash swung gently down his chest, brushing his cock, which made his shaft jerk. Paul was already breathing harder, and the tip of his cock was glistening with moisture.

The woman bent to gather all three of the leashes in her hand. "Now, stand up."

Christian stood and allowed his gaze to shift over to the mirror where he knew Elizabeth was watching everything. Was she enjoying the show? Was she aroused?

His attention flew back to the woman when she grasped his cock and played with him until he was fully erect. She did the same to Paul and Ambrose, one hand working their flesh, the other gripping the ends of their leashes. Paul made a stifled sound and she glared at him.

"You, go and fetch me that whip."

She released Paul's leash, and he went back to the bed and brought both the sturdy riding crop and the longer-tailed driving whip. The woman considered both whips and then tossed the driving whip onto the floor. Christian held his breath as she walked behind them. His head was abruptly jerked backward as his collar resisted the twisting of the leash. She smacked the flat tip of the crop against her palm in a rhythmic motion.

"All of you work your cocks but do not allow yourselves to come."

Christian was glad to touch himself to relieve the gathering ache in his balls. And the pleasure would counteract the pain he was sure lay ahead as the woman thwacked the crop against his buttocks four times and then did the same to the other men. A dull ache spread through his arse and exacerbated the pounding pulse in his cock.

She whipped them again and then dropped the crop onto the floor and came around to the front. She sat in the chair Christian had placed in the center of the room, carefully drew up her black silk skirts, and opened her legs wide.

"You will all get down on your knees and lick me until I come."

Ambrose went first, followed by Christian. Between the two of them, they soon had her wet and moaning. Christian only eased back to let Paul have his turn and concentrated on kissing her thighs and knees instead. She came hard, one hand buried in Paul's hair, the other still clutching the leashes.

Christian's cock was aching in earnest now, but he had always enjoyed delaying his gratification. It made the resulting climax so much better. He only wished he could touch the other men and drive them even higher. So much flesh, so many wet, hard cocks and only one woman to satisfy—although perhaps he should say two, as he was certain Elizabeth was aroused.

"We shall move onto the bed." The woman pointed at Ambrose. "You will carry me."

Ambrose picked her up, and the four of them moved together toward the large four-poster bed that dominated the room. Ambrose laid her gently down on the blue silk counterpane and she thanked him.

"Loosen my stays and undress me."

Christian started on her stockings, kissing and licking her knees and the curve of her shin as he revealed her skin. Ambrose dealt with the lacings on her dress and corset while Paul gathered petticoats and skirts out of the way and finally disposed of the woman's shift.

A tug on Christian's collar forced him to crawl closer to the woman's face. She studied him carefully, one hand under his chin, her thumb tracing his lower lip. He stared back into her dark brown almond-shaped eyes and admired her lushly curved mouth.

"I want to be kissed and sucked and adored. I want to climax at least six times before I let any of you fuck me, and I don't want any of you to come until I tell you so."

Christian tried to nod, but the grip on his chin was too strong. When she released him, he bent his head and kissed her large breasts, then felt Ambrose and Paul move into position and start to pleasure the woman too. It soon became hard to distinguish whose body brushed his, who was groaning and whose cock slid against his in an endless tangle of warm, sweaty lust. He could taste the woman on his tongue, could even taste the leather leashes, which bound them together like rough curling vines.

He tried to remain detached and count her orgasms, but it was hard to concentrate when she dug her nails into his arse or played with his cock until he was dripping and aching and desperate for release. He even remembered to oil his fingers and ease them into her arse, certain that if she really wanted all three of them, she'd not want to be penetrated without some preparation.

Eventually she shoved at his chest and pushed Ambrose away from between her legs. "Let me up."

She sat back against the headboard, her bosom heaving, her

mouth swollen with their kisses, her brown hair disordered on her shoulders.

She pointed at Paul. "I want you in my arse." She pointed at Ambrose. "You in my cunt." She finally turned to Christian. "And you, my pretty, in my mouth."

Christian showed Paul where the oil was to lubricate his cock, and Paul covered himself quickly, his breathing ragged, his shaft now glistening a deep red. He crawled behind the woman and sat against the head of the bed, his knees spread wide to accommodate the woman's broad hips and lower body. She scooted back toward him, and he lifted her over him and slowly rocked himself inside her. Both of them gasped when her buttocks lodged tightly against his groin.

"Now you." The woman beckoned to Ambrose, who crawled between her thighs. Christian couldn't help caressing Ambrose's tight buttocks as he watched his friend slowly and carefully press his cock between the woman's swollen labia.

She moaned and grabbed at Ambrose's shoulder. "You will follow *my* rhythm, not your own. You will only come when I'm ready."

"Yes, Mistress," Ambrose murmured.

She snapped her fingers in Christian's direction. "Come here."

For a moment, he debated disobeying her and her gaze narrowed. She grabbed the end of his leash and yanked it hard until he had no choice but to move or choke.

"I said come here."

He went around to the side where he could see both Ambrose and Paul in profile with the woman sandwiched between them. He knelt up and she reached for his cock and squeezed it hard, her nails digging into his already-oversensitized flesh. His breath hissed out and she smiled before leaning forward and swallowing his shaft whole.

* * *

Elizabeth stared at the entwined bodies on the bed and realized that her heart was beating very fast and that she was actually squirming in her seat. The sight was certainly erotic enough to make any woman wet and wanting and . . . Elizabeth couldn't help but wonder how it would feel to be the woman, to have the power to tell all the men what to do and have them obey her.

The sight of Ambrose's tight buttocks flexing as he drove into the woman was enticing enough, but she also knew that Paul was doing his part and that Christian . . . He had his eyes closed as the woman sucked and played with his cock, one hand gripping the bedpost, the other on Ambrose's shoulder.

Elizabeth suppressed a moan as the woman released most of Christian's cock and just toyed with and nibbled the swollen purple crown. She saw how hard he was trying not to thrust forward with his hips and take control of the situation. Her hand slid to her lap and pushed through the layers of skirts and petticoat to her own needy core. She'd let him fuck her mouth. She wouldn't be able to stop him.

Suddenly, everything appeared to speed up and the woman started to buck and writhe against the men's constraining bodies. Her muffled scream exploded around Christian's cock and he jerked in response. Elizabeth knew he was coming, too, from the savage expression on his face. Ambrose gave one final thrust and went still. Elizabeth couldn't see Paul, but he would be gaining his release as well.

Ambrose moved back and so did Christian. Paul carefully lifted the woman away from him, and she appeared to be talking again and all the men nodded. Elizabeth waited as Paul got off the bed and walked over to the secluded corner of the room to wash himself. Then he brought a bowl of water back with him and started attending to the woman on the bed.

Did she want more, then? It seemed likely. Elizabeth realized she was aching to join them, to have all three men give her the same attention. But . . . she wouldn't want to be in charge. That salacious thought made her pause. What would she want, then?

She jumped as Christian got off the bed and sauntered with effortless grace toward the mirror. His blond hair was tousled, his skin gleamed with sweat, and he was already half-erect again. He had a washcloth in his hand, which he rubbed slowly over his damp muscled chest and groin. Elizabeth stiffened, as he appeared to stare straight at her. One of his hands was cupping his balls and stroking his cock as if he were offering them to her.

His lips moved and she strained to make out what he was saying. He glanced down at his cock and ran his thumb over the crown. "Touch yourself."

Was that what he was asking her to do? She quivered at the thought and shook her head even though he couldn't see her. He played with the end of the leather leash, flicking it over the slit in his cock, biting his lip as if the sensation was both pleasurable and painful. He looked back at her again, his hazel eyes narrowed.

"Fuck yourself."

She understood what he wanted, and even as he mouthed the words, her hand was already gathering up her skirts and burrowing under her petticoats to seek her sex. Her fingers encountered slippery wetness and heat and an already-throbbing clit, and she almost moaned out loud.

Christian's nod and contented smile seemed to suggest he knew exactly what she was doing. He turned back to the woman on the bed, and Elizabeth kept her hand wedged between her thighs. She waited to see what the woman would demand next and shivered as Christian lay flat on his back and the woman mounted him.

She didn't feel jealous. Somehow she knew Christian was performing for her and for her pleasure alone. Elizabeth slid two fingers inside her sex and moved them in time to the men on the bed as the three of them fucked the woman, changing positions as she commanded, using their hands to force another erection as she demanded more and more. The thrill of her own climax made Elizabeth cover her mouth as she screamed out her pleasure.

Eventually, even the woman seemed exhausted and she unbuckled the men's collars. They helped her get dressed again, and Christian bowed deeply as she appeared to compliment them all. Elizabeth leaped to her feet and waited by the black drapery at the door in case the woman wished to communicate with her. But there was no sound other than the gentle chime of the bell as the door into the main hallway opened and closed.

Elizabeth walked back to the mirror and stared at the now-empty room. Where had all the men gone?

"Did you enjoy that, Elizabeth?"

She turned, her hand pressed to her lips, to find Christian had come through the black drapes and into the room, still naked. As he sauntered toward her, she inhaled the intertwined smells of sex and soap and sweat.

He cupped her chin. "Did you do what I told you to do?"

She could only nod and he smiled.

"I'm glad to hear it." His fingers traced the curve of her jaw where the bruises still lingered. "Did you come?"

"Yes."

"Even better." He paused and looked down into her eyes. "Everything I did in there was for show. You know that, don't you?"

She moistened her lips with her tongue. "I wasn't jealous, if that is what you mean."

He leaned closer and licked at the seam of her lips, his tongue as delicate as a butterfly's touch. "I'm glad." His fingers moved to the back of her gown, and he started undoing the buttons. "I want to see you."

She let him take off her gown, and it pooled at her feet. He helped her step out of it and guided her back to sit in the chair. "I know you are sore." He kissed her knee through the filmy muslin of her shift. "I'll be careful."

"I'm not . . ." She moaned as he gently pushed her knees apart and stared at her needy sex.

"God, look at you," he whispered. "All ready to be fucked. Did watching us excite you?"

"Obviously." Elizabeth couldn't help her sharp retort.

He chuckled against her thigh, and his warm breath stirred against her most tender flesh, making her shiver.

He lifted his head to stare at her, his gaze considering. "What did you like the most?"

She yearned to say "you" but hesitated to give him such an easy victory. "It was all wonderful."

He licked her clit, the tip of his tongue curling around her swollen bud like a caress. "What part in particular? Did you like seeing us all in collars and leashes?"

She almost groaned at the new question. "That was certainly unexpected."

She was rewarded for her answer with another slow drag of his tongue over her clit and down to her opening. His tongue dipped inside her, and she wanted to clutch at his hair.

When he looked up at her, his mouth was wet with her juices. "Would you like to lead me around like that?" His finger came to rest on her clit, and she felt the pulse of her need throb against his flesh. "I suspect I would resist you."

A picture of herself in a collar, fighting *him* flashed through her mind and she shuddered. "I would . . . I would not want to do that to you."

His gaze sharpened and he moved his finger from her clit and slid it deep inside her. She held her breath, but he did nothing more. She tried to raise her hips and he held her still.

"What *would* you want, Elizabeth?"

She licked her lips and stared into his suddenly narrowed eyes. Keeping his finger still inside her, he bent forward and kissed her mouth so slowly and thoroughly that she whimpered. He pulled away and bit the tip of her nose. "Do you want my mouth and fingers on your cunt, Elizabeth? Do you want me to make you come?"

She nodded but he did nothing more than stare at her.

"Yes," she whispered reluctantly. "I want you to make me come."

"Then answer my question." He kissed her again. She tried to arch her back and push his solitary finger deeper, but he allowed her no quarter. "What made you wet, what excited you?"

His soft voice made her shiver and want to answer him. He sank down to his knees between her open thighs and regarded his embedded finger. "I want to make you come, but I can't until you tell me the truth."

"I never tell you the truth," she whispered. "You know that."

He licked her swollen clit with the tip of his tongue, back and forth, back and forth until she wanted to scream with frustration. Every time she inched forward, he moved back, keeping her on the brink of a climax that she knew would be amazing.

"Please, Christian."

He looked up at her. "Tell me."

She sighed. "I liked watching you."

He added a second finger to the first and she moaned, but he still didn't move them. "You liked watching me having to do what I was told?"

"That was certainly unusual."

He held her gaze. "I don't enjoy it."

"I know that."

He added a third finger. "And what else?"

"Isn't that enough?"

"I'm not that conceited. I'm sure there is more." His thumb hovered over her clit and she stiffened. "Do you want to climax or not? You're so wet and open that you look like you've already had a man's cock and his come inside you."

In truth, at this moment, she wanted to climax more than she wanted to breathe. She closed her eyes and he snapped his fingers.

"Don't do that."

The cool note of command in his voice made her focus on his face.

"Look at my fingers inside you. Don't you want my mouth there as well?"

"Yes," she choked out. All she had to do was put her own hand on her clit and she would be climaxing right now. But she knew she wouldn't do it, and she guessed he knew it too.

He licked a slow circle around her clit and then down and around his own fingers, making her quiver.

"Tell me."

"I imagined myself in the bed with you all."

"With the client too?"

"No, just me and the three of you."

He added a fourth finger, and the glimmerings of a climax stirred deep inside her.

"Were you holding our leashes?"

She stared down at his embedded fingers that stretched her wide, aware that she was vulnerable and on edge and that she no longer cared.

"No."

His thumb settled over her clit. "Then what?"

"You were holding mine," she whispered unsteadily. "You were all . . ."

"All what?"

"Fucking me."

"As we fucked the client?"

"No." She licked her lips. "I had no say in what you were doing to me."

"We were using you as we wished?"

"Yes."

"And did you like it?"

"I loved it."

With a curse, he pumped his fingers into her, and his mouth dove down to join his thumb on her clit. Elizabeth screamed as the strongest climax of her life roared through her, and she kept coming, her body wracked by the spasms, her back arching as she ground herself against his mouth and fingers.

Christian pulled her out of the chair and down on top of him, expertly bringing her over his erect shaft and letting her set the pace. She came again and he propped himself up on his elbows so that he could take her breasts into his mouth and suckle her in time to his thrusts. Her third climax took him with her, and he groaned as his come was forced out of him in long, hot spurts high inside her.

She collapsed over his chest, her breathing unsteady, her face buried against his shoulder. He held her carefully, aware that she was still bruised from her ordeal and unwilling to add to the soreness she would have on the morrow.

He threaded his fingers into her long, tangled hair and nuzzled her ear. If he'd understood her correctly, his lover entertained fantasies of being dominated. Excitement threaded through him as he considered what to say to her next.

"Elizabeth."

"Yes?"

"You enjoy it when Ambrose, Paul, and I all fuck you?"

"Yes." She moved restlessly against his chest. "And I should not have said anything. You will never let this go, will you?"

"You also fantasize about being taken against your will?"

She pulled back from him. "I didn't say *that*."

He held her wary gaze. "You *said* that you would have no say in what was done to you. Isn't that the same thing?"

"I . . ." She tried to roll away from him, but he held her still. "I have imagined what that might be like."

"Indeed."

This time, Christian let her go and watched as she gathered up her clothes. The thin muslin clung to her skin where he'd left his seed and his sweat. He cupped his balls, and his already-overused cock started to stiffen again, the pain melding into the anticipation of pleasure. The sight of her well-fucked body stirred something deeply primitive in him. He wished he'd bitten her throat and marked her completely as his own. . . .

She glanced at him and then looked away. He made no effort to cover himself or slow the glide of his fingers over his rapidly hardening flesh.

"Do you think I find your fantasies repulsive?"

"I'm not sure." She kept her face averted. "All I know is that you will find a way to use them against me."

"Against you? Surely if I understand what you want in bed, I can better provide satisfaction for you?"

She sighed and her shoulders went down. "Of course. I forget that you manage a house of pleasure. That would be your goal."

His fingers stilled and anger pooled in his gut. "You're not a client. I have no need to please you at all."

She headed for the door. "Then, please, don't bother."

He let her leave, aware that she had exposed herself far more than she would have liked. It would be wise to let her regain her composure before he followed up on her interesting revelations. She didn't know that the thought of her fighting his domination excited him more than anything. He squeezed his cock hard and his come flooded out over his pumping fist. But he would follow up on her fantasies. The temptation was too hard to resist.

15

"Thank you for seeing me today, Mr. Neate. I appreciate it," Christian said.

Mr. Neate looked up from his perusal of Elizabeth's locket and grunted. "It's always a pleasure doing business with you, Mr. Delornay. I never know what you will turn up with next. Although this"—he pointed at the locket—"is quite a simple piece compared to most of the jewelry you bring me."

"It is indeed. You managed to open the clasp?"

"I did. Would you like to see what is inside?"

Christian nodded and Mr. Neate carefully opened the locket to reveal two tiny portraits of a man and a woman. Christian peered at the small painted images. The female bore a striking resemblance to Elizabeth.

"I believe the locket was made in London by a goldsmith named Edwards, Mr. Delornay. The hallmark dates it to about thirty years ago."

Which would tie in nicely with Christian's theory that the locket had belonged to Elizabeth's mother.

"Does Mr. Edwards still practice his trade?"

"I don't believe so. After making some inquiries, I found out that he sold most of his work through Wilson and Farridge, a jewelers in Cheapside. Do you know it?"

"I can't say I've ever been there, but I suspect it will be my next call this morning." Christian closed the locket and handed it back to Mr. Neate. "Did you have any success in deciphering the crest engraved on the front?"

Mr. Neate passed him a sheet of paper. "I managed to draw it out for you. The motto is in Latin."

"So it is." Christian studied the crest. "I'll have to check with the College of Arms to make sure I have it right." He folded the piece of paper and put it inside his coat. "Thank you, Mr. Neate. You have been most helpful."

"A pleasure, sir." Mr. Neate wrapped the locket in a piece of soft cloth and gave it to Christian. "I polished it up a bit and fixed that hinge, so the owner will be able to open it more easily."

"I'm sure she'll be most grateful."

After shaking hands with Mr. Neate, Christian turned to leave the small, cramped shop. He signaled for a hackney at the curb, glad for once that he hadn't chosen to drive himself. The hackney driver would probably know exactly where to find Wilson and Farridge in Cheapside, which would save him valuable time. With the weather looking like rain, he had no desire to wander around an area of London he didn't know and risk either his life or his horses.

He patted the pocket where he'd put the locket and the drawing of the family crest. If it had its own coat of arms, Elizabeth's father's family was an ancient and respected one. He doubted all her relatives were dead and wondered whether they would finally be willing to recognize her. Perhaps they already had and she was simply too proud to respond to them?

He smiled. That was a distinct possibility. His Elizabeth might not acknowledge her rank, but she bore all the hallmarks of a true lady. He frowned as the hackney jolted to a sudden stop and his driver started yelling at some unfortunate man with a cart full of apples who had dared to cross in front of him. She wasn't "his" Elizabeth. She belonged to no man. She'd made that abundantly clear.

He leaned closer to the window and studied the route to Cheapside, aware that the finer streets were disappearing and the roads becoming narrower. The houses were taller and more packed together and the people less genteel. Not that he felt in any danger. He was well able to take care of himself.

The Wilson and Farridge shop front looked as if it had seen better days. The timber-framed building sat low on the ground as if hunched over in a sulk, and the dirty diamond-paned windows and marked oak door hardly hinted at prosperity. But then Elizabeth had said her father was the black sheep of his family, so perhaps his choice of jeweler had suited his straitened circumstances rather than his rank.

Christian got down and asked the hackney driver to wait. After some further words and an exchange of coin, the driver agreed, and Christian was able to pursue his business. When he pushed open the warped door, a bell clanged somewhere in the back of the building. There was no one at the counter, so Christian waited patiently until he heard booted footsteps approaching.

The man who appeared was tall and thin, with a fine shock of pure white hair. He squinted at Christian through his spectacles.

"May I help you, sir? Do you wish to pawn something?"

His suspicious tone made Christian want to smile.

"Good morning. I'm here on another kind of errand. I'm trying to trace the owner of a piece of jewelry. I believe it was made by a goldsmith associated with your shop."

The man sighed and shook his head. "We don't do a lot of jewelry now, sir. It's mostly trade, if you know what I mean."

"This particular piece was bought several years ago. I'm hoping you might have a record of it being made or purchased from your shop."

"We might do, sir. We do have all our records." He regarded Christian with shrewd eyes. "Of course, searching for that information will take me away from my work . . ."

Christian took out his purse. "Naturally, I'm prepared to pay for your time, Mr. . . . ?"

"I'm Mr. William Farridge, the third to bear that name and the third to run the family business."

"A pleasure to meet you, Mr. Farridge." Christian consulted his pocket watch. "Do you think you might find the information for me now, or should I come back later?"

"I have the books in the back. Do you have any idea when the piece of jewelry was purchased?"

Christian took out the locket and showed it to Mr. Farridge. "I understand that it was made by a Mr. Edwards about thirty years ago."

"That would probably be Joshua Edwards. He sold us some beautiful pieces before his death." Mr. Farridge sighed and peered at the locket. "You don't see craftsmanship like this anymore. Give me but a moment and I will fetch the relevant book."

Christian leaned against the countertop and examined the various items on the shelves behind the worktops. He suspected most of them were articles that had been pawned and were either awaiting the return of their owners or a new home. Among the items jostling for position on the crowded shelves were a fine silver christening mug, a pewter tankard, and a full set of wooden false teeth. He hoped the owner of the teeth wasn't suffering too badly from their loss.

"Here we are, sir."

Mr. Farridge returned bearing a large leather-bound book

covered in spiderwebs, which he thumped down on the counter-top. Christian resisted the urge to sneeze as dust flew out.

Mr. Farridge opened the book, pushed his spectacles up his nose, and started turning the pages. Christian tried to look as well, but the spidery handwriting and narrow columns defeated him. He'd need a magnifying glass to make any sense of it.

"Ah! Here it is. One gold locket sold to the Honorable Mr. George Walker." He looked up at Christian and showed him the entry. "It also gives details of the type of gold used, the procurement of the portraits, and the cost of the special engraving on the front that had to be done by our own craftsman in the shop."

Christian strained to make sense of the spiderlike scrawl but had no more luck than he had before. "Thank you, Mr. Farridge. Do you also have the address of the original purchaser? I would like to return this treasure to its rightful owners."

"I'll copy it all out for you." Mr. Farridge got a quill pen, ink, and some paper and scratched away for a few moments. "Here you are, sir. I'm not sure if the family still resides at this address, but these aristocratic folk do tend to stay in their ancestral mansions, don't they?"

"Indeed, they do, Mr. Farridge." Christian slipped the note and the locket into his pocket and drew out a gold sovereign. "This is for your time. Thank you."

He left the shop and got back into the waiting hackney cab. So Elizabeth's father had been an "honorable," had he? If Christian remembered his titles correctly, and it was his business to know them intimately, that meant her father must have been the son of an earl, a viscount, or a baron. Surely such a family would not want a descendant of theirs working in a pleasure house?

But they had abandoned her father, or at least let him walk away from them—that was something to contemplate. Perhaps Elizabeth had heard enough about them from her father to know that they would never welcome her. Christian frowned. But they didn't have to welcome her into their home, did they? Surely a gentle reminder that Elizabeth was their kin might result in an offer of an allowance or a place to stay that would give her some security in life?

Would she be happy with that? He guessed that her independence was as important to her as his was to him. How ironic, then, that both of them were still living off his mother's bounty. He sighed and stared out of the window. What other option did he have? He only knew how to run the pleasure house. If his mother was determined to hang on to it, where did that leave him? At least he was offering Elizabeth a choice.

He forced his thoughts back to the more practical present. He would contact the College of Arms and send his carefully worded advertisement to the newspaper to lure RR out of hiding. The quicker he managed Elizabeth's affairs, the sooner she would be out of danger and possibly out of his life.

The hackney pulled up at the rear entrance of the pleasure house on Barrington Street, and Christian paid the driver and got down. As the horses trotted away, he took a moment to stare up at the familiar white and stone façade. Was that why he was so reluctant to strike out on his own? Was he too afraid of losing the only real home he had ever had? Yet even this "home" didn't belong to him. His parents owned it and he just worked for them. A familiar ache gathered in his chest and he shoved it down. He had to believe that he was perfectly capable of leaving both the pleasure house and Elizabeth. He simply had to.

Elizabeth studied her face in the mirror and scowled. The bruising looked even worse than it had the day before, and her whole body ached as if she had run fifty miles. She picked up the bag of jewelry Ambrose had returned to her and emptied the contents onto her dressing table. It took her but a moment to separate the pieces *she* valued from the pieces *of* value her husband had bought her. If she pawned the jewelry, would she have enough money to get her over to France and back to Armand's château?

She bit her lip. The problem was that she needed at least two good strong reliable men to help her. The Kelly brothers would be perfect. But how was she to recruit such men while at the pleasure house? More to the point, since her recent brush with Gaston, how was she even going to get out of the house by herself to find a pawnshop without raising the alarm?

Frustration threaded through her. She hated being helpless, and here she was trapped in another kind of prison. A kinder one this time, but it seemed that could be just as binding as suspicion and hatred.

Elizabeth fingered the strand of pearls that had once belonged to her mother. These she would wear and cherish until the end of her days. She searched for the locket her father had given her mother on their wedding day and could see no trace of it. Had Armand kept it deliberately to upset her? It would be just like him.

She put the jewelry back into the pouch and stood up. There was no point in worrying about what might happen. She *had* to get back to France before Armand did something unthinkable. Therefore, she had to find a way to make her plan work.

A knock on her door made her pause.

"May I come in?" Christian asked.

"Of course." Elizabeth fixed on a welcoming smile and watched as Christian closed the door behind him. He was wearing a dark brown coat with a black waistcoat and a simply tied cravat. He angled his head to one side and studied her.

"Your face looks terrible."

She bobbed him a curtsy. "Thank you. It might look worse, but it actually hurts much less."

"So I should imagine." He came toward her, put his fingers

under her chin, and turned her face more fully into the candlelight. She thought about how she'd seen him last, naked, his
skin glowing with exertion, his cock hard and ready to pene-
trate her. She also remembered what she'd revealed and fought
an urge to pull away from his all-too-knowing touch.

"I thought you might like to dine up here with me."

"Alone?"

"That was my plan."

"Am I really that hideous?" Elizabeth asked lightly. The last
thing she wanted was to share an intimate evening with Christian Delornay. She was concealing so many secrets that she
feared she'd forget herself and start screaming them at him in a
never-ending scroll.

"You certainly aren't fit to welcome our guests."

"But surely the kitchen staff wouldn't mind?"

His faint smile disappeared. "Elizabeth, are you trying to
avoid me?"

She met his gaze. "I . . . I might be."

"Because of what happened the other night?"

She allowed a hint of bewilderment to enter her smile. "I beg
your pardon?"

"Elizabeth . . ."

She opened her eyes wide at him. In truth, if he thought her
reluctance to dine with him stemmed from her sexual confes-
sions, that suited her perfectly. But it was never wise to capitu-
late too easily. Christian was no fool.

"Don't you have your accounts to do or something?"

"I'm all caught up and I have the evening off."

She manufactured a heavy sigh. "Then I suppose I should
accept your generous offer."

He kissed her hand. "That is very gracious of you. "I'll ring
the bell and ask Madame to send up the first course."

* * *

During dinner, Elizabeth managed both to make small talk with Christian and allow her brain to worry away at the question of how to pawn her jewels. As she nibbled on a lemon shortbread biscuit, Christian drank a glass of brandy. It occurred to her that he must already know she had the jewelry. All she had to do was think up a plausible reason why she needed the money.

Christian cradled his brandy glass in his two hands. "Did Ambrose return your jewelry to you?"

How strange that he was thinking about her jewelry too.

"Yes, he did."

"It still seems that the advertisement was a lure to get hold of your person rather than to return your possessions."

"I thought it might be, but I felt I had no choice but to go."

"Why?" Christian asked. "What was so important?"

She met his gaze. Let him think her mercenary. "My jewelry is important to me."

"It can be replaced."

"Not all of it. There are certain items"—she touched her throat—"like these pearls, that are irreplaceable."

His mouth twisted. "I doubt you would risk your life for them, though."

"Christian, I didn't really believe that my husband's cousin Armand would attempt to capture me. I thought that maybe he had decided to let me go. I even wondered if the jewelry was an attempt to buy me off."

There was a long silence broken only by the crackling of the fire and the ticking of the clock on the mantelpiece. Christian placed his brandy glass carefully on the table between them.

"Don't lie to me."

Elizabeth slowly let out her breath. She kept her gaze on the glass and his long fingers wrapped around it.

"The jewelry is important to me for more than just sentimental reasons." He didn't respond and she continued. "I plan on selling most of it."

"Selling it? For what purpose?"

She shrugged. "So that I can live independently."

"You wish to leave?"

She raised her eyes to meet his. "I can hardly stay here forever, can I?" She attempted a laugh. "Your next lover would not be very happy about that, would she?"

His gaze was cool, his tone arctic. "How kind of you to care about my next mistress, Mrs. Smith. Have you already picked her out for me as well?"

"I am a realist, Mr. Delornay. Our liaison will not last."

"When exactly are you planning on leaving?"

"It depends on several things. I need to have the jewelry valued first."

"And you need to make sure that you are no longer in danger."

"As I said, perhaps the return of my jewelry really does signal the end of the problem."

Christian sat forward. "I don't agree. Your attempted abduction took place after the jewelry had been returned. Why would your cousin bother if he considered he had paid you off?"

Elizabeth had no answer for that. "Are you suggesting I should stay here indefinitely?"

"I'm suggesting you stay here until we have neutralized the threat against you." Christian stood up and threw his napkin onto the table. "I don't think it will take that long and then you can do whatever you wish without any fear for your long and, no doubt, happy future."

Elizabeth looked up at him. What he suggested suited her perfectly, but she suddenly felt guilty. He had done nothing but offer to help and protect her, but she couldn't allow that to influence her decisions. It didn't matter what he thought of her. She had to do what was right.

She stood up, too, and went to him, placed her hands on his shoulders, and gently kissed his mouth.

"Thank you, Mr. Delornay."

He didn't kiss her back, so she kissed him again, running the tip of her tongue along the seam of his lips. With a groan, he opened his mouth and let her in. His response made her press her whole body against his. With a muffled curse, he caught her wrists and brought them behind her back.

"Don't do this."

"Do what?"

"Try and buy your way out of a difficult situation with sex."

"I wasn't! I just wanted to . . ." She shook her head. "Damn you. I *wanted* to kiss you!"

His gaze narrowed. "You never do anything without a purpose. You use your body to bend a man to your will."

Anger warmed her belly and she fought against the grip on her wrists. He was the first man she had ever willingly kissed in over ten years. Didn't he understand that? God, she was so tired of this, so tired of having to pretend. "I have learned how to placate a man, yes. How else was I supposed to survive? I found I had an aversion to being beaten and raped!"

"You assured me that all the men you fucked were gentlemen."

"I . . ." She could only shake her head again, too enmeshed in her own protestations and half-lies to even know where to start.

"Do you think I'll force you?"

"No!" She realized she was shouting, but for once she didn't care. She was sick of being judged and found wanting, sick of being compliant. "I wanted to kiss you!"

He yanked her even closer, his lips a fraction away from hers. "Then do it. Do what you want."

She bit him hard on the lower lip and he hissed in pain. She took advantage of his momentary recoil to work her wrists free of his grip and brought her hand up to slap his face.

The sound was shockingly loud in the silence, but she didn't care. She gloried in it, in the darkening redness on his cheek, in his incredulous expression.

"What in God's name was that for?"

She was beyond caring now. "Because you . . . you . . . don't understand!"

He took a step closer and she raised her fists.

"What don't I understand?"

"*Anything!*"

He reached for her and she batted his hand away, but he kept coming and she let fly with her nails, scraping his cheek. That didn't stop him either, so she launched herself at him, biting and kicking. He avoided her blows when he could, his expression intent, his aim to subdue her with the least possible exertion on his part so obvious that she redoubled her efforts to hurt him, to *really* hurt him, to get past that perfect shell to find the man underneath.

His fingers closed around her wrist, and he twisted it behind her back, bringing her to her knees.

"Let me go!"

He didn't answer, and she tried to get up, only to have him bring his weight down on her back. His mouth settled over her ear, and he bit down hard, making her gasp.

"Is this what you fear, Elizabeth? Being held down, being forced?"

His free hand was already under her skirts, shaping the curve of her buttocks, his long fingers probing her sex.

She couldn't stop him. She couldn't get him off her.

"If you dread this, why are you wet and ready to be fucked?" His finger slid inside her and she fought a moan.

"Didn't you tell me that you liked the idea of a man taking you whether you wanted him to or not?"

She tried to turn her head and sink her teeth into any part of him she could reach, but to no avail. His finger started to pump into her, and his thumb pressed hard against her clit.

"Stop it!" she whispered.

He paused, his breath warm on her throat. "What if I won't stop?"

She gasped as he rolled her onto her back and straddled her. She struggled to free her hands and go for his face again, but he caught them and drew them over her head.

"What if I won't stop? Will you fight me?"

She stared into his hazel eyes and saw his lust and the raw excitement. She'd wanted to get beneath the surface of his accomplished lovemaking, but was this what she wanted? She didn't care. He bent his head and kissed her, and she tried to bite his tongue.

"Don't," he said. He shifted his body so suddenly that she couldn't take advantage of it, his knees now bracketing her shoulders. She shivered as he undid his pantaloons and shoved them down to display his thick shaft. "Suck my cock."

She found herself growling at him, and he merely smiled. His fingers closed on her face, and he used his thumb to prise open her jaws, keeping it there so that she couldn't close her mouth. "Suck me."

She couldn't stop him sliding his cock inside her mouth, and she loved the way he felt, his thick, insistent presence and the sensation that she was never going to fit him all in, that she would choke. Would he care? Would he even notice? She swallowed him in, taking him deep, and heard his groan of approval.

"That's it, let me fuck your mouth. Let me come down your throat."

He didn't wait any longer; he set his own fast pace, and she could do nothing to stop him taking her as he wanted, her mouth used for his pleasure, his body holding her captive beneath him despite her struggles.

Even as he pumped himself into her, she realized her lower body was relatively free. Could she brace her legs and push him away, feel his tender cock grate against her teeth as she forced him to withdraw? Even as the idea came to her, she acted on it, sliding her legs up until her feet were on the floor and arching her back and hips to throw him off balance.

Her sudden movement worked well enough to make him release her jaw and slam his hand on the floor to stop himself falling forward. Elizabeth used the opportunity to slide down under him, releasing his cock as she went and rolling onto her front. She didn't get far. He was on her in less than a moment, but she continued to kick out at him until he recaptured her wrists and restraddled her.

He was panting now, his chest heaving, his smile wild. "Are you done now?"

"No!" she hissed.

"Because you still want to be fucked, don't you?"

She snapped at his shoulder, and his expression grew serious. "I'm not going to stop, Elizabeth. Do you understand that? I don't care how much you fight me—I'm not going to stop."

She glared at his perfect features marred now by the bloodied tracks of her nails and the mark of her hand. He held her gaze, his mouth a hard line, his weight pressing down on her.

"Fight me, Mrs. Smith. *Make* me understand."

He shoved his knee between her thighs and lowered himself on top of her, pushing her legs wide despite her struggles. His pantaloons were still unfastened, his cock erect. She moaned as he shoved himself deep inside her in one sure motion and started to thrust.

"So wet and ready to be fucked," he murmured against her ear. "So wet . . ."

She couldn't move an inch, her legs spread wide, the unforgiving floor underneath her, his cock impaling her again and again as he slammed his full length from tip to root into her. An ache grew low in her gut, and she tried to lift her hips, but he wouldn't let her control anything, wouldn't let her take anything from him but what he chose to allow.

One of his hands remained grasping her wrists; the other worked its way between their bodies and settled over her clit, rubbing her tender flesh in rough, unforgiving circles. Stabs of mixed pleasure and pain made her sex clench and grip his pumping cock. He forced his tongue into her mouth and moved it in the same unforgiving rhythm as his cock and thumb.

She couldn't stop him. She didn't want to stop him. She . . . "Oh, God!" she screamed into his mouth, but he didn't pause as her orgasm broke over her in a devastating wave.

"Do it again," he growled, and she closed her eyes as he continued to fuck her even harder. "Come for me."

She tried to stop the gathering pleasure, but she had no control, no ability to stop him from doing exactly what he wanted. The second climax was even more intense than the first, the third so all-encompassing that she started to cry and thrash around as much as she was able.

He reared over her, his eyes narrowed, and cupped her cheek. "You can fight me all you like, but I'm still going to fuck you." His smile was both triumphant and dangerous. "And you want it."

She glared back at him. "You are a bastard."

"Indeed." He glanced down at her rucked-up skirts to where his cock was still lodged firmly between her thighs. "And you like me just the way I am."

"I do not!"

"You *want* this." He pinched her clit and she came again, gasping and fighting against the thick shaft of his cock. "You *understand* this." He placed his hands on either side of her face and started to pump into her, his hips moving freely, each thrust slamming into her already-sensitive sex. "You *need* this."

She started to come, and this time he came with her, the hot spurt of his seed high and deep inside her. He slowly pulled out and bent to pick her up. She would have protested, but she feared she would be unable to stand unaided.

She held on to his shoulders, and he laid her gently on the bed and stripped her naked. Then he stood back to take off his clothes. She could do nothing but stare at him and watch as his cock thickened. He crawled into bed and looked down at her. "Are you ready to fight me again?"

She stared up at him and shook her head.

"Are you sure about that?" He bent and set his teeth on her nipple, making her catch her breath. She tried to turn away from him, but he wouldn't even allow her that luxury.

"Elizabeth." She forced herself to meet his eyes and he smiled. "I want to fuck you again, but I know what you'll do if I try."

"What will I do?" she whispered.

"Let me." He kissed her forehead. "And I don't want that kind of submission. I prefer it when you fight me."

"I can't right now." She swallowed down a sudden rush of unwanted tears. "I can't even think."

He nodded. "It's all right." He kissed her again. "Good night, Mrs. Smith. I'll see you in the morning."

She watched him leave and then curled up in a ball, her body still shivering from the intensity of their lovemaking—if she could call it that. It felt more like she had been ravished. She closed her eyes and waited to feel ashamed, but the sensation remained disquietingly absent. *Willingly* ravished. She couldn't deny that. How had he known that she would love every scorching moment? She'd attacked him, *hurt* him, and he'd reveled in her anger, given it back to her and encouraged her to show him how she truly felt. That was the biggest mystery of all and the thing that scared her more than any of her issues with Armand. Was Christian trying to show her that she could truly be herself with him? And if that was the case, why was he doing it? Surely she meant nothing more to him than any of his other lovers?

16

"What happened to your face?"

Christian grimaced as his mother enfolded him in a perfumed embrace and considered how to answer her. She cupped his cheek with her gloved hand and tutted in disapproval. "Did you go back to that horrible place? Is Mrs. Smith not enough for you?"

Christian gently removed her hand. "I don't believe that's any of your business, *Maman*. How are you, and where is Philip this fine morning?"

Helene frowned at him and took a seat in front of his desk. "Philip is out with Richard. I wanted to see you before we travel up north to stay with Lisette and Gabriel. Emily is coming with us, as are Anthony and Marguerite. Richard will join us in a week or so." She paused. "I hope you have decided to come at least for Christmas?"

"And spoil such a lovely family gathering?"

"Christian . . ."

He sat down and regarded his mother across the desk. She looked very fashionable in her green muslin gown and matching pelisse, and scarcely old enough to be the managing mother of three.

"It is always a pleasure to see you, *Maman*. Was there anything in particular you wished to discuss with me?"

"There are two things," Helene said. "Firstly, I have some more information about your Mrs. Smith."

"Indeed?"

"I believe I have narrowed down the region of France she came from to Brittany. Apparently, she used the English name Elizabeth Walker when she traveled. I have a man looking into the French families who still reside there. He said he will have answers for me by the end of the week."

"That is excellent news, *Maman*. Mrs. Smith inadvertently let slip the name of her husband's cousin to me last night. He is called Armand."

"I'll pass that information along to my contact in France." Helene wrote the name down. "Have you found out anything else?"

Christian relayed the information he had gathered about Elizabeth's English family, and Helene smiled. "We will soon have her either restored to her rightful place or put the matter in the hands of the best lawyers. Either way, Mrs. Smith will no longer be destitute, in danger, or dependent on our goodwill."

"That is true," Christian agreed.

"Will you miss having her as your mistress, Christian?"

"Naturally, *Maman*," Christian said smoothly. "I will be devastated."

Helene laughed. "You have never mourned a lost lover, my dear. I'm not sure you have the ability."

Christian wanted to disagree with her. In truth, the idea of Mrs. Smith leaving him made him feel curiously unsettled. And how was it that his own mother believed he was such a cold fish?

"There is something else you wished to discuss with me?"

"Oh, yes, while I am away with Lisette, I expect you to send me a weekly report about the pleasure house."

"I intended to do that anyway." Christian fought his usual desire to defend himself.

"I'm sure you did." Helene hesitated. "I expect to be away for at least three months."

"Three months?" That was a surprise. Christian didn't think his mother had ever left the business for more than a couple of weeks. "Are you sure about that?"

She met his gaze. "I'm very sure." She rummaged in her reticule and brought out a sealed letter. "I wish you to read this."

Christian took the letter and broke the wax seal. "It's from your solicitor." He frowned as he continued to read before lowering the paper to stare at his mother. "You're putting fifty percent of the business in my name?"

She nodded. "I think it's time, don't you? Philip has always intended to give you his shares in their entirety. I felt it important that I should give you some of mine too."

"Why now, *Maman?*" Christian asked. "You have always given me the impression that you don't completely trust me."

"I trust *you*, Christian. It's more that I didn't trust you with my business." She sighed. "That probably makes no sense to you."

"But why?" He leaned across the desk, his hands clasped in front of him. "Please, tell me."

"Because you are so . . . self-contained, so contemptuous of those who fail, so *separate.*"

It wasn't the first time she had said those things to him, but it still riled him. "What does that have to do with the pleasure house? It's just a business."

"It isn't just that. The people who come here might appear

to have everything—titles, money, lands—but many of them have other needs they find very difficult to meet in their normal lives."

"I understand that," Christian said impatiently. "We provide them with the means to fulfill those needs."

"Yes, in a business sense we do. But we also provide an emotional release, a place where a duke can grovel on his knees in front of a kitchen maid, or the heir to an earl can spend time with his male lover."

"So?"

Helene studied him. "Your very tone indicates the problem to me. You don't see that part as important, do you?"

"*Maman,* what exactly are you trying to say?"

She shook her head. "And it is all my fault. How could I expect you to understand about love and need when I abandoned you for most of your life?"

Christian shifted restlessly in his seat. "Do we have to bring that up? I thought we'd decided not to refer to it again."

"Yet *you* refer to it all the time. You just choose not to have an open discussion about it."

"There is nothing to discuss."

"You decided that as well, Christian, not me. *You* decided it was better to cut yourself off from me and your father and pretend you didn't give a damn about us."

"I didn't *pretend, Maman.* I meant it." He held her gaze. "I'm not interested in listening to you rehash the past, and I have a perfect right to resent the way you lied to me for the first eighteen years of my life."

"I made the best provision I could considering the circumstances."

"So you always say, but it doesn't change the facts, does it?"

"Christian, if you could just try and understand. I was eighteen. I had no means of supporting myself apart from the pleasure house, and it was hardly a fit place to bring you up!"

"I know all this. Why are you bringing it up again?"

She clasped her hands to her chest, her eyes full of tears. "Because you can't seem to let it go."

He frowned at her. "Of course I can. I'm standing here talking to you now, I'm civil to Philip, and I work myself to death in your bloody pleasure house!"

"But you have cut yourself off from everyone."

"What the hell is that supposed to mean?"

Christian suddenly realized he was unable to maintain his usual calm politeness. Perhaps having persuaded Mrs. Smith to reveal her true feelings had rubbed off on him.

"You don't allow anyone to get close to you, Christian."

"I'm close to Lisette."

"Not since her wedding. In truth, she is very worried about you and asked me to try my hardest to persuade you to come and spend Christmas with her and Gabriel."

"I have no desire to intrude on Lisette's wedded bliss. She knows that," he said irritably. "It's not that I lack affection for her."

Helene sighed. "I'm sure you love her dearly, but . . ."

"But what? She was the only person apart from Marguerite who was there with me in France. She is the *only* person who truly understands me."

"You must feel doubly abandoned, then?"

Christian glared at his mother. "No! Why do you have to make everything about emotions? As I said, I'm very happy for her!"

"I want you to be happy, too, Christian. We all do."

He picked up the letter. "And you think that giving me these shares will make me happy? Offer me one hundred percent of the business, *Maman,* and I'll be more than willing to talk to you."

Helene looked stricken, but he was beyond caring.

He laughed, the sound harsh. "You can't do it, can you? You

can't give up your business as easily as you gave up your children. It's always meant more to you than any of us."

"*Non*, Christian, that's not true. I . . . ," Helene whispered.

He tossed the letter back onto his desk. "I don't want the shares on those terms. I'm not surprised at Philip doing this out of guilt because Richard has returned, but you? I don't want your pity. I'd much rather you considered me capable of running this place."

"We do consider you capable!" Helene rose to her feet, her color high, her reticule clutched in her fist. "Why can't you understand that? Why can't you see?"

Her words reminded him of Elizabeth's impassioned plea the night before. Was he really so incapable of understanding other people's feelings? Had he cut himself off so completely that there was no way back? And why the hell should he care anyway? Trying to understand women such as his mother and Elizabeth led to an emotional marshland he would sink into and never escape.

"I have to speak to Ambrose. Please excuse me."

He stood up and his mother blocked his path. She brought her hand up to touch his cheek, and he flinched away from her.

"Christian," she said fiercely. "There has never been any contest between the needs of my children and the needs of the pleasure house. You and your sisters will always come first to me. *Everything* I did was for you. I would've whored myself out to a thousand men a night if it meant you all lived in safety and security and didn't have to do what I did." Her voice shook. "You have to understand that, at least."

He moved her gently to one side and strode toward the door, ignoring both her attempt to catch at his sleeve and her demand for him to stop. He walked down to the kitchen and paused before he opened the door, realizing he was shaking and that he didn't want anyone to see him like that. He went down another flight of steps to the cellars.

With a groan, he sat down on the bottom step and shoved his hands into his hair. What in God's name was the matter with him? He felt . . . raw, as if he were the one exposing his soul and not Elizabeth. He stared blankly at the whitewashed wall. Was this what she feared when he forced her to admit how she felt? This exposed? This shattered?

If his mother was right about her love for him—and by God, he couldn't completely deny what he'd just seen in her eyes—then what was his life all about? Was he really so stuck in the past, still so angry about her betrayal that he couldn't move on or trust another soul?

Suddenly he missed Lisette so badly that he pressed his hand to his heart. The old Lisette would have at least tried to help him, but he'd pushed her away, hadn't he? Unsure as to whether she would understand his reasons for going to the Demon Club and aware that she would be worried for him.

Elizabeth would probably understand his sexual needs better than Lisette ever could. There were, after all, some things you could not discuss even with your twin sister. He groaned and the sound echoed around the unlit cavernous space. Was that why he both feared and courted Elizabeth at the same time? She'd managed to separate her emotions from her physical self. Was that why he was so determined to break her, to prove that it couldn't be done and to vindicate himself?

He took a deep breath. How pathetic was it that he had finally found a woman who both intrigued and delighted him, and yet he was unable to tell her how he felt. Cutting himself off from everyone and holding himself to a higher standard had isolated him as he had originally intended. But was it really what he wanted? He was no longer sure.

Elizabeth walked into Christian's office and found Madame Helene dabbing at her eyes with a wisp of lace handkerchief.

"I'm sorry, madame. I didn't realize that you were here. Shall I come back later?"

"Oh, no, no, please come in. I wanted to talk to you anyway."

Elizabeth came in and shut the door. "I was looking for Mr. Delornay. The wine merchant is wanting someone to look over his accounts."

"Christian isn't . . ." Madame's perfect features crumpled. "He is very angry with me."

"Oh, dear." Elizabeth guided Madame to a chair and crouched down in front of her. "Are you quite well, ma'am? Can I fetch you a glass of wine or something stronger?"

Madame reached for Elizabeth's hand. "Thank you, but no," she sighed. "I made the mistake of commenting on Christian's scratched face."

Elizabeth felt her cheeks heat up. "Well, as to that . . ."

Madame kept talking. "I asked him not to go to the Demon Club again, and he obviously didn't listen."

Elizabeth remembered the afternoon when Christian had returned with his face scratched and stinking of perfume. "You don't approve of the club?"

Helene shuddered. "It was set up to amuse a group of bored aristocratic gamblers and has turned into the sort of place where no one is safe. I don't even believe the play is honest, so the chances of losing and being forced to engage in sexual acts against one's will is extremely high."

"Mr. Delornay doesn't strike me as the kind of man who would get involved in such underhanded dealings."

"You would think he'd be satisfied with what we have here, wouldn't you?" Helene bit her lip. "But he has always craved the unusual and the forbidden. In truth, I think he goes there to spite me."

Elizabeth had nothing to say to that, her mind busy with the revelation that Christian might have underplayed his explanation as to the Demon Club and what it meant to him.

Madame Helene extracted her hand from Elizabeth's and sat back, her expression concerned. "I did not mean to worry you, Mrs. Smith. I assumed you knew of this club."

Elizabeth got to her feet. "I did know about it, but like you, I was under the impression that Mr. Delornay no longer enjoyed going there."

"I thought so, too, and then I saw his face today, and he didn't deny his association with the club." Madame shook her head. "He just told me to mind my own business."

"That sounds just like him." Elizabeth headed back to the door. It wasn't her place to disabuse Madame of her notions about her son. From what she understood, their relationship was difficult enough at the best of times. "I'll go and ask Madame Durand to bring up some tea."

"That's all right, my dear. I have to go and meet my husband at home." Madame hesitated. "When you see Christian, ask him to reconsider his position about the business, will you? Oh, no, that is hardly fair. I'll write him a note." She looked at the desk. "Do you know where he keeps his pens and paper?"

Elizabeth moved to the desk and started opening the drawers. The top drawer was shut, but the key was in the lock, so she opened it. "Here you are, madame."

Madame Helene wrote her note and placed it on top of another letter that already lay on the desk. "I'll leave this here." She glanced at the clock on the mantelpiece. "Oh, I must be going. Please see that Christian gets this, won't you?"

"Of course I will, madame."

Elizabeth waited until Madame Helene collected her things and left the room before turning to clean up the desk. She stoppered the ink, replaced the pen, and tried to put them back when she noticed something wedged in the back of the drawer.

She opened the drawer as fully as she could and coaxed the metallic object out.

She frowned as she turned the silver bangle around and then read the inscription on the inside. Why did Christian have her mother's bangle in his desk drawer? The door slowly opened and she looked up into Christian's cold eyes.

"Has my mother gone?"

As he walked toward her, Elizabeth continued to study him. "Yes. She seemed upset. Why didn't you tell her that I scratched your face?"

He shrugged. "Because it is none of her business."

"She thinks—"

"I know what she thinks, and it is still nothing to do with her."

His brusque tone made all her warning senses come alive. "Are you feeling quite the thing, Mr. Delornay?"

His smile was lethal and so cold it made her want to hide from his sight. "I'm *feeling* like a man who is tired of impudent females questioning him about matters that don't concern them."

He might as well have slapped her face. She absorbed the unexpected hurt and held up the silver bangle instead. "Then perhaps you might care to explain why I found my bracelet in your desk. This does concern me."

He came around the desk to examine the bangle more closely. "How do you think I got it? I removed it from your jewelry before Ambrose returned it."

"You went through my possessions?"

"You left them in your pocket. If it hadn't been for Ambrose's vigilance, you might never have seen them again. Perhaps you should take more care of your belongings."

His sheer brazen effrontery made her momentarily speechless. "I was almost abducted! I was hurt!"

"I know that."

"Yet you still went through my things."

"And I take full responsibility for doing so." He sat in his chair and looked up at her. "The bracelet has a hallmark and an inscription on it."

"So?"

"It is possible to trace such things back to the jeweler who made them."

Coldness seized up Elizabeth's breathing. "I didn't know that."

He smiled. "I was hoping you didn't." He slid his hand into his pocket and handed her a small velvet bag. "You'll probably want this back as well."

She undid the drawstring and found her missing locket. Wordlessly, she looked up at him.

He shrugged. "You are very like your mother."

She stared down at the now-restored locket and took a slow, deliberate breath. "You had no right to do that."

"Do what?"

"Investigate me."

"I have every right. You are living here at my expense, and I am responsible for you."

She raised her eyes to meet his cool gaze. "How would you feel if I had done that to you?"

"You have no need to go behind my back about anything. I don't lie to your face, Mrs. Smith. I'm not the one trying to keep my identity a secret and refusing to accept anyone's help."

For a moment she yearned to tell him the truth, but his cynical gaze reminded her that he wouldn't believe her even if she did. Who would? She knew her story sounded like she should be locked away in Bedlam forever.

"I cannot tell you the truth." She gathered her courage and her recently discovered anger—anger he'd allowed her to express for the first time in years. "And why should you care anyway? At the beginning of our relationship, you made it abundantly clear that you wanted nothing more from me than sex, and I believe I have provided that to your satisfaction."

He blinked slowly at her and revealed absolutely nothing. "You are quite right. Pray forgive me."

She clutched the bangle to her chest and stalked away from him.

Christian watched her leave and then picked up the note his mother had left for him and threw it unread into the fire. He'd ignore the initial offer of fifty percent of the business as well and hope that it was forgotten. Had he been fighting a phantom enemy all these years, or had the notion of owning the pleasure house outright simply helped protect him from the messy business of emotions?

He stared into the fire and tried not to think of Elizabeth's stricken expression when she'd left him. He'd finally achieved what he wanted and made himself invulnerable again, and for what? The pleasure of seeing those around him walk away? Where was the joy and satisfaction in that?

A knock on the door brought him back into the present, and he looked up to see Ambrose bearing a pile of mail.

"Mr. Delornay, I've heard back from the College of Arms, and they have confirmed the Walker crest and the family's title. Apparently Elizabeth's father was the third son of an earl." Ambrose put the letters down on the desk and went still. "What's wrong?"

Christian took a deep breath. "Nothing is wrong. Why do you ask?"

"You look as if someone has stolen your favorite possession."

"I'm fine!" Christian snapped.

Ambrose took a step back. "Yes, I can see that. I suspect that quarrelling with both your mother and your lover in one morning might be enough to upset even you."

"I don't pay you to spy on me."

"I have eyes, Mr. Delornay. Pardon me for using them. I thought you paid me to be aware of what was going on in this house."

"I do. I don't pay you to meddle in my family's private business," Christian said softly.

There was a moment of silence, and then Ambrose inclined his head a frigid inch. "Indeed, Mr. Delornay. Let me remove my unworthy carcass from your magnificent presence and count my sins in the kitchens where I obviously belong."

He turned on his heel and walked out, slamming the door behind him, and Christian hissed a curse. He only needed for Paul, Emily, and his newly found half brother to turn up and he would succeed in offending every single available member of his extended family.

He reached behind him and took a bottle of brandy from the shelf and contemplated his options. As everyone would now spend the rest of the day ignoring him, he had the perfect opportunity to drink himself into a well-deserved stupor. At least he knew the pleasure house would run perfectly well without his help.

17

Christian woke up with a headache, which was hardly surprising considering the amount of brandy he had consumed the previous day. What was surprising was that he was in his own bed and that his clothes had been removed and taken away. He opened one eye, inhaled, and realized Ambrose was placing a tankard of ale and a large mug of coffee beside his bed.

"Good morning, sir."

Christian struggled to sit up against his pillows as Ambrose opened the curtains to let in some light.

"Good morning, Ambrose."

"Will you be requiring breakfast, sir?" Ambrose asked, his expression wooden, his manner that of the perfect deferential servant.

"No, I think the ale and coffee will suffice." Christian cleared his throat. "Did you put me to bed last night?"

"I believe that was one of the Kelly boys, sir. I asked him to assist you after I ascertained that you were unable to walk un-aided." Ambrose took out some clothes from various drawers and laid them on the bottom of the bed. "Do you require a bath, sir?"

"Perhaps later," Christian said. "Ambrose, I . . ."

But before he could complete his sentence, his friend had bowed and left him alone. Christian stared at the door and sighed. Apologizing to Ambrose was always difficult. In truth, apologizing to anyone had always been hard for him. It was no wonder most people saw him as an arrogant, cold bastard.

He glanced at the clock on the mantelpiece and realized it was almost twelve. Despite his headache, he drank the ale and then the coffee and forced himself to wash and get dressed. He approached the kitchen warily, but there was no sign of Elizabeth, his mother, or Ambrose, so he was able to check the newspapers without interruption.

His eye was caught by a reply to the advertisement he had put in the paper to flush out RR. The bastard had agreed to meet "Elizabeth" at the same newspaper office at three that afternoon. Christian smiled grimly. At least he could do something to move matters along.

He walked back to his study and found the information Ambrose had received from the College of Arms. The family address corresponded with the address the jeweler had given Christian for Elizabeth's father. The current title owner, Michael Walker, the Earl of Spentham, appeared to be the older brother of Elizabeth's father.

Christian spent some time contemplating the best way to tackle the Walker family and decided that a letter from a pleasure house might not be the most favorable approach. Instead, he drafted a letter and included with it a note to his father's solicitors asking them to act for him in the matter. He also stressed the need for a speedy resolution to the matter and that cost was not an issue.

He wrote the name of the solicitors on the back of the sealed letter and went back down to the kitchen where Seamus Kelly was watching the door. It took him but a moment to send Seamus on his way with a few coins and instructions on how to find the solicitors' offices on Columbia Road.

When Christian turned back into the kitchen, Ambrose was there talking to Madame Durand. Christian waited until they had finished and cleared his throat.

"Ambrose, may I speak to you in my study?"

"Of course, Mr. Delornay."

He followed Ambrose to his office, closed the door behind them, and leaned against it.

"I'd like to apologize for my behavior yesterday."

Ambrose met his gaze and nodded, his expression inscrutable.

Christian sighed. "Ambrose, I mean it. I had no right to speak to you like that. You *are* family."

"I am not and I never will be." Ambrose's smile was sweet and full of regret. "You were right to correct me. Sometimes I forget my status here."

"Please, the fault was entirely mine. I allowed my mother to upset me, and then I compounded my errors by getting annoyed with Mrs. Smith when she found her silver bracelet in my desk and rightly called me out on it."

"Ah."

"None of which was your fault, of course, so getting angry with you was not fair."

Ambrose regarded him closely for a long moment. "Your mother means well."

"I know that."

"So does Elizabeth."

"Now that is a different matter altogether. She lies to us, Ambrose, and I don't understand why. She told me yesterday that even if she did explain herself, I would never believe her."

"I got that impression from her too. She seems to believe

that whatever she has done has put her beyond help or redemption."

"Mayhap she murdered her husband."

"If that was the case, surely there would be no need for all this subterfuge? Her husband's family would simply call in the authorities to deal with her."

"Then what?" Christian frowned. "She said it comes down to money, and I assume there is some truth in that. But there must be something else. . . ." He looked up at Ambrose. "By the way, I'm going to attempt to meet up with the infamous RR today at the newspaper offices. I'll need someone to pretend to be Elizabeth."

"Perhaps Marie-Claude will help out. She is fond of Elizabeth."

"Everyone is fond of Elizabeth," Christian muttered.

Ambrose gave a reluctant laugh. "Actually, Elizabeth reminds me of you, your mother, and the kitchen cat—self-contained, imperious, and willing to kill if necessary."

Christian glanced at his watch. "I've asked my solicitors to contact Elizabeth's family, and my mother will have new information as to the French side of the business by the end of the week. Hopefully we will have this all cleared up soon."

"And Elizabeth will be free."

"I hope so."

Even as Christian said the words, he hated them. He didn't want her to be free. He wanted her naked, under him, and swearing never to leave him. But if he tried to keep her, wouldn't he be just as bad as all the other men in her life? She had to make her own choice. Judging from their current combative relationship, he doubted she'd want to stay within a mile of him.

"Mr. Delornay?"

"Yes, Ambrose?"

"I fear to say anything to upset you, but I believe you have come to care for Mrs. Smith."

Christian took his time looking up into Ambrose's all-too-familiar face. "Yes, I do believe I have."

At precisely three o'clock, Christian and Marie-Claude, wearing Elizabeth's black bonnet and pelisse, entered the newspaper offices. There was no sign of anyone else waiting, so Christian found a seat for Marie-Claude and inquired of the clerk at the counter as to the correct time.

As he conversed with the clerk, the outer door opened and a man came in and headed straight for Marie-Claude. It took Christian only a second to turn around and block his path.

"Richard? What in God's name are you doing here?"

His half brother looked as surprised as Christian felt as he nodded in the direction of Marie-Claude. "Good afternoon, Christian. I'm here to meet with a client of mine."

Christian pointed at Marie-Claude. "This woman here? You are RR?"

"Indeed. Are you acquainted with her?" Richard frowned. "I wish I'd known that earlier, as it would have saved a lot of unnecessary bother." He started to walk toward Marie-Claude, but Christian grabbed his arm.

"That isn't the woman you seek. I arranged this meeting because I wanted to meet the man who was attempting to abduct my acquaintance."

"*Abduct* her? What are you talking about?"

Christian stared grimly into his half brother's puzzled face. "Perhaps we should adjourn to somewhere more private and lay our cards on the table."

"I'm more than happy to do that." Richard put his hat back on and headed for the door. "I have a hackney cab waiting outside."

Christian arranged for Ambrose and Seamus Kelly to escort Marie-Claude back to the pleasure house and then got into the cab with Richard. They didn't speak on the journey as Christian tried to comprehend his half brother's bizarre involvement in a matter so close to his own heart. The cab pulled up at Philip's town house and Christian sighed. He could only hope his mother and father were out and wouldn't get to hear about this matter. He doubted they would be able to keep their opinions to themselves.

Richard left his hat and gloves with the butler in the front hall. Christian decided to hold on to his in case he had to leave quickly. Richard glanced at him as they walked deeper into the house.

"Would you object to coming up to my bedchamber? It is the only place where we might talk undisturbed."

"And escape the notice of our esteemed parents?"

Richard's quick smile reminded him of Emily. "They are rather prone to interfering, aren't they?"

"You have no idea," Christian replied as they started up the stairs. "They practically ruined Lisette's wedding."

"I heard you had a hand in that as well."

Christian acknowledged the hit. "I didn't say that I was above meddling in my sister's affairs, did I?"

Richard opened the door into his bedchamber and Christian stepped inside. The fire was still lit, and the pleasant aromas of sandalwood and bay rum warmed the air. Christian took a seat by the fire and waited until Richard took off his cloak and joined him.

"I must ask what you meant about the lady almost being abducted," Richard said.

Christian sat back. "And I must ask you to explain your involvement with this case."

Richard considered him for a long moment. "All right. I'll go first. A French family wishing to trace a woman who had disappeared from their château hired me through the British embassy in France. As she was English, the family was concerned she had either been abducted or had fled back to England. They asked me to find her and bring her safely home to France."

"Why would anyone ask you to do such a thing? I thought you didn't have an occupation."

"I spent several years on the Continent and speak most of the languages fluently. I also made a lot of friends." Richard shrugged. "Since the war, I've been asked to trace missing soldiers and family members, first by friends and later by members of the government. There is no formal arrangement and usually no payment involved, apart from some traveling expenses."

"You do it out of the goodness of your heart?"

Richard half smiled. "I do it because I lost someone I loved in France during the war, and I hate to see others suffer when I could be helping them."

Christian sighed. "And now I feel small-minded and petty and put in my place. Of course, you would be a hero, wouldn't you? Does our father know about your work?"

"Of course not. And, please, don't tell him." Richard sat forward. "Now perhaps you might tell me your interest in this matter. How do you know Madame Elizabeth?"

"I am acquainted with her. That is all you need to know," Christian said, and Richard's eyebrows rose. "Apart from the fact that my mother is also involved with this and will not take kindly to anyone trying to hurt or abduct her protégé."

"That is hardly helpful, Christian."

"I'm not inclined to help you when you are in cahoots with Elizabeth's enemies."

"But they are not her enemies. They simply want her to return home."

"By *force?*"

"What exactly happened?"

"After your last meeting, she was followed out of the office and her deceased husband's valet tried to abduct her." Christian paused long enough to judge Richard's incredulous expression. "Are you still insisting you didn't know anything about this plan?"

"Of course I didn't!" Richard retorted. "I was engaged through the embassy!" He ran a hand through his short brown hair. "Was she all right?"

"She is now. Luckily I'd sent a man to watch her, and he was able to get rid of the valet."

"I'm glad she was unharmed. She struck me as a very pleasant and upstanding woman."

"She is. I want to meet the man who gave you this commission. I believe he might be called Armand. Is he currently in England?"

"I'm not sure."

Christian looked askance at his half brother. "You're not sure?"

"I wrote to tell him of Elizabeth's refusal to return and suggested that if he wanted a speedy conclusion to the problem, he might prefer to come to England and see her for himself."

"And he agreed?"

"He did. I haven't heard anything since then, but I'm expecting him any day now."

"I want to meet him, Richard."

His brother's brown gaze clashed with his.

"Why?"

"Because Elizabeth's continued good health is important to me."

"You are involved with her?"

"You could say that."

Richard sat back and crossed his legs. "Her family seemed quite sincere in their desire to have her back."

"They aren't her family. They are her husband's family. I believe she has relatives here. I intend to restore her to her rightful position in English society."

"And you call me a hero," Richard muttered. "Look, I will bring my client to meet you when he arrives, but I insist on being present."

"That is acceptable to me." Christian rose to his feet and clasped a hand on Richard's shoulder. "I appreciate your cooperation."

"I don't want any harm to come to anyone you care about."

"Then keep my mother and father out of my business."

Richard chuckled as he escorted Christian to the door and down the stairs. "I was thinking more of our mutual female acquaintance, but I understand your concerns, and I'll do my best."

Elizabeth was approaching the kitchen when she heard Ambrose's and Marie-Claude's voices raised in an argument. When her name was mentioned, she slowed her steps and paused at the door. She peered through the crack and saw Marie-Claude taking off a black pelisse and hanging it on the back of a chair.

"I need to get this coat and bonnet back to Elizabeth's room before she notices they have gone. Do you know where she is?"

"I don't, Marie-Claude, and I repeat, please do not tell her about what occurred."

"I'm hardly likely to do that when I still don't understand it myself. What on earth was Mr. Richard Ross doing at the newspaper offices? Surely Elizabeth would have known who he was? He looks just like Mr. Delornay!"

Elizabeth put her hand over her mouth as several things fell into place. Christian must have attempted to contact RR by himself, and the mystery man had turned out to be his very own half brother. No wonder RR had looked familiar—she was sharing a bed with his sibling!

Had Christian known all along that his brother was involved, or had he been surprised to see him there? Or was it even worse than that? Elizabeth swallowed hard. Had Christian engineered the whole situation to get her to betray herself? Surely if he already knew about her French family, he would have done something about it before now. She bit her lip. She had no doubt that Richard Ross would share everything with Christian.

Should she try and run? Take her jewels to the nearest pawnshop and head back to France to confront Armand and steal back everything he'd taken from her? She had a terrible sense that if she didn't act soon, all her choices would be taken away.

"Elizabeth, are you all right?"

She jumped when Ambrose put his hand on her shoulder.

"What happened at the newspaper office today?"

Ambrose looked pained. "I can't tell you. I promised Mr. Delornay."

"Why would Mr. Delornay's half brother be aiding my enemies?"

"You heard that?"

"Yes, I was just coming to find you."

He squeezed her shoulder. "Why don't you have a cup of tea and wait for Mr. Delornay to return? I'm sure he'll be happy to answer any questions you have."

She shook off his hand. "You know that he will do no such thing. He is as reluctant to share information as I am."

"Which is what put you in this predicament in the first place," he reminded her gently.

"I have to leave," she burst out. "I have to find someplace to pawn my jewels and get back to France."

"I can't let you go," Ambrose said, his brown eyes full of regret. "You are still in danger."

"How do you intend to stop me?"

He shrugged. "I'll lock you up if I have to."

"You wouldn't dare!"

"Elizabeth, I would do anything to keep you safe. By now

I'm sure your assailant has probably worked out where you live. I can't let you leave here."

Elizabeth thought quickly. "Will you at least escort me to a pawnshop to sell my jewelry?" There was always a chance she could lose him in the crowded streets of the city.

"No, because I don't trust you," Ambrose said. "In truth, I'm not going to let you out of my sight until Mr. Delornay returns." Elizabeth glowered at him, but he didn't even flinch. "Now come into the kitchen and have some tea."

18

Christian walked into the kitchen of the pleasure house deep in thought and was surprised to find quite a reception committee awaiting him. Ambrose and Paul flanked Elizabeth, and Marie-Claude sat opposite her. None of them were smiling, and Elizabeth looked particularly grim. Christian took his time taking off his hat and gloves and placed them on the table before finally sharing a gaze with Ambrose.

"Is there something wrong?"

Marie-Claude made an impatient sound. "We'd all like to know what Mr. Richard Ross was doing at the newspaper offices."

"I'm sure you would." Christian smiled at her and returned his gaze to Elizabeth. Something about the determined slant of her mouth set him on edge. "I'm sure you'll understand if I wish to converse with Mrs. Smith about the matter first before I share any more details."

Marie-Claude waved a dismissive hand. "Of course, Mr. Delornay."

"Would you like to come into my study, Mrs. Smith?"

"If Ambrose will allow it." Elizabeth sniffed. "He's scared that I'm going to bolt." She rose and patted her skirts.

"She wanted to leave and I told her she couldn't," Ambrose explained, and Christian nodded.

"Thank you, Ambrose." He inclined his head to Elizabeth. "Mrs. Smith?"

She walked ahead of him down the hallway like a queen and sat down in one of the chairs in front of his desk with a thump. Rather than retreating behind his desk, he took the seat next to her.

"What exactly did Ambrose tell you?"

"Absolutely nothing. The only reason I knew there was an issue was because I overheard Marie-Claude wondering about Mr. Ross's presence at the newspaper offices."

"Ah." Christian considered what he might reveal and how best to coax information out of her. "Is that why you were trying to run away?"

"I wasn't running away. I was simply planning on returning home."

"A home you hate."

"*Yes.*" To his consternation, her eyes filled with tears. "I left too quickly. I behaved selfishly."

"If there are legal matters that need to be attended to, rest assured that we can deal with them from here. All you have to do is tell me or my solicitor exactly what the issue is."

She stared at him and slowly nodded. "Perhaps that would be for the best."

He raised his eyebrows. "I beg your pardon?"

"I'm agreeing with you. Why do you sound so surprised?"

"Because you only agree with me when you are planning something else entirely."

She met his suspicious glare, her gray eyes now clear and guileless. "Perhaps I have run out of ideas."

"I doubt that." He reached across and took her hand. "Elizabeth, I—"

"It would help if you took me to pawn my jewels tomorrow."

"For what purpose?"

"So that I can reimburse you for any services your solicitors provide. I don't want to be dependent on you for everything."

"I understand that." He paused. "I know a man with a shop on Cornhill who will give you a fair price for your jewels."

She seemed to relax. "Thank you."

"By the way, my half brother, Richard Ross, sends his compliments."

"Did you know he was involved in all this?"

"No. It was a complete surprise to me." He was glad to be able to tell her the truth about something. "Richard has lived on the Continent for years, so I hardly know him myself."

"May I ask how he got involved?"

"Apparently, he works to restore the lost to their loved ones."

Her small smile made him hold her hand tighter. "I was neither lost nor taken from my loved ones. I was the fool who ran away."

"He did not know that. I told him about the abduction attempt and it made him far more willing to help us."

She fixed her gaze on their clasped hands. "You will send me back to Armand, then?"

He waited for a long moment until she looked up at him, her beautiful face still and afraid.

"No," he said softly. "I will not."

"What if you cannot prevent it?"

"That isn't possible. There is always something you can bargain with."

"I do not deserve your help, Mr. Delornay."

The sudden strengthening of her voice made him uneasy. "Did you kill him?"

"My husband? No, but there were times when I thought about it."

"I'm not surprised." He paused. "Even if you had killed him, I would still support you."

She reached forward and cupped his cheek. "That is because underneath all that bluster you are a good man."

"Bluster?" He tried to smile. "I'm a man who has allowed his troubled past to dictate his future. In retrospect, I'm not sure whether that was a wise decision at all."

"We all carry our pasts with us, Mr. Delornay. We all have regrets."

He turned his face until his mouth met the palm of her hand and kissed it. Yet again, her words echoed his mother's. He pushed that old hurt down and focused on the present. "Come to bed with me, Mrs. Smith."

She didn't reply, but when he rose and held out his hand, she placed hers in his and followed him to the door.

Elizabeth let Christian take her to his bedroom and close the door behind them. None of the staff would dare bother him now. Poor Marie-Claude would have to wait until morning for her explanation. Elizabeth felt as if she stood on the edge of a precipice. She had to leave before Christian found out all her secrets, and yet she didn't want to go. He'd said he'd absolve her of anything, but she wasn't so sure about that. Some things were simply unforgiveable, especially to a man with his history. She doubted Jean-Pierre and Evangeline would ever be able to forgive her for leaving them behind.

She waited in the center of the room for Christian to join her. If she managed to get the money tomorrow, she would be able to leave that night. There were always times at the pleasure house when all the staff was occupied, and she would take any opportunity she could. Tonight was hers, though—hers and Christian's. She intended to make it as memorable as she could so that during the long, lonely years ahead she could remember how Christian had forced her to feel and breathe and exist again.

"Elizabeth?"

She looked up into his concerned hazel eyes and rose on tiptoe to kiss him on the mouth. Such a beautiful man, and such a pleasure to be taken by him . . . He kissed her back slowly and languorously, as if they had all the time in the world. She tried to deepen the kiss and pressed herself against him, but he would not be hurried.

Eventually, he caught hold of her wrists and pinned her hands to the small of her back so that all she could do was concentrate on his never-ending kisses and moan his name.

"There's no need to rush, Elizabeth. We have all night."

She tried to bite his lip, and he withdrew his mouth from hers and stared down at her. "My terms tonight, Mrs. Smith, not yours. I want you screaming and begging for me to fuck you. I want you desperate."

"I'm already desperate," Elizabeth whispered. "I want—"

He put his fingers over her lips. "I'll give you what you want—you know that. Do I have to tie you down?"

She tried to pull out of his grip and he smiled. "It seems that I do." He led her toward the bed, and she didn't resist him. "Sit."

He went to his chest of drawers and returned with several long black silk scarves, which he laid on the bed beside her.

"Do you not wish me to undress?"

He put his hands around her waist and laid her flat on her back in the middle of his vast bed. "I don't think so." He busied himself tying her hands to the bedposts with the long scarves, stretching her arms wide and making the seams on the thin muslin of her bodice strain. He eyed her breasts appreciatively but made no move to touch them.

He took off her kid slippers and then tied the scarves around her ankles and attached them to the bed frame as well. The scarves were tight but not unbearably so, and she could move a little if she wanted. He leaned over her and kissed her gently on the lips.

"You can fight me as much as you want now and you still won't win. I'll be able to do whatever I want to you."

She shivered as he kissed her nose and straightened to remove his coat, cravat, and waistcoat. She could see the thick outline of his erect cock through his breeches and thought about how he would taste and feel when she finally had him inside her mouth or sex.

He sat beside her and removed his riding boots, bracing himself against the bedpost to detach the tight-fitting leather from his stockinged foot. She tensed as he rolled over and covered her mouth with his own, teasing and tormenting her with his clever tongue and teeth. His hands stayed maddeningly at her shoulders. There was nothing she could do to encourage him to explore her body except kiss him back with all the ferocity she was capable of.

When his hand slid lower and finally cupped her corseted breast, she moaned into his mouth. He did nothing but hold her in his palm like a ripe fruit and continue to kiss her. His other hand settled over the junction of her thighs, the heavy pressure igniting a pulse of interest in her clit.

More kisses and then the slightest movements of his hands shaping and tweaking her breasts, rubbing the many layers of fabric against her mound until she thought she would die if he didn't so something more, something more *definite*.

"Please . . . ," she whispered, and he lifted his mouth from hers to stare down at her.

"Be silent, Elizabeth. I'd gag you, but I need your mouth."

"But . . ."

His hands stopped moving and she wanted to sob.

"My terms, Mrs. Smith. You can have your turn later—if you have the energy left to fight me."

His mouth fastened over hers, and she sighed as he started to touch her again. Eventually she lost track of the time as his kisses deepened and the bone-deep ache he was creating low in her sex grew and grew until she climaxed. She hadn't known it was possible to climax without being penetrated.

He watched over her as she trembled and cried out his name, his expression inscrutable, his fingers under her chin so that she had to look at him. He straddled her waist and brought his hands underneath her to loosen her dress. He then dragged it down over her shoulders, exposing the swell of her breasts within the tight confines of her corset. She shivered as he shoved his fingers down and found her nipples, pinching and pulling them until she felt the ache all the way to her sex.

His bent knee pressed against her skirt-covered sex, making her arch her back into the grinding pressure and close her eyes as she started to come again. She felt him smile against her mouth as she spasmed and shook, his fingers finally releasing her nipples and returning to her back to release her corset, making it gape at the front.

"Very nice, Mrs. Smith, but we're not done yet."

She knew better than to attempt a reply this time and lay quietly as he slid a pillow under her upper body, raising her slightly. He knelt over her, one hand slowly unbuttoning his breeches to reveal his stiff cock. Wetness gleamed at the swollen tip, and Elizabeth instinctively licked her lips.

He smoothed a hand up the length of his shaft and then brought his wet fingers to Elizabeth's mouth. "Don't worry. I'll give you all the cock you'll ever need."

He gathered her breasts in his hands, positioned his cock between them, and started to thrust, each motion making her flesh wet. His thumbs settled over her already-sensitive nipples. "Bend your head and lick me."

She realized it was possible to reach the crown of his cock with her tongue, and she willingly obliged him. His salty taste slid against her lips, and her sex clenched on nothing and wanted everything.

"Ah . . ." He pulled back and she watched as he came all over her breasts.

He climbed off her and went back to the chest of drawers. Elizabeth waited anxiously until he returned to the bed, her gaze fixed on the items in his hands. He showed her the clamps and the two narrow phalluses.

"I know you like these." She didn't even nod and his smile widened. "I enjoy you being tied up, Elizabeth. But I think I prefer it when you are fighting me with every ounce of your energy."

He carefully folded up her skirts and stood looking down at her exposed sex. She gasped as he flicked her swollen clit with one finger. "You're already wet and ready to come again." His finger moved lower and circled her opening. "You're ready for my cock too."

He retrieved the oil from the nightstand, anointed one finger, and pressed against her arse, opening her tight bud with the gentle insistent glide of his probing finger. The jade phallus was barely two fingers wide, and Elizabeth wondered why he had chosen it. He of all men knew she'd taken much larger cocks inside her than that. But she couldn't even ask him or he might stop touching her altogether.

The jade felt cold against her heat and far more rigid than a man's cock. She hissed out a breath when Christian's tongue licked at her clit.

"I'm going to slide the other one inside your cunt. Don't come."

She held still as he slid the jade home and then sat back to admire her. Tentatively she squeezed her internal muscles. Although she could sense the phallus, it was more a provocative sensation than a feeling of fullness. God, if only she could move. She realized she was straining against the restraints.

Christian looked down at her. "What's wrong, Mrs. Smith? Not enough cock for you?"

She wanted to snarl at him, and concentrated on channeling her feelings into her gaze. He broke the contact by bending his head and slowly licking his way around her sex, sucking her labia into his mouth until she could feel them swelling and throbbing. Of course, he clamped them, capturing both the intensity of the feeling and the heat in each throbbing piece of flesh. Her clit came next, the sting of the clamp and the gradual increase in pressure as he screwed it tighter made her writhe against her bonds and made him laugh.

Every part of her *needed;* every pulse of her heart was echoed in her sex and in her nipples. He reared above her, his gaze roving over her exposed flesh, her desire reflected in his narrowed stare. Suddenly he rolled on top of her and caught her face in his hands. He kissed her with a brutal possessiveness that took no prisoners and claimed her as his own. His cock thrust against her clothing, and she cried out, wanting him lower, wanting him buried deep inside her. But just the pressure of his body was enough to make her climax, and she shook with it, her wail of mixed pleasure and denial screaming into his mouth, leaving her shaken and breathless.

By the time she opened her eyes, he was busy untying her wrists and ankles. She lay stretched out as he'd left her, her mind too confused to understand, her body still desperate to be taken.

Christian glanced down at Elizabeth. By God, she looked glorious, her sex decorated for his pleasure, her mouth swollen from his kisses, and her nipples two hard points of need. He slowly tucked his reluctant cock back into his breeches and did up the placket.

She watched him from the bed, her gray eyes full of passion and gathering bewilderment.

"I think I've proved beyond doubt that you are quite capable of climaxing, Mrs. Smith, don't you?" He bowed. "Would you like me to carry you back to your own bed?"

Her hand shot out and grabbed his thigh, preventing him from moving anywhere. He obligingly held still while she struggled to roll over amidst the ruin of her clothes and the tangled scarves.

"You can't mean to leave me like this?"

He frowned down at her. "I can do what I damn well like."

"You can't!"

Her grip intensified and this time he managed to pull away from her. He took a step back and she launched herself at him. He fell to the floor, bringing her down on top of him. She tried to slap his face, and he blocked the blow, keeping hold of her wrist. With his free hand, he dragged her gown and petticoats off her, then twisted her underneath him to finish the job and rid her of her corsets and shift.

"What's wrong, Elizabeth?"

She squirmed underneath him and tried to kick him. His body reacted and his cock jerked against his breeches.

"You are . . . selfish!"

He raised his eyebrows. "I made you come several times. I came only once. How is that selfish?"

"Because I want you inside me!"

He slipped his hand between them and roughly fondled her sex, his fingers catching on the clamps. "Here?"

"God, yes!"

"Right now?"

She tried to bite his right shoulder and he quickly unbuttoned his breeches. He shoved his knee between her thighs, opening her wide. He touched the phallus embedded in her cunt and slid two fingers in above it. Her eyes widened as he stretched his fingers. "I'm not taking this out. If you want me so much, you'll take my cock in here too."

He positioned his cock where his fingers worked her and pressed deep along the line of the dildo. His shaft jerked at the hard, soft contrast of her forgiving flesh against the unyielding stone. He stayed deep, using his hips to drive him forward and her urgent response to meld them together into an earth-shattering climax.

Before she even finished coming, he picked her up, put her back on the bed, and placed his mouth over her clit, sucking her hard into his mouth. Her fingers tightened painfully in his hair and she moaned his name. He removed the dildo and stabbed his tongue repeatedly inside her, using his fingers to drive her into another convulsive climax.

His cock was hard again, so he reversed his position and fed it into her willing mouth, letting her suck him to his demanding rhythm while he pleasured her cunt. But it wasn't enough. It could never be enough. He pulled out and rolled her onto her front, shoving his cock back inside her in a fast, unforgiving drive that had her thrashing around. He held her steady, one arm wrapped around her breasts, the other teasing, tweaking, hurting her clit until she came for him again and he came, too, in thick hot waves that seemed to go on forever.

With a groan, he gathered her close to his chest and lay on his back, letting her fall over him like a blanket. She felt right tucked against his heart. He'd never thought he'd find a woman like her. Did she understand that on some level? He still wasn't sure.

Much later, she stirred in his arms. "What do they offer at the Demon Club that is better than this?"

He slowly opened his eyes and stared up at the canopy over the bed. "There is nothing better than this."

She stayed silent for so long that he thought she had gone to sleep.

"Then why do you go there?"

He opened his mouth to tell her to mind her own business and then closed it again. Would she understand? Had anyone ever actually asked him *why* he went rather than simply condemning him for going?

"At first, I enjoyed the novelty and unpredictability of the place. If you lose a game of cards, you gain a point. When you reach five points, you have to offer your sexual services to anyone who wins the next hand at any of the tables."

"It sounds horrible." She shivered and moved closer to him.

"I rarely lose at cards, so I've never reached five points. For a while I was the major recipient of a lot of sexual favors from both men and women, most of whom were reluctant participants at best."

"You probably liked that."

He paused to consider her words. "I suppose I did. I like a challenge in bed. I like a fight. But after a while even that palled. I knew that I was taking advantage of those poor souls rather than engaging in a mutually agreed upon pleasurable sexual act.

"I also became aware that there was a certain set of men who were intent on manipulating the gambling either for personal gain or revenge. I refuse to fuck anyone for someone else's personal vendetta."

"Your mother doesn't think the place is honest."

Christian kissed the top of Elizabeth's head. "She is extremely aware of all the competition to her pleasure house and is very knowledgeable about the unpleasantness behind such businesses."

"But she worries about you too."

He felt his peace evaporating. "Do we have to talk about my mother?"

Elizabeth sighed against his chest. "Why do you dislike her so?"

"I don't dislike her."

"Is it because she is so successful? A lot of men do not like women to make a success of their lives. And from what I understand, your mother did it against incredible odds."

"Did she tell you that?"

"No, but I think everyone else who works here has told me some version of the story of how she started the pleasure house."

He rolled away from her and stared up at the ceiling. "She certainly got what she wanted."

"I know. A secure future for her children." She hesitated. "I can only admire her determination to succeed against all the odds."

"Don't forget, in order *to* succeed, she gave up her children."

Elizabeth came up on her elbows and looked down at him, her long hair brushing his skin. "But she reclaimed you as soon as she could."

"Not exactly. We came looking for her and found out she wasn't a housekeeper but a brothel keeper."

"That must have been horrible for all of you."

"All of us?"

She hesitated. "Mostly for you and your sisters, but I can understand why your mother lied."

"I can't," he muttered.

"Because she was trying to protect you from what she had to do." She kissed his nose. "A mother's love is quite ferocious." Her voice faltered. "I doubt I would be so brave if I were in her shoes. In truth, I know I wouldn't be."

He tried to make light of it. "I'm sure, unlike my mother, you'd never put yourself in the position of having to choose."

She stiffened. "How do you know that?"

He shrugged. "Because I'm like you. We are survivors. We're too stubborn to need anyone else or care to sacrifice ourselves."

"That's not true." She touched his stubbled cheek. "Everyone needs someone."

"Even you?"

He realized he was holding his breath. He couldn't really see her face in the darkness, but he knew she was looking at him. He almost flinched when her mouth found his and she kissed him. Desire flowed through him so quickly that he was instantly aroused again. She moved over him, her sultry core brushing the tip of his straining cock, and took him in. He sighed as she started to move over him, rising and falling, gripping and releasing his cock with every upward and downward motion.

He put his hand around her neck and drew her down until his mouth could latch onto her breasts. She whispered his name and he felt her come all around him. His beleaguered cock couldn't last against such power, and he joined her, his climax deep and sure inside her.

She collapsed over him and he held her there, his cock still inside her, her head tucked against his shoulder.

"Thank you, Christian."

He closed his eyes and realized that for the first time in a long while, he was at peace. She understood and accepted him in some fundamental way that had never happened before. It only occurred to him as he was drifting off to sleep that Elizabeth hadn't answered his question after all. . . .

19

"Mrs. Smith?"

"Yes?" Elizabeth turned as the butler who guarded the front door of the pleasure house beckoned to her. She'd been about to start her morning tour of the house to make sure everything was in place for the incoming guests.

"There is a lady here demanding to see Mr. Delornay. I've already told her that he isn't available, but she refuses to leave."

"Do you wish me to speak to her?"

The butler looked relieved. "If you would, Mrs. Smith. I put her in the morning room to your right."

Elizabeth opened the door into the morning room, and the woman who paced the hearth swung around, her face falling as she registered that only Elizabeth was there. She started to pout.

"Where is Christian?"

Elizabeth curtsied. "I do apologize, ma'am, but Mr. Delornay is out on business this morning. Do you wish to leave him a message?"

"Who on earth are you?" the woman demanded, tapping her foot.

"I'm Mr. Delornay's assistant," Elizabeth said as she mentally catalogued the expense of the woman's clothing, her fragile beauty, and the fact that she wore a wedding ring. "I can assure you that anything you wish to pass on to Mr. Delornay will remain strictly confidential."

"I'm Lady Kelveston. I'm sure Mr. Delornay has spoken of me." The woman drew closer, and Elizabeth tried not to inhale her cloying perfume. "When will he be back?"

"I'm not sure, my lady. I only know he intended to visit his solicitors."

"I can't afford to wait around here all day," Lady Kelveston whined. "How typical of Christian not to be available when he is wanted. Do you know the woman he intends to bring to the orgy with him?"

"I wasn't aware of any orgy, my lady. Mr. Delornay is a very private man."

For a second, Lady Kelveston's eyes narrowed and her gaze ran over Elizabeth. She sighed, opened her reticule, and drew out an engraved card. "Give him this and tell him I am looking forward to seeing him."

Elizabeth took the invitation card without looking at it. "Of course, my lady. I'll see that he gets it."

"You may also tell him that we have some surprises in store specifically for him."

Lady Kelveston didn't bother to express her thanks or finish the conversation before she headed for the door. Elizabeth remained where she was until she heard the front door shut. She turned the card over and read the invitation. It was from the Demon Club and requested Christian's presence for a night of sin on the following Sunday.

Elizabeth studied the engraving and recoiled from the strong scent still clinging to it. She remembered that scent. It had been all over Christian the last time he'd obviously been to the Demon Club. Deep in thought, she retraced her steps back up the stairs and into Christian's study.

It was quiet in there, and she was grateful for both the space and the privacy. Lady Kelveston's tone had been proprietary when she'd spoken of Christian. But Elizabeth remembered that Christian hadn't seemed particularly enamored by the woman who had covered him with perfume and scratched his face. She sat at the desk and laid the invitation on the blotter.

She couldn't believe that Lady Kelveston was the reason why Christian frequented the Demon Club. His reluctant explanations the night before had hinted that he now attended the club to right wrongs, not to indulge in sexual games. She believed that. He'd seemed quite sincere after the passion of his lovemaking.

She thought about his mouth on hers and pressed her fingers to her lips. Her perfect lover. She'd finally found him, and she already knew she'd have to leave him. Would he miss her? She'd thought not, had congratulated herself that at least he'd escape unscathed. But after last night, she was no longer sure. There had been something in his voice and in the way he had possessed her so thoroughly that had spoken of deeper and unacknowledged needs.

Oh, God, she wanted to stay with him. To share his sharp wit, his bed, his *life,* to show him that he could fulfill all her needs and that she could do the same for him. Elizabeth put her face in her hands and groaned. And yet hadn't he said they were both too independent to need anyone else? He'd also suggested that women, like his mother, who put anything ahead of their children were unnatural. She'd tried to show him with her words and her body that that wasn't so, but perhaps she had failed.

It was too late to change her destiny now. She had to get back to France, rescue Jean-Pierre and Evangeline, and take them to safety. What happened to her after that was irrelevant. She had to make up for the damage she had inflicted on her husband's family.

She took a deep breath and raised her head, only to find that Christian had come quietly into the room and was watching her. She looked at his familiar face, his aristocratic cheekbones and fine hazel eyes now brimming with disquiet. Such memories would have to last her a lifetime.

"Is everything all right, Mrs. Smith?"

She summoned a smile from God knew where and vacated her seat. "Yes, Mr. Delornay. Did you need something?"

He continued to watch her from the doorway, one shoulder wedged against the frame. "I said I would accompany you to the jewelers this morning. Are you ready to go?"

"Yes. I'll just fetch my bonnet and coat." How ironic that his kind act would hasten her on her journey away from him.

She went to hurry past him, but he stopped her with a gentle hand on her elbow and looked down into her eyes. "Are you sure that you are all right?"

"Yes. It has been a busy morning."

"And a busy night." His slight smile made her want to weep. "I'll wait for you in the hall."

Later that afternoon, as the other members of the pleasure house staff milled around the kitchen talking, Christian sat and contemplated his coffee. Ambrose took the seat opposite him and he looked up.

"Elizabeth is with Marie-Claude on the second floor."

"Good," Christian said absently. "I've told the entire staff to keep an eye on her, but you never know what a desperate woman will do."

"Then why did you agree to let her pawn her jewelry?"

"I had to do something to stop her running off in a panic

yesterday. I'm convinced she means to leave for France as soon as she can."

"I think she does too. Whatever she needs to recover from her husband's family is obviously important to her."

"We should find out tomorrow what that is. Richard sent me a note to tell me that Elizabeth's cousin, Armand, has arrived at Dover and that he'll bring him to meet me here."

"Do you think we can keep her here that long?"

Christian knew his smile wasn't pleasant. "I'll tie her to my bed, if necessary. She'd enjoy that."

"You want her to stay, don't you?"

"Yes, I do, but I'm not going to make her decisions for her. She's had enough men in her life trying to control her without me adding to it."

"That must be hard for you."

Christian laughed. "You have no idea. When I said I'd happily tie her to my bed, I meant it."

"I believe she cares for you, sir."

"She seems to have made a lot of conquests here," Christian said dryly. "You, me, Paul . . ." He frowned. "Where is Paul, by the way? I haven't seen him for the last couple of days."

Ambrose slapped his hand on the table. "Damnation, I meant to tell you about this the other day before we got caught up in Elizabeth's issues."

"Is Paul sick?"

"No, he came by to tell me that he'd been accepted as a member of the Demon Club."

"*What?*"

"That's exactly what I said." Ambrose sighed. "He seemed excited by the prospect."

"Who in God's name offered him membership?"

"I believe it was Kelveston or his wife, or maybe both of them."

Christian shook his head. "I don't have time for this."

"Time to rescue Paul from his own stupidity? You don't have to, sir. When he is not on these premises, he is not your responsibility."

"Ambrose, the Demon Club is not like the pleasure house. The play is deeper and the dealers are crooked. The club owners pick their intended victims very carefully and make certain they eventually lose enough games to find themselves in the punishment cage. They could hurt him very badly, very badly indeed, and I think he suffered enough in the war, don't you?"

"Ah." Ambrose smiled and Christian stared at him.

"What in God's name is amusing about that?"

"It explains why you go there. You've never been able to resist a challenge, have you?"

"Why I go there is hardly the point. We need to stop *Paul* going there."

"Why?" Ambrose asked. "He is an adult. He will find out fairly quickly what he's let himself in for and decide whether he likes it or not. Isn't it time we all stopped helping him clear up his mistakes?"

Christian met Ambrose's dark gaze. "Maybe you are right. I just feel responsible for him because of Gabriel."

"And you have already done your part. The rest is up to Paul. Surely your main concern at this moment is Elizabeth? I must say I'm very interested in finding out the truth."

"So am I." Christian finished off his coffee. "But somehow I suspect Elizabeth will hate it."

He went back to his office. The invitation card to the Demon Club orgy Lady Kelveston had hand-delivered still sat on his blotter. He contemplated her scrawled signature for a long moment and wondered what Elizabeth had made of her. He doubted the two women had much in common. Melinda liked a man to dominate her while Elizabeth liked to fight back.

He put the card in his drawer without sending a reply. Part

of him wanted to decline the invitation and tell the Kelvestons to go to hell, but then who would protect innocents like the unfortunate Miss Retton from the likes of Kelveston and his cronies? Better him than any of those other bastards.

A soft knock on the door brought his head up. Elizabeth came in and he found himself smiling at her. She was dressed in a soft blue muslin gown that somehow made her eyes look even grayer. She was always beautiful, but at this moment, she looked far too anxious for his liking—her normal calm façade had deserted her.

"Mr. Delornay, there's something I forgot to tell you."

He folded his hands on the desk and wondered what the hell she was up to now. "And what might that be?"

"When Lady Kelveston called to deliver your invitation, she asked me to give you a message."

"Indeed."

"She said that she was looking forward to seeing you at the Demon Club, *personally,* and that she had arranged some little surprises just for you."

Paul . . . Christian groaned. "Damnation."

"I'm not quite sure what she meant, but she seemed very excited by the prospect."

"I'm sure she was."

"She also wanted to know who you were bringing as your guest." She hesitated.

"I'm not even sure that I *am* going, let alone if I intend to bring a guest." Christian busied himself tidying his pens.

"Did you intend to take me?"

"I thought you might enjoy it. Originally, I believed it might shock you, but now I'm not so sure."

Elizabeth smiled. "I'm quite hard to shock, Mr. Delornay. In truth, I think Lady Kelveston dismissed me as a potential rival the moment she set eyes on me."

"Because she is a fool."

"A fool, maybe, but a woman scorned is a dangerous thing."
He finally met her gaze. "She is no rival to you."

She raised her chin at him in quite her old challenging way.
"I was not aware that I was in a competition."

"Don't worry, you're not."

She turned toward the door and Christian stood up. "Where
are you going now?"

"I'm going back to help Marie-Claude. I didn't want to forget to relay Lady Kelveston's message to you before I . . ." She
blushed. "Before I forgot it."

She hurried out and this time Christian didn't stop her. She
didn't realize it yet, but he *would* be stopping her leaving for at
least another twenty-four hours until this matter was settled
between them.

He pulled the invitation card out of the drawer and set about
writing an acceptance note. Despite everything, he couldn't
allow Melinda Kelveston and her husband to use Paul simply
to get at him. He'd face them once and for all and make sure
Paul came to no harm.

20

"Mr. Delornay? Mr. Ross and his guest are here," Ambrose said.

Christian sat up straight and adjusted his cravat. "Please send him in, Ambrose, and find Mrs. Smith and ask her to join us."

"Yes, Mr. Delornay."

Christian stood as the door opened and Richard came through followed by a shorter, dark-haired man dressed in the height of fashion.

"Good morning, Mr. Delornay. May I present the Comte de Saint-Brieuc?"

Christian bowed and the other man followed suit.

"*Monsieur,* I believe I have to thank you for taking such good care of my late, lamented cousin's wife."

"I've done my best," Christian replied, his gaze fixed on the man Elizabeth had been frightened enough of to run away from. He was younger than Christian had anticipated and quite unremarkable in any way. "She is an extraordinary woman."

"Indeed, she is." Armand sighed. "Although I fear my cousin's demise upset the balance of her mind more than any of us realized."

"Indeed?" Christian took his seat, and the other two men followed suit.

Armand shrugged. "Why else would she run away?"

"That is a very good question, sir, and one I hope you are able to answer for us."

"It is a little complicated." Armand spread his hands. "I fear she did not understand the legalities of the situation and became agitated as women are prone to do."

There was a knock at the door and Ambrose ushered Elizabeth in. Christian had plenty of time to both judge her shock at facing Armand and ignore the accusing glance she shot him.

"Elizabeth!" Armand leaped to his feet and hurried toward her. "I am so glad to see that you are well. We have all been so worried about you, the children particularly."

"*Children?*" At first Christian didn't even realize he was the one who had spoken.

Armand turned back to him, a glint in his eye. "Indeed, a boy and a girl." He lowered his voice. "As I said, Elizabeth must have been momentarily crazed to abandon her children like that."

Christian felt like someone had punched him in the gut. He ignored Armand and fixed his gaze on Elizabeth, who was as pale as the paper on his desk.

"You have children."

She swallowed convulsively. "I—"

"Don't worry about that, my sweet. That is all behind us now that you are to be restored to the bosom of your family." Armand patted her arm and she flinched away from him.

Christian couldn't take his gaze off Elizabeth as she sank down onto the nearest chair. He forced himself to gather his wits.

"It hasn't yet been decided whether the dowager Comtesse de Saint-Brieuc wishes to return home."

Armand placed his hand on his heart. "Of course she wishes to come home. What kind of mother would abandon her own offspring?"

"She's hardly abandoned them, sir," Richard said quietly. "I assume they are quite safe and well cared for at the château."

"But a mother's love," Armand exclaimed. "Monsieur Delornay, I appeal to you."

Christian forced a smile. "I'm not the best judge of that, sir."

Elizabeth brought a hand up to her mouth and closed her eyes. She looked completely defeated.

"Perhaps I should just go with Armand."

Christian fought for his usual detachment but found it impossible to maintain. "You'll stay here until this matter is decided properly, *madame*."

Armand cleared his throat. "As Elizabeth's closest male relative and future husband, I believe I am the one who should make that decision."

"Are you certain you are her closest relative?" Christian countered. "I believe there might be others here in England who hold a higher claim than you do."

Richard stood up and came between the two men, but he addressed his remarks to a now red-faced Armand. "Perhaps it would be better to wait until we have all the facts before us, sir." He turned to Christian. "When do you think you will hear from Madame's family?"

"Fairly soon, Mr. Ross."

"What exactly does that mean?" Armand asked fretfully. "I have to get back to France. I have a position to maintain."

From the corner of his eye, Christian noticed that Elizabeth looked as if she might faint. He was hardly surprised. Being exposed as a mother who had abandoned her children would be hard on anyone. He couldn't help but recall his own mother's appalled expression when he and Lisette had barged into this very room all those years ago.

"I'm expecting to hear within the next week. Are you willing to wait that long?" Christian asked.

"If I must," Armand sniffed.

"In the meantime, Madame will remain here where she is safe."

"What do you mean?" Armand raised his eyebrows.

Christian met his gaze head-on. "We would hate for there to be any more accidents to her person."

Armand shrugged. "I assume you are referring to Gaston's attempt to coax Elizabeth back to us. He can be a little impetuous at times, but it is just because he is so loyal to our family."

"*Impetuous?*"

Armand had nothing to say to that and offered instead a typically Gallic shrug of his shoulders.

"One other thing, sir," Christian interjected smoothly. "Do you perhaps have copies of the late Comte's will? If Madame's English family does join us, I'm sure her solicitors will be eager to make sure she is adequately provided for."

Armand frowned. "Elizabeth is going to marry me. There is no reason for her lawyers to see anything."

Christian couldn't bring himself to look directly at Elizabeth, but he raised his voice a fraction. "Madame, do you intend to marry Armand?"

"No, Mr. Delornay, I do not."

Christian smiled at the now-seething Frenchman. "Well it seems nothing is quite settled after all. Perhaps we would be wise to wait until all the legalities are over and let *Madame* decide exactly where she wants to live and with whom." Christian nodded at Richard. "I'll send you a message when my solicitors receive an answer to my letter. Perhaps you would be willing to bring the comte back with you in a few days? I'm sure we will be able to resolve this to everyone's satisfaction."

He went to the door and caught Richard's eye as he went past him. He kept his voice low. "I need you to find out everything you can about the Saint-Brieucs, particularly about the last holder of the title and his will."

"I'll do my best," Richard murmured.

Christian waited a second until Richard and Armand disappeared before turning back to Ambrose. "Go to my solicitors, tell them that matters have now become urgent and find out if they have any information for us."

"Yes, Mr. Delornay." Ambrose hesitated. "Do you want me to escort Elizabeth upstairs?"

"I'll handle Mrs. Smith," Christian said. "Go on. I'm not going to tear her limb from limb."

Ambrose reluctantly started down the hallway, his gaze worried, and Christian turned back to his office, where Elizabeth awaited him. He went in and closed the door softly behind him, then crossed the room to sit at his desk. He needed a physical barrier between him and Elizabeth; he knew that.

"Well, Mrs. Smith. Or should I say, Madame la Comtesse de Saint-Brieuc?"

"I'm still Elizabeth. That part at least was true." She looked up at him and smiled, and he felt the falseness of it slam like a knife into his chest. So she was going to play her part through to the bitter end. Good, because by all that was holy, he needed the protection of the role already assigned to him.

"I apologize for bringing you face-to-face with your intended like that, but I thought it for the best."

"I do not intend to marry Armand, Mr. Delornay."

"Ah, that's right." He paused. "What exactly do you intend to do, then?"

She shrugged as though the matter was of very little importance. "I suppose if he understands that I will never marry him, I'll go back to France."

"I'm sure your children will be very relieved to hear that." He hated the snap in his voice but couldn't suppress it.

She glanced at him and then away. "I knew you would find that unforgiveable."

"Abandoning your children?" He gave her a smile as false as her own. "Why on earth would you think that? I'm sure your arguments on this matter will echo those of my mother. She always insists that she didn't abandon us—that she made sure she left us with every material comfort a child could desire."

Pain flashed across her face but was gone so quickly that he wasn't sure if he'd seen it or only hoped for it in his own fevered imagination.

"This is why I didn't tell you the truth, Mr. Delornay. I knew it would enrage you."

He raised his eyebrows. "Hardly that. It just confirms my opinion that not all women are suited to be mothers."

"I . . ."

For a moment he thought she was going to argue with him, but she closed her mouth and shook her head instead.

"Whatever the outcome, Madame, I suggest we wait until we hear from your English relatives before you decide to trot dutifully back with Armand to France."

Her chin went up at that. "My, Mr. Delornay, you have been busy meddling in my affairs. I thought I told you my father's family had no interest in me at all?"

He held her gaze, aware that, despite the coldness and sense of distance settling over him again, he wanted nothing more than to strike out at her and hurt her as much as she was hurting him. "You told me many things, Madame, most of them false. How was I supposed to know when you spoke the truth?"

She rose from her chair, one hand gripping the back of it as if she needed the support. "If you give me Armand's direction, I can leave the pleasure house right now, sir."

"I do not have it, and as I've already said, you will remain here until everything is sorted to my satisfaction."

"But this isn't your affair, Mr. Delornay. It is mine."

"You are still employed here."

"Then I'll resign."

"You'll stay here, Madame la Comtesse. It is still the safest place for you."

She met his hard gaze, and he realized she was close to tears. Despite everything, he wanted to go to her, enfold her in his arms, and tell her that everything would be all right.

"I'm so sorry, Mr. Delornay."

He bowed. "There is absolutely nothing to be sorry about, Madame. I'm delighted to have been of service to you in your time of need."

"Don't say that." She took an impulsive step toward him and then faltered as if whatever she saw in his eyes frightened her. "You didn't deserve to get caught up in all this."

"It has been an interesting adventure, has it not?" He shrugged. "Almost as amusing as attending a badly written play. But all things must come to an end."

Ah, that was better; he sounded almost like his old self again. "Perhaps next time you consider abandoning your home and your children, you'll think about the consequences before you disrupt so many lives. It always amazes me how selfish beautiful women can be."

She stiffened. "I knew you wouldn't be able to resist comparing me to your mother."

"I can hardly help it, can I?"

She took a sudden step toward him, her hands fisted at her sides. "Because we're both willing to do anything to safeguard the future of our children?"

He stared down at her. "Don't you dare tell me what I think. I understand my mother far better than you ever will."

"I don't think you do. You still view her as you did as a child."

"And you think your opinion means anything to me?" He summoned a dismissive smile. "Like knows like, Madame. Of course you would defend my mother. You are just like her."

The color left her face and she went still. All he could hear was the clock on the mantelpiece ticking and her harsh intake of breath.

She smiled and the beauty of it made him want to close his eyes. "Yes, Mr. Delornay. I am exactly like your mother, and I wouldn't change that for *anything*. For once you are absolutely and completely right."

Elizabeth managed to get to her bedchamber before she started to cry, but it was very close. She sank down onto the rug before the fire, pressed her hands to her eyes, and sobbed until she was shaking and gasping. Armand had made her look like a madwoman and just the sort of mother Christian would despise. And, God, with his history, he'd taken the bait perfectly. What defense did she have? Whatever the circumstances, he'd already judged and condemned her.

As she began to run out of tears, Elizabeth turned to the warm fire in the grate and stared into the flames. It didn't change anything. She'd already known she would lose Christian whatever happened. No man would want to be burdened with a woman like her. She'd lied far too often and far too well to encourage anyone to trust or believe in her. She hadn't expected Christian to withdraw his support from her so completely, though; she hadn't realized how much she'd come to rely on him either. . . .

She pushed that thought away and concentrated on what she could salvage. Armand was in England, which meant the children were alone at the château. Had his mistress, Louise, stayed behind to guard them, or had she accompanied Armand? Would

Louise care whether the children were taken? Elizabeth had to assume she would, seeing as they represented the future of the Saint-Brieuc dynasty, and Louise was very conscious of her role in that future.

Elizabeth got up and washed her hands and face. She should know never to depend on anyone else by now. She had the money to return to France and the desire, so she would simply continue with her plan later that night. She changed her crumpled dress, gathered a few possessions in her largest reticule, and went to the door. She knew Christian wouldn't let her work in the pleasure house, but she could at least sit in the kitchen and keep Madame Durand company before she left.

She tried to open the door and realized it was stuck. After a couple of minutes of fruitless jiggling, she realized that the door wasn't jammed at all. Someone had deliberately locked her in.

"Mr. Delornay, I have some news for you."

Christian was sitting in the kitchen trying to forget the expression on Elizabeth's face when he'd likened her to his mother. Did she really think he needed to grow up? If so, she was a fool. "What is it, Ambrose?"

Ambrose sat next to him. "Your solicitors said they have received a reply from the Walker family, and they are intending to meet with you and your representative on Monday, if that is acceptable."

"That will be perfect," Christian said. "By the way, I've locked Mrs. Smith, I mean Madame la Comtesse, in her room. Don't let her out."

"Locked her in?" Ambrose frowned. "Why?"

"Because I don't want her running back to Armand."

"Why would she run now when everything has been discovered?"

"I'm not sure." Christian went still. "That's a very good question."

"I don't think she likes Armand very much, do you? I can't imagine why she agreed to marry him."

"I'm not sure if she did or whether she was just told that it would happen."

"He didn't strike me as a very pleasant individual."

"He was extremely unpleasant," Christian said slowly. "So why didn't Elizabeth take issue with what he said?"

"Because she knew he spoke the truth?" Ambrose hesitated. "If she really did leave her children in France, you are the last person she'd want to know about it."

"Because I'm irrational on the subject?"

"Not exactly *irrational*. You have a perfect right to hold strong views on the matter," Ambrose said carefully.

"You think I'm wrong about my mother, don't you?"

Ambrose simply looked at him.

Christian swirled the contents of his wineglass and contemplated the ruby reds. "Is that why Elizabeth didn't argue with Armand? Did she assume I wouldn't defend her because of my relationship with my mother?"

"I don't know, sir," Ambrose said. "I expected her to defend herself a little more strongly, but once he brought up the subject of her children, she seemed to crumble." He sat up straight. "Mayhap she fears what he will do to them if she argues. By bringing them up straight away, he managed to subtly threaten her."

"She left them, Ambrose. Why would she care what happened to them now?"

"You know it's not as simple as that." Ambrose hesitated. "I don't think your mother stopped caring about you for one moment."

Christian stared at the wine. Ambrose was probably the only person apart from Lisette brave enough to voice that particular opinion. Did he have a point? Had his mother cared for him in the only way she knew how?

He remembered her coming to visit him, Marguerite, and Lisette in France once, how the nuns had had to tear him away from her embrace and how hard she'd cried when they'd made her leave. . . .

And how did that relate back to Elizabeth anyway?

"She told me that nothing was ever that simple."

"Who did?" Ambrose asked.

"Elizabeth." He raised his gaze to Ambrose. "There is something I'm missing, isn't there? How in God's name am I going to get her to tell me what it is?"

"Couldn't you just ask her?"

Christian laughed. "She'd just lie."

"But who is she trying to protect when she lies—herself or the children? And what is she trying to protect them from—their cousin or herself?"

"I have no idea, Ambrose, but I suspect there is a lot more to find out than we realize." He rose to his feet. "In fact, I think tomorrow night I'll allow Mrs. Smith to escape if she wants to."

21

"You had no right to lock me in my room!" Elizabeth said tightly.

Christian leaned against the bedroom door and regarded her closely. It was Saturday evening, over twenty-four hours since she'd first been locked in her room, and she was still angry and sick at heart.

After their last horrible encounter, she could hardly bear to look at Christian. She had to convince him to set her free. She cleared her throat.

"Mr. Delornay?"

"You've already told me that you intend to return to France with Armand, so there really isn't any need to contain you." He flung open her door and bowed low. "Please accept my apologies. I'd prefer it if you kept to the pleasure house. Despite your cousin Armand's protestations, Gaston might still be lurking outside, ready to dispose of you and save everyone a lot of bother."

Elizabeth stared at him. "Why have you changed your mind so easily?"

His cold smile reminded her of the first time they'd met when she'd been unable to understand or read his face at all.

"I'm quite capable of reassessing my risks, madame. As you pointed out, this really isn't my problem. I'm just keeping you safe until you return to your rightful position."

There was nothing in his polite, social tone to indicate that he cared for her. Nothing at all and it hurt. God it hurt more than she could possibly have imagined. But it was for the best. She was the only one who was supposed to feel any regret for the lost opportunity of meeting and loving a man like him.

She curtsied to him and walked toward the doorway where he still lingered. She waited for him to move away but he didn't.

"What are the names of your children?" he asked quietly.

She stared at the top button of his gray waistcoat and slowly took in a breath. She would not cry in front of him. She would *not*. "Jean-Pierre and Evangeline."

"Do you miss them?"

She pressed her lips tightly together and refused to look up at him. She supposed he deserved his revenge, but she would be damned if he expected her to discuss the children.

"I only ask because I don't understand. You do not strike me as the sort of woman who would abandon her responsibilities so easily."

She had to finish this before she leaned into his deceptively slender chest and told him the whole sordid tale. With all her remaining courage, she looked up at him.

"But you don't really know me at all, do you, Mr. Delornay? Perhaps there is a reason why your mother and I got along so well. Perhaps I told her what I refused to tell you and that's why she let me stay."

He grabbed hold of her wrist, and the coldness in his hazel eyes turned to ice. She fought an urge to step back from such frozen fury. Instead she smiled as sweetly as she could and he let go of her.

"Damn you to hell, madame."

She put some distance between them. "Of course I'll stay in the pleasure house today, Mr. Delornay. Is there anything in particular you would like me to do?"

"Stay out of my sight?" he suggested.

"Naturally, sir." She curtsied again and sailed past him into the hallway, her smile instantly dying, her hand pressed to her aching heart. She would find solace in the kitchen. Surely Madame could do with an extra pair of hands? And if Christian came by, there were plenty of places to hide.

When she entered the kitchen, Ambrose looked up from his perusal of the newspaper, got to his feet, and studied her intently.

"Madame la Comtesse."

"Elizabeth will still do nicely." She sat and waved him back to his seat. "Are you angry with me as well?"

"I'm more surprised than anything." He folded the newspaper and gave her his full attention.

She held up her hand. "Please don't tell me I don't look like the sort of woman who could walk away from her children. Mr. Delornay has already been over that."

"I'm sure he has. But now I quite understand why you were reluctant to reveal what happened to you."

"As soon as I realized he was at odds with his mother and why, I knew he would never understand what I was forced to do."

"Forced?" Ambrose asked.

Cursing herself for revealing even that, Elizabeth took the opportunity to rise and ask Madame Durand for some coffee. By the time she took her seat again, she was determined to be more careful.

"Where is Paul? I haven't seen him for days."

"Paul is . . . busy elsewhere."

"With the military?"

"I'm not sure." Ambrose seemed to find the topic of conversation as uncomfortable as she had found the last one.

"If Paul isn't here and I'm no longer available, what are you doing about the room of desires?"

"We've recruited one of Marie-Claude's protégées, Henrietta, to help out, and Mr. Delornay and I will continue to play our parts when necessary."

"Henrietta is an excellent choice. She is completely unshockable."

Ambrose smiled. "That is certainly an advantage." He reached across the table and took Elizabeth's hand. "We will miss you, Mrs. Smith."

"I'll miss you too. You have been very kind to me."

He patted her hand. "You needed it."

"I will never forget you, Ambrose." Although the rise of her emotions was debilitating, and she would need all her strength later, it was a relief to be able to say how she really felt.

"You don't have to go with him, Elizabeth," Ambrose murmured. "Stay here and let us help you."

She stared into his worried brown eyes. "I can't. I wish I could, but I've realized I have no choice." She forced a laugh. "I never did have a choice. I have to go back. I'm fairly sure Mr. Delornay, at least, will be glad to see me leave."

"That's the most ridiculous thing I've ever heard."

"What do you mean?"

"You know he cares for you."

"I know nothing of the sort."

"If you leave him, I fear he'll never recover."

She pulled her hand away from between his. "Don't be ridiculous, Ambrose. He'll never be able to forgive me for this."

He shook his head. "I've never met a more stubborn pair of fools in my life. Why can't you just—"

She held up her hand to stop him speaking. "Because we can't. Please don't do this," she whispered.

He stared at her for a long time. "Elizabeth, you can't always run away. You do know that?"

She nodded and he sighed and rose to his feet. "I have work to do. Perhaps I will see you later? I'm sure Mr. Delornay told you not to leave the pleasure house."

"I'm going to stay here and help Madame Durand." Elizabeth smiled. "She says I will come in useful this afternoon when she needs someone to slice apples and blackberries for her pies."

By ten o'clock that night, Madame's pies were cooling in the larder and she had retired to bed, leaving Elizabeth in charge of the kitchen. Not that there was much to do. The buffet staff already knew where to get the supplies to replenish the food, and Elizabeth merely made mulled wine as required.

There had been no sign of Paul, Ambrose, or Christian for hours, and Elizabeth was beginning to hope she would be able to leave after all. She'd already packed her reticule and had it with her in the kitchen. The last obstacle was Seamus Kelly, who was guarding the back door.

Dubiously, Elizabeth regarded his broad back. Would he even know that Christian had told her not to leave the premises? Surely it would be better if she sent him elsewhere while she slipped out the back door? He was such a sweet man that she didn't want to get him in trouble.

"Seamus? Could you help me for a moment?"

He turned his pleasant, freckled face toward her and smiled. "What can I do for you, Mrs. Smith?"

She waved vaguely in the direction of the kitchen range. "I need some more of the Spanish red wine to add to the spices and orange peel for the posset. As there is no one else here, could you possibly go down to the cellar and bring me up another two bottles?"

Seamus shifted from one massive foot to the other. "I'm supposed to be watching the door, ma'am."

"I know you are, but I'm too afraid to go down into the cellars myself." She pretended to shiver. "It is so dark down there. I promise to watch the door for you."

His smile was indulgent. "All right, then, ma'am. Just call out if anything happens and I'll be back up them stairs in a flash."

She squeezed his massive arm. "Thank you, Seamus."

He blushed and mumbled something unintelligible as Elizabeth unlocked the cellar door. She propped the door open with an old rusted warming iron and watched as he descended the stairs. As soon as he disappeared from view, she grabbed her coat, bonnet, and reticule and ran for the back door.

The bitter cold hit her immediately, but she didn't stop to fully button her coat. It was imperative that she get as far away from the pleasure house as possible before they discovered she was missing. Her booted feet slipped on the icy cobblestones as she ran through the mews yard at the back of the house, past the stables, and then down onto the narrow street below.

Her breath formed an icy swathe around her as she paused to seek her bearings. She'd studied the area well enough to know that if she wanted to find a hackney cab, she needed to get out of the residential region of Mayfair and into the more commercial parts of the city.

Footsteps echoed on the cobblestones behind her, and she started moving, barely resisting the temptation to look back. Her fingers were cold, and even as she increased her pace, she belatedly tried to button her coat one-handed. Her aim was to get as far as one of the coaching inns on the edge of the city and leave for Dover on the morrow.

"Madame la Comtesse."

Gaston's triumphant voice echoed behind her. Her fingers closed on the handle of the knife in her pocket. Stupid of her not to listen to Christian's warnings, but she'd assumed he'd been lying to make her stay. But not everyone lied as easily as she did. Not everyone was prepared to sacrifice everything to survive.

She kept walking. Either he'd have to come after her or she'd escape him. She *was* tired of running away, and she'd realized recently that Gaston was a coward and a bully. He ran at her and she swung around to confront him, knife in her hand. He screamed as the blade sliced into his outstretched hand, and his French became vile and guttural.

She ignored his threats and concentrated on the job at hand. She didn't need to kill him; she just needed to stop him following her. Rage flooded through her and she drew back her arm again.

"Go away, Gaston, or I'll kill you." He cringed and flung up his hands before his face. "Do you really think I came out here alone? There are at least two men following me, and they will not care whether you die."

His head whipped around and she maintained her confident smile. "Do you want me to scream for help and prove my point?" His teeth drew back in a snarl as he glared at her. "Are you really that keen to die for Armand, Gaston? He has no intention of paying you for killing me. He denied all knowledge of your plans."

"Liar!"

"I saw him on Friday. I'm sure he told you." She deliberately looked over his shoulder back toward the mews of Barrington Square. "I see Seamus Kelly coming. He'll beat you to a pulp. Run away while you have the chance and talk to Armand before he betrays you to the authorities anyway."

Gaston spat in her direction and muttered in French before

turning on his heel and running for the shadows. Elizabeth took a deep breath and ran in the opposite direction, the bloodied knife abandoned on the street, her thoughts in chaos.

To her relief, a hackney cab was dropping a party of men off on the corner of the square. One of the men paused long enough to ask her directions and open the door of the cab for her. She thanked him profusely.

"Where do you want to go, ma'am?" the driver shouted.

"The Greyhound Coaching Inn in Carshalton," Elizabeth shouted back as she stepped up into the cab, and the gentleman helpfully shut the door for her.

"That's a long drive, ma'am. Do you have the necessary coin?"

Elizabeth held up a crown. "Indeed I do, sir, and I'll pay you well for your time."

He turned around to grin at her, and she noticed he lacked one of his front teeth. "Fair enough, then. Let's be on our way."

Christian ran down on the cobbled street beside Seamus Kelly, who was still apologizing.

"Seamus, it's all right. She can't be more than a minute in front of us."

He frowned as he heard the sound of French insults being thrown. "Damnation, is Gaston onto her already?"

By the time they reached the cobbled lane that lay between the mews and the square below, there was nothing left but a bloodied knife lying in the center of the road. Seamus slapped Christian on the back.

"The lady went down to the right. I saw her. You go on. I'll follow whoever else was here."

Christian didn't need a second urging; his mind filled with images of Elizabeth being stabbed, of her dying somewhere he couldn't reach her. He heard the sound of a hackney cab and headed in that direction. By the time he reached the corner of the square, the cab was already moving away and he had no chance of catching it.

He paused and cursed out loud, his chest heaving, his gaze roving the square. A burst of laughter caught his attention. Diagonally across the garden in the center of the square, a group of men was walking toward the house on the opposite corner. Christian took off after them and prayed that he was right.

It seemed to take forever for the hackney cab to reach the coaching inn. At times, Elizabeth wondered if they had gotten lost, but the driver was whistling cheerfully and she had no choice but to believe that he knew where he was going. She'd chosen the inn after talking to many of the tradesmen who frequented the kitchens of the pleasure house. She'd wanted a place that was decent but not too high in the instep, as she would be appearing there without luggage and in the middle of the night.

By the time they reached the coaching inn, Elizabeth was barely able to keep her eyes open. She accepted the driver's help to get down and, after she gave him the whole crown, his escort into the taproom. The landlord came to greet her, his careful gaze taking note of both her solitary state and her lack of baggage.

Before she could speak, the driver nodded at the landlord. "Lady's carriage broke an axle. Left her maid in hysterics and her luggage all over the London Road. Thought she'd be better off here than standing in the street waiting for her carriage to be fixed."

Elizabeth stared at her unlikely hero and he winked.

The landlord bowed. "Indeed, ma'am. Should we be expecting your husband as well?"

"No, sir, I'm a widow." Elizabeth drew back her veil and gave the landlord the benefit of her most bewitching smile. "I just need somewhere to lay my head for the remainder of the night so that I can forget my horrible ordeal." If the hackney driver could manufacture a tale, the least she could do was go along with it.

"Yes, ma'am. We have a suitable bedchamber for you at the back of the house so you won't hear all the comings and goings. I'll take you up."

Elizabeth turned to the hackney cab driver. "Thank you, sir."

He winked at her again. "Pleasure to help a pretty lady. Now keep safe, you hear me?"

"I will."

She followed the landlord up the narrow staircase and to the end of the timbered hallway. He opened a door and she followed him in. He bent to light the fire and then some of the candles.

"I'll send someone up with some hot water. Do you require any refreshments?"

"No, I thank you." Elizabeth sank into the chair closest to the fire and held out her hands to the blaze. "I'm just glad to get in from the cold."

"Indeed, ma'am."

"Thank you." She smiled at him again, and his face softened. Christian was right. Beauty did give her some advantages, and on this occasion she was quite happy to exploit them.

He left her in the warm glow of the fire, and she took off her soaked boots and stockings and put them close to the fire to dry. A knock at the door revealed a maid with the promised hot water, a glass of warm milk, and a nightgown. Elizabeth gratefully accepted everything and asked to be woken before dawn.

After washing her hands, she sat in the chair, tucked her feet up under her, and slowly sipped at the milk. There was a hint of honey and chamomile, which she assumed were to help her sleep. When she finished the milk, she took her time unpinning her hair. Her head was aching and the bed looked more comfortable every time she thought about it.

The stable clock struck one, and she finally crawled into bed. The sheets were well starched and fresh, the pillow rather hard, but by this time, she didn't care at all.

It hardly seemed more than five minutes before the maid was shaking her awake and offering to help her dress. Elizabeth hurried through her morning preparations, drinking scalding coffee and munching on soft white bread and butter as the maid laced up her corset and helped her with her hair.

A cockerel was crowing as she left the inn, which somehow seemed fitting, and the sun still hadn't risen. She made her way to the ticket office for the mail coaches and managed to purchase an inside ticket for the next transport, which was due within the hour. She spent the remaining time in the communal taproom, the veil on her bonnet down, her reticule clasped firmly in her hands.

When the coach arrived with all its usual hustle and bustle, she got to her feet and went outside into the cold bright morning to join the busy throng around the vehicle. She ignored the shouting and jostling as best she could, part of her still disbelieving that she was actually going to leave England for good. She didn't expect to return. If her plan failed, Armand would find a way to dispose of her. She shuddered at the thought that he might give her to Gaston.

Just as she was about to board the coach, a hand closed tightly on her elbow. She turned her head and found Christian at her side, his smile firmly in place, his expression concerned.

"Madame, I am so glad I found you before you boarded the coach. You are needed back at home."

She tried to pull out of his grasp, but his hold was inexorable. Voices behind her started to grumble, and she felt the pressure of the other bodies eager to get on the coach shoving against her.

"Excuse me, madame." Christian yanked on her arm and pulled her out of the throng. "Perhaps you'd care to discuss this matter with me in the inn."

"Let me go."

She didn't bother to lower her voice, but it hardly mattered. In this melee, no one cared whether she was being held against her will. All they cared about was getting on the coach and sending it on its way.

"Do you have any luggage, ma'am?" Christian inquired, his voice far more civilized than his grip on her arm.

"No." She glared at him through her veil, but he didn't seem to notice. "Let go of me, Mr. Delornay, or I will cause a scene."

"No one will hear you in this racket, and if you try it, I'll simply put you over my shoulder, carry you into the inn, and say you've fainted."

"You wouldn't dare," she hissed.

"Try me." His smile was feral. "I'm tired of being lied to. It's past time for you to tell me the truth."

She allowed him to draw her away from the posting inn and toward the much-quieter environs of the church graveyard. He let her pull out of his grasp and walk ahead of him. Frost still shone on the grass, and the dark foliage gave everything a crisp and otherworldly feel. Christian studied the squat Norman church tower and then dropped his gaze to the slender woman in front of him.

His hunch that the jolly revelers in the square must have given their hackney cab to Elizabeth had paid off. Even in their drunken state, they'd heard her destination quite clearly and had been happy to share it with him. He hoped to God it wasn't the only piece of luck he would have. He was damned if he was going to allow Elizabeth to disappear until she had heard from her own family and from him.

"Tell me the truth, Elizabeth."

His quiet command made her stop walking and stare down at the frozen ground. "You know that I like to lie, Mr. Delornay."

"Yes, I know that. You lied when you told me you intended to go back to France with Armand. You also lied when you tried to pretend that the children meant nothing to you." He moved closer. "Why bother to run away if you'd already decided to return with Armand?"

She shivered as the wisps of his frozen breath trailed over her shoulder and he continued talking. "I thought about it for a long time last night, and I realized that your aim must be to get to the children without Armand's knowledge while he is stuck here."

She didn't reply but he saw her stiffen and decided he had nothing left to lose. "I wish to make a bargain with you."

She slowly turned around. "A bargain?"

"Lift your veil. I want to see your face." He nodded as she obliged him. "It concerns a trade. If you do something for me, I will help you recover your children from Armand."

"What kind of trade?"

Ah, at least she hadn't turned him down flat. "Paul has become deeply involved with the Demon Club. I need your help to extract him from their claws."

"Paul is an adult. Isn't he entitled to take his sexual pleasures where he wants?"

Christian grimaced. "Let us just say that he wasn't invited into the club on his own merits. Certain interested parties used him to lure me back. I'm afraid they intend to hurt him quite badly."

"And if you go to his aid, aren't you doing exactly what they want?"

He met her wary gaze. "Not if you are with me. I think that if we work together, we can all survive this mess and walk away unscathed." She bit her lip and he kept talking. "If you help me, I'll do everything in my power to ensure that Armand doesn't keep those children from you."

"There is nothing you can do."

"At least let me try. And if we can't come to a legal solution on Monday, I swear I'll accompany you to France and help you steal the brats."

She stared at him, her face pale. "Why?"

"Because"—he paused—"I wish someone had helped my mother keep her children." *God, where had that come from?* "Perhaps I wish you to have the choices my mother was denied."

She stayed silent for so long that he thought she'd turned to stone like the grave markers behind her.

"I accept your terms, Mr. Delornay."

He realized he was smiling. "Just like that?"

She shrugged. "I've missed my seat on the stage to Dover, and the ship will sail without me. And I doubt you were going to let me go anyway."

He regarded her seriously. "I have no intention of letting you go." *Ever,* his mind added, but he wasn't stupid enough to voice that wish quite yet. Much depended on what happened over the next few days.

He held out his hand. "Shall we return home, then? I've already rented a carriage to take us back to Mayfair."

She sighed and walked across to take his arm. "Perhaps we can discuss how you intend to extricate Paul from his predicament on the journey home."

"Indeed we can. I have several ideas." He glanced down at her. "You might even end up enjoying yourself."

22

Later that night, Elizabeth considered the gown Christian had asked her to wear. It was a transparent white muslin that clung to her shape as if it had been dampened down. He'd also told her not to wear any petticoats underneath, which hardly helped. A pink satin sash did nothing but emphasize the scanty nature of the bodice and the revealing expanse of her bosom.

"It's perfect."

Elizabeth swung around to find Christian regarding her complacently.

"This gown? It is quite indecent."

He came closer and his all-too-familiar clean, laundered scent washed over her. "It is perfect for our purposes. You look like a debutante."

"A debutante who is eager to bed every man in sight, perhaps."

"Which is a fantasy much beloved by the kind of gentlemen who frequent the Demon Club." He paused to tuck an errant curl behind her ear. "I want them to think that you are young and vulnerable." She shivered as his fingers trailed along her jawbone. "Are you afraid?"

"A little," she admitted.

"Good, you should be. These people are not pleasant or civilized. When they enter the Demon Club, they become animals and that certainly doesn't involve respecting other people's sexual choices." He hesitated and then kissed her gently on the mouth. "I won't let anyone hurt you. If my plan goes awry, I'll leave Paul to his own devices and make sure you are safe."

"Thank you for that, at least." She pulled away from him before she gave in to the temptation to kiss him back. "Shall we go?"

Christian ignored both the raucous greetings from acquaintances and the naked bodies in the hallways, and ushered Elizabeth toward the largest salon in the Demon Club. He'd told her to keep her cloak on and was glad of it when he realized that the level of excitement was already high and climbing fast.

Kelveston was sitting in state on a dais flanked by his wife and the four other founders of the club. Below them, other members danced and fondled each other in a scene worthy of a Roman orgy. The golden cage by the fire was even more full of unhappy debtors than usual. Christian spotted Paul's blond hair and disgruntled expression quite easily.

Melinda Kelveston wore the glittering face paint and earrings of a Roman woman and a toga that exposed one of her breasts. Her smile widened when she saw Christian approaching, and she stood up and waved at him.

He walked around the edge of the dancers to the side of the raised dais and bowed. "Good evening, Lady Kelveston, Lord Kelveston, gentlemen."

Kelveston nodded. "I'm glad you could come, Delornay. We are all hoping to get our revenge on you tonight." He laughed and glanced at the other men. "At the card table, obviously."

Christian smiled. "Obviously. May I present my companion, Miss Sylvia? She has recently arrived from France."

He drew Elizabeth forward and pulled off her cloak. She didn't protest and stood there as the men and Melinda all stared at her. To her relief, Melinda didn't seem to connect the lady she had met at the pleasure house with the scantily attired woman at Christian's side.

"She's a pretty piece, Delornay. I'll give you that," Kelveston said.

"And despite her garb, quite an innocent," Christian replied. "In truth, she has no idea what is going to happen to her to-night."

Kelveston licked his lips. "Then she'll go in the cage—agreed?"

"Indeed. But she's still mine." Christian grabbed Elizabeth's arm. "Come along, my dear."

Kelveston and his cronies followed as Christian marched Elizabeth toward the golden cage. He waited while one of the footmen unlocked the door.

"What are you doing, sir?" Elizabeth squeaked, and clung on to his arm.

"Putting you in the cage." He kissed the top of her head. "Now be a good girl and behave yourself. If I'm lucky, I'll win you back. If not, you'll be fucked by someone else and you'll enjoy it."

"I don't want to go in a cage! You never said—"

He removed her clinging fingers from his arm and threw her bodily in, nodding to the footman to slam the door shut and lock it behind her. She stayed at the bars, pleading with him, but he ignored her and turned back to Melinda, who was ap-plauding.

"She'll calm down in a while," he said airily.

"Oh, I hope not! I love it best when they are terrified." She looped her arm through his. "Now that you are free again, do you want to find something to drink before we start playing?"

"Indeed, my lady. It would be a pleasure."

* * *

Elizabeth watched Christian stroll away with the predatory Lady Kelveston hanging on his arm and fought the temptation to hiss at them like a cat. Instead, she pretended to be overcome and allowed herself to fall to the floor, moaning as someone neatly caught her. She opened her eyes to see Paul's grim face over her.

"What in God's name are you doing here?" he murmured.

Elizabeth allowed him to steady her and draw her close to his chest. "Rescuing you."

"I don't need rescuing. I got here all by myself."

"Apparently not. Mr. Delornay believes there was a conspiracy to get you into the club and this cage to tempt him back."

"He would think that."

"And on this occasion I believe his suspicions are correct. They'll hurt you to enrage him."

"Damnation!" Paul groaned. "Can't I do anything right?"

"It's not your fault. Lady Kelveston wants Christian back in her bed. I also suspect Lord Kelveston and his friends are planning to cheat at cards and get Christian in the cage so that they can ravish you both."

"Which means I am superfluous, as usual." He frowned. "But what does this have to do with you?"

She patted his cheek. "I'll explain that part later. Now here is what Mr. Delornay wants us to do . . ."

Christian kissed Melinda as slowly and lasciviously as he could. He'd decided to treat her as if she was a guest at the pleasure house, meeting her demands as impersonally as he met all his guests' needs. It made him think of Elizabeth and all the men she had endured. Would she be able to do what he'd asked of her tonight? She suddenly seemed fragile, and he suspected he was responsible for at least some of that.

Melinda stunk of wine and stale perfume, and the acrid taste of her made him want to puke.

"Did you see who else was in the cage, my darling?" Melinda inquired.

"I can't say I really looked, my lady."

Melinda giggled. "Your friend Paul St. Clare is in there."

"He's hardly my friend," Christian replied. "He's someone I fuck occasionally at the pleasure house."

"Oh, I think he is much more than that," she cooed. "He has connections to your brother-in-law and some of the most exulted members of the *ton*. It would be a shame if his particular sexual predilections were exposed here for all to see and gossip about."

Christian barely managed to smile. "He'll survive."

She dug her fingernails into his coat sleeve. "I'm not so sure about that. My dear Kelveston is very keen to fuck him, and his mood is very dark tonight." She was watching him closely and not quite as drunk as she appeared.

He laughed and kissed her cheek. "Then Paul is indeed a lucky man."

Hoping he had convinced Melinda that Paul meant nothing to him, he led her back to the main salon where the card tables were being set up and to her seat on the dais. Kelveston was conversing with some of his friends, but he paused when he saw his wife and Christian.

"Delornay, you will join me at my table."

"If you insist, my lord." Christian paused. "Although it might be entertaining if we made this into more of a competition."

"Go on," Kelveston said, his brow furrowing.

"We play until the pool narrows and the stakes rise until only the best are left."

"I like the sound of that." Kelveston beckoned to the oldest of the club founders. "Boris, do we have rankings for everyone who is playing tonight? Would it be possible to divide them up into two pools and match the weaker players against the stronger?"

Boris withdrew a long sheet of paper from his pocket and put on his spectacles. "I don't see why not, Kelveston. I'll separate out the players, and while I'm doing that, you can tell the butler to rearrange the tables."

Christian spared a single glance for the occupants of the cage and discovered that Elizabeth was as far away from Paul as she could possibly get. He hadn't *quite* told her she'd be put in a cage, so her indignation hadn't been entirely feigned. He'd win her back, though; he was quite certain of that.

It took quite a while to organize the drunken masses into some semblance of order, and even longer for Kelveston to explain the change in the rules. Each win meant a player got to pick one debtor from the cage to sexually service him or her. The favor could be taken immediately in front of the others or postponed until the player was out of the game.

Christian took a seat at the first table and nodded at his companions. Two of them were so drunk they could barely hold their cards, and the third was a nonentity. If the cards hadn't been tampered with, he would win quickly and easily. The only other ponderables were who would Kelveston and Melinda choose from the cage? It was highly possible that they'd choose Elizabeth or Paul just to enrage him.

But they didn't know his lovers as well as he did. Neither Paul nor Elizabeth would shatter if they were compelled to fuck someone else. At least he hoped they wouldn't. He dealt the cards as quickly as he could and inspected his hand as he realized something still mired his calm. He didn't want anyone else fucking Elizabeth. Pushing that concern down, he concentrated on the game. At this point, he really had no other alternative.

* * *

Elizabeth narrowed her gaze and stared across at the gaming tables. Christian might have told her that she was going to be thrust into a cage! Some of the inmates were openly weeping or lamenting their fate, and it wasn't just the women. Whispers circulated as to what terrible sexual fate might await them all, especially if they were unlucky enough to be won by Kelveston or Delornay.

She tried to ignore the panicked whispers, but it was difficult. For the first time in a long while, she was worried that she would be forced to perform sexual acts with strangers. It seemed that learning to trust Christian had stripped her of her usual defenses. A shout went up from one of the tables, and her throat dried as the footman approached the cage with his set of keys.

To her dismay, it wasn't Christian who appeared behind him but the unpleasant Lady Kelveston, whose gaze skimmed the contents of the cage like a starving wolf. She stared at Elizabeth for a long moment, and then her gaze moved on and she pointed an imperious finger at Paul.

"Him, the blond with the brown eyes."

Paul winked as he strolled past Elizabeth, but she found she couldn't smile back. Lady Kelveston walked across to the nearest chair, sat down, and flipped up her toga to reveal her perfectly bare sex.

"Lick me."

Paul got down on his knees and lowered his head between Lady Kelveston's bare thighs. She shoved her hand into his thick hair and pulled hard until he flinched.

"Make me come."

Elizabeth didn't want to watch Paul, but it was hard to look away. Her attention was finally jerked back when the cage door opened again and Christian stood there. She attempted to stand, but his gaze swept over her and settled on another, much younger woman.

"Miss Retton? You are in here again?"

Miss Retton started to cry and Christian held out his hand to her. "Stop sniveling and come here."

Elizabeth realized she was glaring at Christian, but he didn't look at her at all. She sank back into her corner, her breathing uneven. *Damn him to hell.* The thought of having to watch Miss Retton pleasuring Christian made her fingers curl into claws. She wouldn't watch him. With that thought, she lowered her eyes and stared down at her interlocked fingers.

A gasp made her look up, but it wasn't from Christian. It was Lady Kelveston, her head thrown back, her mouth open as she climaxed under Paul's skilled mouth and hands. Miss Retton sat on a chair by the wall, her hands in her lap, her expression still terrified. Elizabeth looked for Christian, but he was already sitting back at the card table engrossed in another round of the game.

Indignation stirred low in her stomach. In his quest to outdo Lord Kelveston, did he intend to gather as many unwilling lovers as he could? And what then? Did he mean to pleasure them all in some almighty orgy?

Time passed and as players dropped out, the crowd around the card tables grew. Unlike Christian, Kelveston chose his victims and either fucked them or made them suck his cock before sending them on their way. Ten other people were released from the cage, two of them chosen by Christian, who continued to ignore Elizabeth.

For the first time, she began to doubt his motives. Had he brought her here to save Paul or to further his own sexual legend? Paul seemed quite happy keeping Lady Kelveston occupied. He was fucking her now while she knelt on the chair, her bottom raised in the air, his hands firmly grasping her hips.

Four of them were left in the cage now, and the card tables were down to the last two. Kelveston was on one and Christian the other. Elizabeth knew that it would eventually come down to the two men. She could only hope Kelveston wouldn't cheat. There was something about the set of his mouth and the hard black shine of his eyes that made her uneasy.

Applause sounded and Kelveston got to his feet, grinning. He headed for the cage and nodded at the footman. "Let's see what's left, shall we? Stand up, all of you."

Elizabeth reluctantly rose to her feet and tried not to catch Lord Kelveston's stare.

"You, Sylvia or whatever your name is, Delornay's whore. Come here."

The footman reached inside and pulled a reluctant Elizabeth out of the cage. She tried not to shudder as Kelveston locked his arm around her waist and bent his head to nuzzle her throat. It wasn't the first time a man had treated her thusly, so why was it so difficult to stand there and let him paw her?

"She's mine, Kelveston," Christian said. He stopped in front of her repulsive captor, his expression as relaxed and charming as ever. "We agreed that she would be mine first, did we not? You can certainly try her out later."

His gaze met Elizabeth's. She latched onto the calm certainty in his eyes as if he were the only thing that could save her. And perhaps he was. He'd taken away her ability to accept men such as Kelveston and left her with nothing but anger and her own pride.

Kelveston's hand slid up from her waist to fondle her breasts. "I don't remember agreeing to anything except putting her in the cage, Delornay. I got here first, and I get the first choice. You can watch me fuck her if you like."

Christian sighed. "With all due respect, my lord, I don't like it at all."

There was a sudden hush around the two men, and Melinda pushed Paul out of her way so that she could see better, her expression avid.

"My club, my rules, I'm afraid, Delornay."

Christian considered him for so long that Elizabeth almost forgot how to breathe.

"Seeing as how we both won our games and there is only one left to play, how about we keep Sylvia for the ultimate winner?"

"Why would I do that, Delornay?" Kelveston's hand slid between Elizabeth's thighs. "Surely a bird in the hand is worth more than one in the bush?"

Christian smiled and gestured at Miss Retton and the other debtors he had freed from the cage and not yet touched. "Winner takes all?"

Kelveston studied the debtors, his gaze lingering on the still-sobbing Miss Retton. "Yes, and the winner has to fuck Sylvia in front of everyone." His grip on Elizabeth tightened and she fought a whimper. "Even if you win, there'll be no hiding away tonight to savor your conquests, Delornay."

"Agreed," Christian replied. "And I'll want Paul St. Clare as well."

"You are very confident."

Christian shrugged, the gesture very French. "I'm an excellent cardplayer."

"We'll see about that." Kelveston snapped his fingers at the nearest footman. "Go and fetch a new pack of cards from my study."

Melinda pouted at her husband. "What if I don't want Paul to leave me?"

Kelveston released Elizabeth and then bowed to his wife. "When I win, my lady, you can do with him what you will. I'll be more than happy to participate."

"I'm playing, too, my lord. Boris has yielded his place at the table to me." Melinda smiled. "Perhaps you'll all have to come begging to me for your pleasures after all."

Elizabeth could only wonder how Christian felt facing both Kelvestons at the same time. It obviously had been planned and didn't bode well for the final game or for the outcome. There was nothing she could do about it now except pray that Christian's skills were as good as he thought they were.

Christian walked over to Elizabeth and took her arm. She looked up at him and he smiled and spoke in an undertone only she could hear. "Don't fail me now. Kelveston will try anything to win this last game."

She swallowed convulsively. "I'll do my best."

"Good."

He led her toward the card tables where a footman was replenishing the candles and the brandy bottles.

"Kneel beside my chair."

Most of the crowd had dispersed, moving on to more exciting pursuits like fucking each other or drinking. Unfortunately, those who were left were mainly close friends of Kelveston's and even more likely to be after Christian's blood.

Christian beckoned Paul forward and directed him to kneel beside the chair Lady Kelveston would occupy. He took a moment to bend close and smooth Paul's hair. "Tell me if you see them cheating. Use the same method we use at the pleasure house."

He'd already taught Elizabeth the system Philip had developed to identify card thieves and cheats in the most inconspicuous way possible. Helene had always preferred such unpleasantness as confronting cheaters to happen after the game had finished and in the privacy of her office. It meant less of an open scandal for the person concerned and more of an opportunity for them to right the wrong before Helene used her contacts to blacken their name forever.

The fourth man took his seat at the table. Christian barely nodded at him and received a frosty look in return. Lord Norton had no love for Christian, having been banned from the pleasure house for cheating at cards, a coincidence that, considering the circumstances, didn't escape Christian's attention. He was deliberately being set up to fail. There was no longer any doubt of it. Thankfully he'd brought his own luck. All he could hope was that he was good enough to keep one step ahead of his opponents.

Melinda Kelveston took her seat and patted Paul on the head. "I can see why you like him, Christian. He is very skilled."

"Indeed he is."

Christian watched as the footman delivered a new pack of cards to Lord Kelveston, who broke the seal and placed the pack on the table. He continued to watch as Kelveston shuffled the deck and soon confirmed his suspicions that the cards had been tampered with. Kelveston was fingering the cards so carefully that it was obvious he was learning the pack. Now all Christian had to do was work out the system and hope to God that he could turn it to his own advantage.

He bent to kiss Elizabeth's head. "The deck is crooked," he breathed. "Be on your guard."

As Christian started to play, Elizabeth pretended to cover her face with her hands. In reality, she focused her attention on Lord Kelveston, who sat on her right. If she was very careful, she might just see his cards. She soon noticed that when he dealt from the deck, he ran his forefinger over the back right-hand side of each card. She couldn't quite see how he finagled the cards to the right people because he was so fast, but she was certain that he was doing something.

Christian sat back in his seat, his gaze calm, one hand occasionally stealing down to touch her hair or her face. His deliberate gestures might have seemed possessive or designed to infuriate Lord Kelveston, but she knew they meant much more than that.

Paul was keeping watch on the other side of the table, his

deceptively sweet gaze fixed adoringly on Lady Kelveston but encompassing every motion Lord Norton made as well.

The first two hands went to Kelveston, and Elizabeth felt her stomach tighten. However, Christian seemed unperturbed, his smile relaxed, his conversation still light. She concentrated even more carefully on Kelveston and finally caught a clear glimpse of his cards. She reached out to Christian's chair and tapped a series of numbers out on the wood.

A moment later, she noticed Paul doing the same and she could only hope that Christian had the ability to keep all the numbers straight. Each player drew another card, and Elizabeth checked Kelveston's cards again—only this time they weren't the same. Three of them had changed suit. She tapped again, suddenly aware that Melinda Kelveston was watching her. Elizabeth produced a hasty sob and Lady Kelveston laughed and looked away again.

Christian dropped his hand down onto her shoulder and she almost jumped. His fingers slid lower until they delved beneath her bodice, and he pinched her nipple hard. She gasped and tried to pull away from him, making the other occupants of the table chuckle.

"That's the way, Delornay. Make her think about what's coming," Kelveston shouted.

Christian straightened and removed his hand from her body. At the same time she realized he'd stuffed some of his playing cards inside her corset. She hunched her shoulders and prayed they wouldn't fall out.

The play continued, and Kelveston started to get restless, his replies shorter as Christian started to win. He even snapped at Lady Kelveston when she inadvertently played the wrong cards and glared at Lord Norton, who seemed too drunk to understand that their carefully laid plans were going awry.

Christian yawned, stretched out his foot, and deliberately

kicked Paul, causing him to knock into the petite Lady Kelveston, who fell off her chair with a screech. Paul was quick to catch her and receive her gratitude. While the other men set her chair back on its feet and fussed around her, Christian removed the remainder of the deck and replaced it with an identical one from his pocket. Now all that was left of the marked deck was in the other three players' hands.

When everything had been restored to rights, Christian bowed. "My apologies, my lady. It was entirely my fault."

Melinda blew him a kiss. "It is all right, Christian. You can make it up to me later."

Christian smiled and returned his attention to his hand. Would Kelveston notice the differences in the decks, and if he did, what would he do about it? With two different sets of cards now in play, it would be difficult for him to call Christian out for cheating without revealing his own more deliberate attempt.

But would Kelveston care? This club was his creation, his world, and he believed he owned everything and everyone in it. But in the world of the *ton*, a man's reputation meant everything. If Kelveston was prepared to ruin Paul, Christian was quite happy to reciprocate and had the connections to follow through. Christian glanced at his remaining cards. He could finish this in less than five minutes. After that, it was up to Kelveston.

He touched Elizabeth's dark hair and played with a curl that had escaped her chignon. Even if Kelveston didn't contest his win, they still had to get out of the club in one piece. He played his last two cards and watched Kelveston's face flush an unbecoming red.

"My game, I believe, Lord Kelveston?" Christian smiled right into his opponent's enraged eyes.

"You, you . . . ," Kelveston hissed.

"Thank you, my lord. I accept your compliments." Christian stood up, bringing Elizabeth with him. "I should have insisted that you be put in the cage if I won."

Kelveston lunged at him and Christian stepped back. "Is there something wrong, my lord? We wouldn't want rumors to get about that you are a bad sport, now, would we? Or any rumors about other guests."

Kelveston suddenly seemed to recall that they had an avid audience and that his wife was clinging to his arm. He visibly controlled himself and unclenched his fists.

"We're not done yet, Delornay."

"In what way, sir?"

"You agreed to fuck the whore in public."

"I believe I did." Christian felt Elizabeth stiffen against his side. "And I'm quite happy to oblige you." He squeezed her hard. "In truth, I'm looking forward to it." He bent his head and kissed her on the mouth. "Feel free to scream and object, my dear."

She held his gaze and immediately pulled out of his grasp and tried to slap his face. Kelveston laughed as Christian grabbed her wrist and yanked her close. He talked as fast as he could.

"Elizabeth, I can't avoid this. Can you stand it? If I don't give them this at least, we'll all end up in that cage or under a sea of bodies. If you can't, tell me now and I'll make sure Paul gets you away."

For a frozen second, Elizabeth ignored the jeering and urging of the crowd gathering around them and just stared at Christian. He was offering to save her at his own expense. Warmth flooded through her. How had she come to deserve that? The least she could do was save them both.

She shoved herself away from his chest and brought her hand up again to slap his cheek. His head recoiled as the crack of flesh on flesh reverberated around the room.

"How dare you!" Elizabeth screamed.

His eyes narrowed and all the warmth deserted his face. He reached out a hand, grabbed the front of her bodice, and yanked hard. The sound of the muslin ripping set off a roar in the salon that made Elizabeth's ears ring. She staggered backward, one hand holding up the ruins of her dress, the other held out to ward him off.

He started toward her anyway. "You'll pay for that."

She turned to run and the crowd obligingly parted for her. He caught her easily and brought her down onto her knees, one arm folded back up against her spine, his fingers hard on her wrist. She shuddered as he nipped her ear.

"Fight me, Mrs. Smith," he murmured. "Let's give them a show they'll never forget."

He tried to shift his grip on her arm, and she used his forward momentum to slip out of his grasp and crawl away from him. He easily caught her again, bringing her crashing down on her stomach, his long frame stretched over her. She felt the pressure of his growing cock against her bottom.

He wrapped a hand in her hair and yanked her head back until she had no choice but to join her mouth to his. She still tried to bite him and the crowd applauded.

He whispered against her mouth, "I'll keep Paul close, and that should stop most of the fools here trying to touch you."

"What about Kelveston?" she gasped as he kissed her hard, his hand tugging on her hair.

"He might be a problem. Could you bear him in your mouth?"

"If he doesn't mind me biting his cock off."

"Let's make sure he doesn't touch you, then."

Christian rolled her onto her back and straddled her. She kept trying to escape him, leaving ugly welts on his hands and face with her nails, but he wouldn't be deterred. And her body was waking up and wanting the fight, wanting to be taken without finesse, with the directness Christian alone had shown her she needed.

Holding her captive between his knees, Christian unbuttoned his satin pantaloons and the crowd went wild. His cock sprang free and he ran his hand up and down it, spreading the wetness. He brought his hand to her chin and cupped it, rubbing the crown of his cock against her tightly closed mouth. His wetness soon coated her lips. She couldn't move away because of his tight grip.

She heard Kelveston laugh and urge Christian on, his bad humor seemingly forgotten.

"Paul?" Christian said. "Hold her hands still for me. She's got claws like a wildcat."

Paul knelt down by Elizabeth and drew her arms up over her head, making her back arch. Christian slid his thumb along her jaw and forced her to open her mouth a fraction. She continued to glare at him as he increased the pressure, widening the gap until the crown of his cock edged inward.

"Suck me."

Elizabeth frantically shook her head, and he brought his other hand down to stop her moving at all. His finger and thumb closed over her nose, and she had to take a breath or suffocate. He laughed as she gasped out a breath, and he shoved his cock in until she could feel the salty wetness dripping onto her tongue and then running down her throat.

"That's better."

He relaxed his hands and let her breathe normally as he started to pump his shaft in and out of her mouth. With Paul still holding her wrists, Christian rotated his position until his back was to Paul. His hands were now free to wander over her breasts, to pinch and pull her nipples until she was writhing with the combination of pain and pleasure he aroused in her.

He yanked up her skirts to the cheers of the Demon Club and went to ease his cock out of her mouth. As he withdrew, she set her teeth on him and his breath hissed out as she deliberately nipped his foreskin.

"Goddammit, she's a feisty one. She's drawn blood!" Kelveston exclaimed.

Christian cupped his cock and balls, and Elizabeth knew he was making sure that Kelveston and the others got a good look at the small bleeding wound on his crown and considered whether they wanted to risk the same. He took his weight off her and stood up.

"What's wrong, Delornay? Are you too scared to continue?" Kelveston jeered.

Christian's smile was cold. "Let go of her hands, Paul." He stared down at Elizabeth and she saw the carnal invitation in his eyes.

"I'll give you twenty seconds to run."

She scrambled to her feet, met his gaze, and took off. The enthusiastic club members started bellowing like hounds on a foxhunt, but she hardly heard them. If she could just get closer to the door before Christian caught her again . . .

She screamed as he crashed into her from behind and she fell. Before she hit the unforgiving marble steps, he wrapped his arms around her and rolled them both over, his body taking the impact of the fall. He kept moving, and she was under him again, his knee spreading her legs wide, his body covering hers while his cock slid home.

He caught her flailing hands and held them at her sides while his hips thrust and retreated, driving his cock deep inside her. She no longer cared about the audience; all she cared about was Christian fucking her, making her his own, protecting her even when, to most of the men, it probably looked like he was doing exactly the opposite.

His flesh slapped against hers and she felt the pressure to come low in her belly. He shortened his strokes, grinding against her clit until she could no longer fight him, only scream as he fucked a climax out of her that was shocking both in its intensity and its duration.

Before she'd even finished coming, he flipped her over and entered her from behind, his fingers roaming over her breasts and her clit urging her onto another plateau of pleasure where she could only take what he gave her and try not to beg for more.

His fingers slid into her tangled hair and he drew her head back. "Suck his cock. Bite him."

Paul appeared on his knees in front of her, and she gladly accepted the thickness of his cock in her mouth. Better than Lord Kelveston, better than any stranger.

Christian groaned and pumped harder, pushing her against Paul, making her shudder between the two thrusting bodies. She came again and this time Christian came with her, his seed shooting high and hot inside her. Paul pulled out and blew her a kiss.

"Go, I'll take care of the rest."

"Are you sure?" Elizabeth managed to gasp.

"Indeed. It will be a pleasure."

As Christian recovered, Paul turned to Lord Kelveston with a lascivious grin and crawled across to him. He raised his head and licked the front of Kelveston's tented pantaloons. Kelveston grabbed for his blond hair, and Melinda shrieked as Paul shoved his hand up her skirts and brought her down to the ground.

The last thing Elizabeth saw before Christian picked her up and stumbled toward the door was Kelveston unbuttoning his placket, his expression intent, and the rest of the crowd pairing off and fucking as if she and Christian had set off a trail of gunpowder that had just ignited.

She buried her face against Christian's chest as he continued to head for the front door. No one stopped them, and Christian paused only long enough to find her a cloak and to button up his pantaloons. A moment later they were in his coach and on their way home.

Elizabeth opened her eyes and stared down at Christian. He didn't say anything and she touched his cheek.

"I'm fine, Christian."

"Are you sure?" He swallowed hard. "I was worried that I was a little . . . extreme."

She shifted on his lap until her wet core rested against the swell of his burgeoning erection and rubbed herself against him until he cursed and disposed of the necessary clothing so that he could thrust upward and inside her. She rode him hard, craving the rough words and caresses he showered on her and the hard pace of his need. He slid a hand between them and made her come and then made her come again until she was sore and begging him to stop, to never stop, to keep fucking her until she died of it. . . .

When they reached the pleasure house, he simply lifted her in his arms, took her to bed, and started fucking her all over again.

23

Christian winced as he shaved and the blade caught all the scratches Elizabeth had inflicted on him the previous night. He feared he was going to look rather disreputable to the Walker family lawyers, but there was nothing he could do about it. He smiled into the mirror. Each scratch was a badge of honor.

His smile faded as he considered all the possible outcomes of the upcoming meeting. He still had no idea what Elizabeth would choose to do. Would she go back to France after all? He sensed that whatever happened, she would not abandon the children, and where did that leave him? He knew that was self-ish, but having finally found a woman he could love, he was reluctant to lose her.

But love was all about compromise, wasn't it? Hadn't his parents' experiences taught him that? They'd waited almost twenty years for their particular happy ending. He wasn't quite prepared to go that far, but he'd be damned if he'd force Elizabeth into anything too quickly. He hadn't even told her that he loved her yet. Last night she'd shown him exactly what sort of a woman she was, one prepared to go to hell and back to save her children and her friends. With that revelation firmly in mind, he made his way down to his office.

Ambrose was already there sifting through an unusually large pile of mail. There were also several bouquets of flowers on the desk.

"I'm not sure quite what you hoped to accomplish last night at the Demon Club, sir, but you and 'Sylvia' seem to have created quite a stir." He handed Christian a pile of envelopes. "You received any number of congratulatory notes and invitations to every kind of entertainment imaginable." He nodded at the flowers. "These were sent by admirers of Sylvia who want her to be their mistress and are offering all sorts of incentives."

Christian groaned. "I didn't think about that. My whole purpose was to get Elizabeth and Paul out without injury and have something to hold over Kelveston."

"And what happened to Paul? I didn't see him come in with you last night."

"I didn't see you either, Ambrose." All Christian's attention had been on the woman he'd held in his arms. "Paul chose to stay at the Demon Club while we escaped."

"He refused your help?"

"No. In truth, he sacrificed himself for us. Not that it looked like much of a sacrifice. He seemed to be enjoying himself immensely."

Ambrose gathered up the remainder of the mail. "Do you want to read any of this drivel?"

"Not particularly. Although, save any that are addressed to Elizabeth. She might find them amusing." He glanced at his watch. "What time are we expecting the Walker family solicitors and Armand Saint-Brieuc?"

"In about fifteen minutes, I believe," Ambrose replied.

Christian continued to stare at him. "Ambrose," he said slowly. "How can Armand be the new Comte de Saint-Brieuc if his brother had children, one of whom is male?"

"I'm not sure, sir." Ambrose looked puzzled. "Perhaps there are different inheritance rules in France."

"Not that I know of," Christian said. "It does beg the question of why Armand wants Elizabeth back with those children so desperately. Do you think he plans to kill the lot of them and claim the title?"

"Hardly, sir. Especially now when he has all this attention directed at him."

"Then what exactly is going on?"

The front doorbell clanged. "I don't know, but I think we're about to find out." Ambrose gathered the mail and headed for the door. "I'll fetch Elizabeth."

The first to arrive was Christian's solicitor, Mr. Erickson.

"Good morning, Mr. Delornay."

"Good morning, Mr. Erickson, and thank you for attending this meeting," Christian replied.

"I was hoping to see you today anyway, so everything tied in quite nicely."

Christian frowned. "Why was that?"

Mr. Erickson opened his case and handed Christian a bulky envelope. "Your mother and father asked me to deliver this to you."

Christian slowly opened the package and read the letter on the top from his mother before examining the official-looking documents. He looked dazedly up at Mr. Erickson.

"My parents have signed the pleasure house over to me in its entirety."

"Indeed." Mr. Erickson smiled and held out his hand. "Congratulations, Mr. Delornay. I hope you intend to keep your business with our firm."

"Naturally," Christian managed to reply, although his thoughts were still with the unbelievable news the solicitor had just confirmed. His mother had given him the pleasure house. He could do with it as he wished—sell it, burn it to the ground, or run it as he saw fit. He swallowed down an unheard of desire to cry. His mother had given him his freedom. And what had he discovered? That his mother's love for him indeed had no end and that his love for Elizabeth meant the pleasure house was nothing more than a place to do business.

"Mr. Delornay?"

He jumped at the sound of Ambrose's voice. "Yes?"

"Mr. Ashley is here."

Christian rose to welcome the solicitor for the Walker family. He seemed quite happy to deal with Christian and immediately apologized for the absence of the Earl of Spentham, who sent his apologies and hoped to meet with his newly discovered relative on the following day at his London town house.

When the door opened again and Elizabeth appeared, Christian was the first to stand up, take her hand, and introduce her to Mr. Ashley and Mr. Erickson.

"May I present the dowager Comtesse de Saint-Brieuc to you, Mr. Ashley? You might know her better as the daughter of the honorable Mr. George Walker."

"Indeed, Madame la Comtesse, it is a pleasure. The earl did not know of your existence until we heard from the Ross solicitors. He was both shocked and surprised to hear that his younger brother had a daughter."

Elizabeth smiled and shook the proffered hand. "I'm not sure my father ever thought to contact anyone in his family after he left England and married my mother."

"I'm sure he had his reasons, madame, but may I assure you that the present earl and his wife are more than willing both to extend the hand of friendship to you and acknowledge the connection."

"That is very kind of them."

Mr. Ashley bowed low. "Due to his prior commitments at

the House, his lordship was unable to get here this morning, but I have an invitation from him asking you to call tomorrow afternoon at three."

"I would be delighted to meet him, sir."

Christian enjoyed watching Elizabeth at her most sweet and beguiling. The combination of her beauty and charm turned most men into blathering idiots. Luckily, he wasn't one of them, but it didn't mean he couldn't appreciate her skills.

"The earl wanted me to be here this morning in case any issues arose with the disposition of your deceased husband's will. I am more than happy to act on your behalf, madame."

"Thank you." Elizabeth patted Mr. Ashley's hand and he turned pink. "I appreciate that."

Ambrose appeared at the door and beckoned to Christian, who rose and murmured an apology as he excused himself.

"What is it, Ambrose?"

"Mr. Ross wants a word with you. I've put him in your mother's office."

"Where's Armand?"

"He's coming in his own carriage. Mr. Ross wanted to get here before him."

Christian entered his mother's study and was struck by both the familiarity and the differences in it to his own. A faint trace of his mother's perfume remained, and he pictured her sitting at her desk smiling at him. She'd given him the pleasure house. . . . He found himself nodding a welcome to his half brother.

"What is it, Richard?"

"I have some details about the Saint-Brieuc will."

"How did you get those?"

Richard shrugged. "As I said, I have a lot of contacts in France and a few favors owed. Luckily they paid off." He laid out a sheet of paper on the desk. "If there really are children involved in this mess, I don't see how Armand can be claiming the title, do you?"

"That was my exact thought," Christian said. "What does the will say?"

"It leaves the title and estates to the last comte's heir, Jean-Pierre."

Christian met Richard's calm gaze. "Then what exactly is Armand after?"

"I have no idea. The guardianship of the boy is left to three people—Elizabeth, Armand, and a woman called Louise Dinard. Do we know who she is?"

Some vague memory stirred in Christian's brain, but he couldn't quite retrieve it and he shook his head. "Armand was trying to pressure Elizabeth into marrying him. Perhaps he thought that would increase his power over the boy."

"But it still doesn't account for the fact that Elizabeth ran away from two children she loved or that Armand is using the title." Richard raised his head. "Unless he believes the children are bastards . . ."

Christian considered everything Elizabeth had told him about her husband. "How old is Jean-Pierre?"

Richard consulted the document. "He is almost six."

"Six . . . oh, Christ, *no*." He thought of Elizabeth, of all those men, of the impotent old man she had married . . . Christian let out a breath as Ambrose knocked on the door. "What is it now?"

"The Comte de Saint-Brieuc is here."

"Good."

Christian retrieved the papers from Richard and headed for the door.

Armand had taken a seat as far away from Elizabeth and Mr. Ashley as the space allowed, and he already looked irritated. Christian cast him a lethal glare. Whatever was going on, he would not let Armand win.

Christian took the seat behind his desk and Richard sat to his right. Ambrose leaned casually against the door.

"Monsieur le Comte," Christian said. "Have you met Mr. Ashley? His firm of solicitors represents Elizabeth's uncle, the Earl of Spentham."

Armand's expression stiffened and he glared at Elizabeth. "You did not tell me that your uncle was an earl."

"I did not think it any of your business, cousin," Elizabeth replied, and Christian wanted to kiss her.

"As you can see, *monsieur*, Madame is not without friends." Christian drew a breath. "Now perhaps you can explain to us why you are claiming the title of Saint-Brieuc while the late comte's will leaves that to his son, Jean-Pierre."

Armand looked startled. "How did you gain access to that information?"

"How I gained it is immaterial," Christian said. "The question still remains. I understand that you, along with Madame Elizabeth and another woman, were named joint guardians of the heir."

Armand stood up and started pacing the hearth rug, his hands clasped behind his back. "I am reluctant to share my family's private issues with strangers."

"We are hardly strangers, sir. And I'm sure we can guarantee that nothing you say will leave this room." *Unless it has to,* Christian silently added.

"Very well, then." Armand regarded them all and then dropped his gaze to Elizabeth, who found herself tensing. "Madame, you can avoid this shame if you choose to leave with me now and marry me."

"I cannot, Armand." Elizabeth shrugged. "Say what you will."

"My cousin, the late Comte de Saint-Brieuc, failed to father any children."

"So whose children are they?" Christian asked.

Armand pointed dramatically at Elizabeth. "They are her

bastards. Children she *forced* upon my poor impotent cousin and pretended were his legitimate offspring."

Elizabeth rose and Christian did, too, as if he meant to intervene. "You are blaming me, Armand? Is that how much the title means to you?" She struggled to draw a breath. "What about the children?"

Armand shrugged. "What about them?"

Elizabeth shook her head. "How can you be so callous?"

He smiled. "I offered to marry you, Elizabeth, and go along with your little charade, but you turned me down. What did you expect me to do? Meekly allow those bastards to take what is rightfully mine?"

"And theirs!" She swung around on him, her fists clenched. "Armand, I love those children as if they were my own. I can't allow you to do this to them."

"Hold on a moment." Christian's interception was sharp. "Elizabeth, what exactly do you mean?"

Her gaze shifted between the two men. Armand was already smiling, thinking he'd won and that she'd never betray the children. Christian was staring at her as if he wanted to look into her soul.

Suddenly, he came around the desk, grabbed her hand, and whisked her out into the hallway. She leaned back against the wall, and he framed her face with his hands.

"Elizabeth," he said quietly, urgently. "Whatever happened, if you want to keep your children, you can. We'll go and fetch them today. I'll sell the pleasure house. I also have an estate in the countryside—we can live there quite happily. Be assured that my family will welcome them whatever their lineage or status in life."

She looked into his eyes, and something inside her melted. He was no longer judging her choices. In truth, he was offering to give up everything he had ever wanted or valued just for her.

Somehow he had come to understand her dilemma and he was offering her a way out.

She cupped his cheek. "They aren't my children."

"*What?*"

"I had to pretend they were mine. They *feel* as if they are mine because I brought them up. But they belong to Armand and his mistress."

"Louise Dinard, the third guardian."

"Yes, she was my husband's mistress for years as well."

"Then what is going on? Why doesn't Armand want his own child to inherit?"

"I thought he did. That was the agreement we all swore to uphold." She swallowed hard. "But when Armand realized he didn't have sole guardianship of the children and complete control of the money, he grew angry. He also knew I would contest his decisions on the estate."

"Which is when he decided to marry you and silence your voice."

"Exactly. When I refused, he threatened to kill one of the children." She shuddered. "I had to run away and pray that with me gone, he wouldn't carry out his threat. The decision nearly destroyed me, and I've regretted it ever since."

"I'll bloody kill him." Christian pushed away from her, but she caught his arm and stared into his furious face.

"No, you can't do that." She stroked his cheek. "If I swear that the children are my husband's true heirs, they will inherit as they were supposed to. But I will never be allowed to see them again, and I fear for their continuing safety." She took an agitated breath. "I can't bring myself to marry Armand, but if I agree they are my bastards, they will be dispossessed and at a disadvantage for the rest of their lives."

"Let alone the damage to your reputation," Christian added.

She shrugged. "That seems rather unimportant compared to the rest of it."

He held her gaze. "Do you love them?"

"Yes. More than anything." *But you*, she added silently.

He shrugged. "Then there is nothing to worry about. Your reputation will be ruined and you can settle down with your children quite comfortably with me."

"With you?"

He kissed her very slowly. "Naturally." He hesitated. "You know that I would do anything in this world to make you happy?"

"Yes. I'm not sure why, seeing as I have done nothing but deceive you since we met."

He kissed her again, this time more slowly and possessively, until she was pressed fully against him from knee to chest.

"You never deceived me for a moment." He paused to smile at her. "Like knows like, Mrs. Smith, and your lies helped me uncover the truth."

"What truth?" she whispered.

"That everyone deserves to be loved."

"Even you?"

"Even me. I love you." He hesitated. "You do love me, don't you?"

"Yes."

He let out his breath, and she saw everything she needed to in his eyes. "Thank God for that. And this time I know you are finally telling me the truth."

"How do you know?"

"Because I'm finally ready to believe it."

He took her hand and she realized that he was shaking. "Shall we go and confirm your notoriety to the world at large and let Armand get away with his schemes? There are still some legal matters to deal with, but we can probably leave those to Richard and the solicitors."

"I wonder if the Walker family will be quite so keen to acknowledge me after this?" she sighed. "I suspect not, but having never had them in my life, I can hardly mourn their loss."

"You might be surprised, Elizabeth. Many English families have dealt with the most atrocious scandals and managed to pretend otherwise. Go and meet them tomorrow and tell them whatever version of events you think fit. After that, the decision is up to them."

"We will still have to go to France and talk to Louise. If we tell her what Armand has done to dispossess his own children, I suspect she'll allow herself to be compensated with a handsome sum of money."

"Will she be angry with Armand?"

"I believe she will. She is extremely jealous of me and hated the thought that Armand wanted to marry me and not her."

"Enough to make his life miserable until the end of his days?"

"Probably. Or she'll take the opportunity to leave him for another man." She fought down a sudden urge to cry and studied his beautiful if slightly battered face. "Thank you, Mr. Delornay."

"You are welcome, Mrs. Smith."

Together they walked back into the room, and Elizabeth happily prepared to have her reputation ruined. She wasn't quite certain what the future would bring, but at least she had hope. The children might end up being restored to her, and she had Christian Delornay's complicated and devoted love. She smiled and held her head high. Sometimes losing one's reputation was definitely worth it.

EPILOGUE

Christian studied the elegant architecture of the Saint-Brieuc château and motioned for Seamus Kelly to knock on the door. Elizabeth stood beside him, her expression so fragile and defenseless that he sought her hand and gave it a comforting squeeze. They'd left the solicitors arguing over the financial arrangements that allowed for Armand to secure the title and for Elizabeth to take the children, and made for the coast.

Christian had decided it was far more important to fulfill his promise to Elizabeth and secure the children anyway.

"Elizabeth, when we get inside, go and find the children. Let me deal with the rest."

She squeezed his hand in reply, and when the door finally opened, she slipped past the butler and headed straight for the stairs, her skirts caught in her hand.

Christian smiled at the flustered butler. "Good morning, is your mistress at home?"

"Madame Dinard is here, but—"

"Excellent." Christian pushed past the man and headed for

the nearest open door. He'd brought four stout men from the pleasure house to protect Elizabeth and the children, and they all crowded in after him. "Ask Madame to receive me, immediately."

It took him no time at all to convince Madame Dinard of both Armand's duplicity and the comfort a large payment in gold would bring to her grieving heart. Frenchwomen were remarkably shrewd and clear-sighted about relationships. He'd had all the necessary papers prepared in London, so all she had to do was sign them and relinquish the children to Elizabeth for perpetuity.

By the time Christian returned to the entrance hall, there was a commotion on the stairs above. He looked up to see Elizabeth coming down with two small hands in hers. When she caught sight of him, she smiled, and the beauty of it made him swallow hard.

"Jean-Pierre and Evangeline, this is Mr. Delornay."

"Good afternoon, sir."

Although the boy spoke in heavily accented English, he still studied Christian suspiciously. The little girl buried her face in Elizabeth's skirts.

Christian held out his hand and spoke in French. "It is a pleasure to meet you both. I have heard so much about you from your mother." He looked up at Elizabeth and saw she was close to tears, before turning his attention back to the children. "Are you game for an adventure with your *maman?*"

Both of the children looked at him. "With *Maman?*" asked Jean-Pierre. "We don't want to lose her. It was horrible." His lip trembled. "Madame Dinard said she was dead."

"I promise that we will keep you safe for the rest of your lives." Christian put his hand on his heart. "You will never have to be without her again."

Please turn the page
for an exciting sneak peek of
SIMPLY VORACIOUS,
the next sizzling installment
in Kate Pearce's
House of Pleasure series,
coming in August 2012!

1

"Are you all right, ma'am? May I help you?"

Lady Lucinda Haymore flinched as the tall soldier came toward her, his hand outstretched and his voice full of concern. She clutched the torn muslin of her bodice against her chest and wondered desperately how much he could see of her in the dark shadows of the garden.

"I'm fine, sir, please . . ." She struggled to force any more words out and stared blindly at the elaborate gold buttons of his dress uniform. "I'm afraid I slipped and fell on the steps and have ripped my gown."

He paused and she realized that he had positioned his body to shield her from the bright lights of the house, and the other guests at the ball.

"If you do not require my help, may I fetch someone for you, then?"

His voice was soft and he had a slight Russian accent.

"Could you find Miss Emily Ross for me?"

"Indeed I can. I have a slight acquaintance with her." He

hesitated. "But first may I suggest you sit down? You look as if you might swoon."

Even as he spoke, the ground tilted alarmingly, and Lucinda started to sway. Before her knees gave way, the soldier caught her by the elbows and deftly maneuvered her backward to a stone bench framed by climbing roses. Even as she shrank from his direct gaze she managed to get a fleeting impression of his face. His eyes were deep set and a very light gray, his cheekbones impossibly high and his hair quite white.

She could only pray he didn't recognize her. No unmarried lady should be loitering in the gardens without a chaperone, but somehow she doubted he was a gossip. He just didn't seem to be the type; all his concern was centered on her rather than making a grand fuss and alerting others to her plight. He released her and moved back as if he sensed his presence made her uneasy.

"I'll fetch Miss Ross for you."

"Thank you," Lucinda whispered, and he was gone, disappearing toward the lights of the ballroom and the sounds of the orchestra playing a waltz. She licked her lips and tasted her own blood, and the brutal sting of rejection. How could she have been so foolish as to believe Jeremy loved her? He'd hurt her, and called her a tease. . . . Had she led him on as he had said? Had she really deserved what he had done to her?

Panic engulfed her and she started to shiver. It became increasingly difficult to breathe and she struggled to pull in air. Suddenly the white-haired stranger was there again, crouched down in front of her. He took her clenched fist in his hand and slowly stroked her fingers.

"It's all right. Miss Emily is coming. I took the liberty of hiring a hackney cab, which will be waiting for you at the bottom of the garden."

"Thank you,"

"I'm glad I was able to be of service."

With that, he moved away, and Lucinda saw Emily behind him and reached blindly for her hand.

"I told my aunt I was coming home with you, and I told your mother the opposite, so I think we are safe to leave," Emily murmured.

"Good."

Emily's grip tightened. "Lucinda, what happened?"

She shook her head. "I can't accompany you home, Emily. Where else can we go?"

Emily frowned. "I'll take you to my stepmother's. You'll be safe there. Can you walk?"

"I'll have to." Lucinda struggled to her feet and Emily gasped. "What's wrong?"

"Oh my goodness, Lucinda, there is blood on your gown."

"Just help me leave this place." Lucinda grabbed hold of Emily's arm and started toward the bottom of the garden. She could only hope that Jeremy had returned to the ball and would not see how low he had brought her. She would never let him see that, *never*. With Emily's help, she managed to climb into the cab and leaned heavily against the side. Her whole body hurt, especially between her legs where he had . . . she pushed that thought away and forced her eyes open.

It seemed only a moment before Emily was opening the door of the cab and calling for someone called Ambrose to help her. Lucinda gasped as an unknown man carefully picked her up and carried her into the large mansion. Emily ran ahead, is-suing instructions, and then led the way up the stairs to a large, well-appointed bedchamber. The man gently deposited Lucinda on the bed and went to light some of the candles and the fire.

Lucinda curled up into a tight ball and closed her eyes, shut-ting out Emily and everything that had happened to her. It was impossible not to remember, and she started to shake again. A cool hand touched her forehead and she reluctantly focused on her unknown visitor.

"I'm Helene, Emily's stepmother. Everyone else has left, including Emily. Will you let me help you?"

Lucinda stared into the beautiful face of Madame Helene Delornay, one of London's most notorious women, and saw only compassion and understanding in her clear blue eyes.

Helene smiled. "I know this is difficult for you, my dear, but I need to see how badly he hurt you."

"No one hurt me. I slipped on the steps and . . ."

Helene gently placed her finger over Lucinda's mouth. "You can tell everyone else whatever tale you want, but I know what has happened to you, and I want to help you."

"How do you know?" Lucinda whispered.

"Because it happened to me." Helene sat back. "Now, let's get you out of that gown and into bed."

She talked gently to Lucinda while she helped her remove her torn gown and undergarments, brought her warm water to wash with, and ignored the flow of tears Lucinda seemed unable to stop.

When she was finally tucked in under the covers, Helene sat next to her on the bed.

"Thank you," Lucinda whispered.

Helene took her hand. "It was the least I could do." She paused. "Now do you want to tell me what happened?"

"All I know is that I am quite ruined."

"I'm not so sure about that."

Lucinda blinked. "I'm no longer a virgin. What man would have me now?"

"A man who loves you, and understands that what happened was not your fault."

"But it was my fault, I went into the gardens with him *alone,* I let him *kiss* me, I *begged* him to kiss me."

"You also asked him to force himself on you?"

"*No,* I couldn't stop him, he was stronger than me and . . ."

"Exactly, so you can hardly take the blame for what happened, can you?" Helene patted her hand. "The fault is his. I assume he imagines you will be forced to marry him now."

Lucinda stared at Helene. "I didn't think of that." She swallowed hard. "He said we needed to keep our love secret because my family would never consider him good enough for me."

Helene sighed. "He sounds like a dyed-in-the-wool fortune hunter to me. What is his name?"

Lucinda pulled her hand away. "I can't tell you that. I don't want to have to see him ever again."

"Well that is unfortunate, because I suspect he'll be trying to blackmail his way into marrying you fairly shortly."

Lucinda sat up. "But I wouldn't marry him if he were the last man on earth!"

"I'm glad to hear you say that." Helene hesitated. "But it might not be as easy to avoid his trap as you think. You might be carrying his child. Does that change your opinion as to the necessity of marrying him?"

Lucinda gulped as an even more nightmarish vision of her future unrolled before her. "Surely not?"

"I'm sorry, my dear, but sometimes it takes only a second for a man to impregnate a woman." Helene continued carefully. "I can give you an herbal potion to make sure that will not happen, but the choice is yours."

"I will *not* marry him."

"Then let us pray that you have not conceived. The consequences for a woman who bears an illegitimate child are harsh." Helene's smile was forced. "I know from Emily that you are much loved by your parents. I'm sure they would do their best to conceal your condition and reintroduce you into society after the event."

Lucinda wrapped her arms around her knees and buried her face in the covers. Her despair was now edged with anger. If she refused to marry her seducer, she alone would bear the disgust of society, while Jeremy wouldn't suffer at all. It simply wasn't fair.

Eventually she looked up at Madame Helene, who waited patiently beside her.

"Thank you for everything."

Helene shrugged. "I have done very little. I wish I could do more. If you would just tell me the name of this vile man, I could have him banned from good society in a trice."

"That is very kind of you, Madame, but I'd rather not add to the scandal. I doubt he would relinquish his position easily, and my name and my family's reputation would be damaged forever."

"And, as your father is now the Duke of Ashmolton, I understand you all too well, my dear." Helene stood up. "But, if you change your mind, please let me know. I have more influence than you might imagine."

"I'd prefer to deal with this myself." Lucinda took a deep, steadying breath. "I need to think about what I want to do."

Helene hesitated by the door. "Are you sure there isn't another nice young man who might marry you instead?"

Lucinda felt close to tears again. "How could I marry anyone without telling him the truth? And what kind of man would agree to take me on those terms?"

"A man who loves you," Helene said gently. "But you are right to take your time. Don't rush into anything unless you absolutely have no choice. In my experience, an unhappy marriage is a far more terrible prison than an illegitimate child."

Lucinda looked at Helene. "Emily told me you were a remarkable woman and now I understand why. I'm so glad she brought me here tonight."

"Emily is a treasure," Helene replied. "I only tried to offer you what was not offered to me—a chance to realize that you were not at fault, and a place to rest before you have to make some difficult decisions. Now go to sleep, and I will send Emily to you in the morning."

Lucinda slid down between the sheets and closed her eyes. Sleep seemed impossible, but she found herself drifting off anyway. Would any of her partners have noticed that she hadn't turned up for her dances with them? Would Paul be worried about her? She swallowed down a sudden wash of panic. If anyone could understand her plight, surely it would be Paul. . . .

Paul St. Clare prowled the edge of the ballroom, avoiding the bright smiles and come-hither looks of the latest crop of debutantes. Where on earth had Lucky gone? She was supposed to be dancing the waltz with him, and then he was taking her in to supper. It was the only reason he was attending this benighted event after all.

Unfortunately, since the death of the sixth Duke of Ashmolton, speculation as to the new duke's potential successor had alighted on Paul, hence the sudden interest of the ladies of the *ton*. He'd grown up with the vague knowledge that he was in the line of succession, but he hadn't paid his mother's fervent interest in the subject much heed until the various male heirs had started to die off in increasing numbers.

And now, here he was, the heir apparent to a dukedom he neither wanted nor felt fit to assume. It was always possible that the duke would produce another child, if unlikely, because of his wife's age. But Paul knew that even beloved wives died, and dukes had been known to make ridiculous second marriages in order to secure the succession. Paul's own father, the current duke's second cousin, had only produced one child before he died in penury, leaving his family dependent on the generosity of the Haymores for a home. In truth, Paul considered Lucky's parents his own, and was very grateful for the care they had given him.

Paul nodded at an army acquaintance, but didn't stop to chat. All his friends seemed to have acquired younger sisters who were just dying to meet him. In truth, he felt hunted. If he had his way, he'd escape this gossip-ridden, perfumed hell and ride up north to the clear skies and bracing company of his best friend, Gabriel Swanfield. But he couldn't even do that, could he? Gabriel belonged heart and soul to another.

Paul stopped at the end of the ballroom that led out onto the terrace, and wondered if Lucky had gone out into the gardens. He could do with a breath of fresh air himself. He was about to pass through the open windows when he noticed a familiar figure standing on the balcony staring out into the night.

Paul's stomach gave a peculiar flip. The sight of his commanding officer, Lieutenant Colonel Constantine Delinsky, always stirred his most visceral appetites. Of Russian descent, Delinsky was tall and silver-eyed, with prematurely white hair that in no way diminished his beauty. Paul always felt like a stuttering idiot around the man.

Delinsky was looking out into the gardens of the Mallorys' house with a preoccupied frown. Paul briefly debated whether to disturb him, but the opportunity to speak to someone who wouldn't care about his newly elevated status was too appealing to resist.

"Good evening, sir."

Constantine turned and half smiled. "Good evening, St. Clare. I didn't realize you were here tonight. Are you enjoying yourself?"

"Not particularly," Paul said. "I find all these people crammed into one space vaguely repellant."

Again, that slight smile that made Paul want to do whatever he was told. "I can understand why. As a soldier, I always fear an ambush myself."

"Are you waiting for someone, sir?" Paul asked.

"No, I was just contemplating the coolness of the air outside, and deciding whether I wished to stay for supper or leave before the crush." Delinsky's contemplative gaze swept over Paul. "Did you come with Swanfield?"

"Alas, no, sir. Gabriel and his wife are currently up north taking possession of his ancestral home."

Constantine raised his eyebrows. "Ah, that's right, I'd forgotten Swanfield had married."

"I'd like to forget it, but unfortunately the man is so damned content that I find I cannot begrudge him his happiness."

"Even despite your loss?"

"*My* loss?" Paul straightened and stared straight into Delinsky's all-too-knowing eyes.

Delinsky winced. "I beg your pardon, that was damned insensitive of me."

"Not insensitive at all. What do you mean?"

Delinsky lowered his voice. "I always believed you and Swanfield were connected on an intimate level."

Paul forced a smile. "There's no need for delicacy, sir. Gabriel was happy to fuck me when there was no other alternative. He soon realized the error of his ways, or more to the point, I realized the error of mine."

Delinsky continued to study him, and Paul found he couldn't look away. "Perhaps you had a lucky escape, St. Clare."

"You think so?"

"Or perhaps the luck is all mine."

A slow burn of excitement grew in Paul's gut. "What exactly are you suggesting, sir?"

Constantine straightened. "Would you care to share a brandy with me at my lodgings? I find the party has grown quite tedious."

Paul wanted to groan. "Unfortunately, I accompanied my family to the ball. I feel honor bound to escort them home as well."

"As you should." Constantine shrugged, his smile dying. "It is of no matter."

Paul glanced back at the ballroom and then at the man in front of him. Despite Delinsky's easy acceptance of Paul's reason for not leaving with him, Paul desperately wanted to consign his family to hell and follow this man anywhere. Gabriel was lost to him. He needed to move past that hurt and explore pastures new. And when it came down to it, he had always lusted after Constantine Delinsky.

"Perhaps you might furnish me with your address, sir, and I can join you after I've dispensed with my duties."

"It really isn't that important, St. Clare."

"Perhaps it isn't to you, but it is to me," Paul said softly. "Give me your direction."